Praise for Alissa York and

THE NATURALIST

NATIONAL BESTSELLER

"I fell so hard in love with this book because it convinced me of something I need to know and forever remember, which is that the human heart will always, inevitably, be revealed and that the human heart, when working well, is a wild heart—and that giving in to one's wild heart is not incompatible with human decency. *The Naturalist* will join those few other books on my shelf that remind me how to live." Miriam Toews, author of *All My Puny Sorrows*

"Alissa York taps the wisdom and intelligence that belongs to all nature. Her writing on animals is simply unparalleled: her love and understanding as clear as her prose, which is elegant, polished, selfless, and wild. This book is the best of adventures, a genuine journey upriver into another world—embark!" Marina Endicott, author of *Close to Hugh*

"[T]he Naturalist showcases . . . York's admirable powers of description." *The Globe and Mail*

"A captivating tale." *Ottawa Citizen*

"Her writing . . . [is] evocative, intricate and saturated with sensory detail." *The Calgary Herald*

"York's writing is graphic and impressionistic, sharp-edged and sensual." *Quill & Quire*

"The descriptions of the natural world are magical. . . . I enjoyed the flow of the novel and the entanglement of characters: there's more to it than trees and monkeys, and you'll have to pick it up for yourself!" *Citizens' Press*

"York's prose is vivid and sensual." *NOW* (Toronto)

ALSO BY ALISSA YORK

Any Given Power
Mercy
Effigy
Fauna

THE
NATURALIST

ALISSA YORK

VINTAGE CANADA

Published by Vintage Canada, a division of Penguin Random House Canada
Limited, in 2017. Originally published in hardcover by Random House Canada,
a division of Penguin Random House Canada Limited, in 2016.
Distributed in Canada by Penguin Random House Canada Limited, Toronto.

Vintage Canada with colophon is a registered trademark.

www.penguinrandomhouse.ca

Library and Archives Canada Cataloguing in Publication

York, Alissa, author
The naturalist / Alissa York.

ISBN 978-0-345-81500-2
eBook ISBN 978-0-345-81501-9

I. Title.

PS8597.O46N38 2017   C813'.54   C2015-905780-9

Book design by Jennifer Lum

Cover images: (Amazon dolphin) © Kevin Schafer / Getty Images;
(handwriting) © Liligraphie / Dreamstime.com;
(rainforest) © ranplatt / iStockphoto.com

Interior image: (vintage frame) © Digiselector / Dreamstime.com

Printed and bound in the United States of America

2 4 6 8 9 7 5 3

Penguin
Random
House

VINTAGE CANADA

for Ricardo and Chrissy Sternberg
(um brasileiro, uma americana, dois canadenses)

and as always
for Clive

PHILADELPHIA

2ND OF JULY, 1867

1

Iris has locked herself in. Rachel lays her ear to the door. "Iris? Are you awake?"

A rustling of bedclothes. "Walter?"

Rachel's heart contracts. "Iris, it's me, it's Rachel."

"—*Walter.*"

Rachel listens to her mistress cry for as long as she can bear it, then turns and follows the corridor to the stairs. Descending into the front hall, she notes the glow of gaslight beyond the high windows; somehow night has fallen, the lamplighters come and gone. Mrs. Pryce has forgotten the wall lamps—little wonder, with all she's had to do. Rachel moves mechanically from one fixture to the next, turning up the gas. She could step through to the parlour, but somehow it seems wrong to seek comfort at such a time. Crossing to the vestibule, she sits down on the mahogany bench.

The street light is kind here, warmed by its passage through the stained glass sunrise above the front doors. She regards herself in the long mirror. Warm light or no, she looks washed out, a good deal older than her nineteen years. Little sprite, Papa used to call her—a name still suited to her body, if not her soul.

Hard to believe two years have passed. She can picture it clear as day: her first trip to the city when she wasn't pinned to her father's side. This time, while Robert Weaver made his way round the livestock pens at the Western Market, his daughter would see to business of her own. Or near enough. Annie had charged her with a list of so-called necessaries. It seemed no spoon, no blanket in the house was fine enough for the child to come.

Rachel was to rejoin her father at the Arch Street Meeting House at two o'clock; until then she was at liberty—within limits. The map he'd given her was marked with his own dark lines, borders to keep her from wandering near docks and taprooms, theatres and worse.

Greene Booksellers on Chestnut Street stood within the inked boundary, but Rachel knew entering a bookshop entailed crossing a different, more deeply etched line. She told herself the Bible Depository sign on the storefront made it all right, though it was only one advertisement among many. Perhaps she might happen upon a volume of illustrated parables—a gift in anticipation of the baby, to soften things between Annie and herself.

The window display was crowded, yet her eye lighted immediately on a single book. Propped open on a wooden stand, it showed a colour plate of a milk snake. A common-enough sight in the barn, the creature curved like a letter of some alphabet she had yet to learn.

"*Coluber eximius,*" she read aloud. Her forehead resting against the shop window, she strained to make out the text on the facing page. It began plainly enough—"Characters. Head short; snout rounded; body above milk coloured . . ."—but soon there was much she didn't understand. It was doubtful whether her own small funds would stretch to cover a present for herself as well as for the half-brother or -sister to be. Still, it couldn't hurt to inquire.

The man behind the counter was heavily whiskered, more of a smithy by type than any bookseller she might imagine. He raised an eyebrow, doubtless in response to her telltale bonnet and plain grey cloak.

"Morning, miss." His tone was gentle, similar to the one Papa used when he moved among the herd. It gave her courage.

"Good morning." She drew the door closed. "Thee has a book in thy window. A book about snakes."

Both eyebrows now, along with the edge of a smile. "Not just snakes, miss, turtles and all sorts. Mr. Holbrook's *North American Herpetology*. I'm afraid I have only the fourth volume in stock."

"I see." The parables forgotten, Rachel made a mental count of the coins in her purse. "I wonder if I might look at it?"

"You might look at a full set if you care to."

The voice made her jump. She turned to find herself in the presence of a tall, slender woman in forest-green silk. Her hair was the colour of honey, piled up under a small dark hat. Her eyes were palest hazel, an unsettling greenish-gold.

"We have all five volumes in our library at home." The woman stepped forward to place a stack of books on the counter. "Along with just about every other title in the natural history line. Mr. Greene can vouch for that, can't you, Mr. Greene?"

"I can indeed, Mrs. Ash."

Rachel couldn't help but mark the change that had come over the bookseller: his black eyes shone like a boy's.

The woman held out a slim, gloved hand. "Iris Ash."

Rachel extended her own. "My name is Rachel Weaver."

"Delighted to make your acquaintance." Iris Ash held her gaze. "And do you esteem reptiles in particular, Miss Weaver?"

No one had ever asked her such a question. "I like . . . all creatures."

"All creatures?" Iris Ash shared a look with the bookseller. "Even spiders?"

Rachel pictured the keeper of the web outside her bedroom window, the delicate mosaic on its back. Even the dark-bodied wolf spiders were something to see, slipping up through the kitchen floorboards to hunt. "Yes," she said, "even spiders."

"Do you hear, Mr. Greene?"

The bookseller grinned at them both.

"You must come home with me and peruse our library, Miss Weaver. It isn't far."

"Oh. Thee is very kind—"

"Nonsense, it's been ages since Mrs. Pryce had a guest to make tea for." She reached for Rachel's arm, finding her elbow through her cloak and giving it a squeeze. It didn't seem possible, but there it was, writ plain across that beautiful face. Iris Ash was lonely.

All five volumes. Rachel stole a glance at the clock behind the counter: not yet noon. Annie's list wasn't nearly long enough to eat up a whole two hours.

It was indeed only a few blocks to the house—though "house" was scarcely the word for it. As they came to stand before the massive front doors, Rachel heard herself ask, "Thee lives here?"

"Ridiculous, isn't it? Just myself, Mr. Ash and the long-suffering Mrs. Pryce in all these rooms." Handing her parcel of books to Rachel, Iris Ash fished a key from her bag.

Inside, Rachel stood staring. The impossibly lofty ceiling, the staircase winding up and away. The walls were crowded with paintings, each more compelling than the last.

As her eye travelled from frame to frame, Rachel became sensible of a theme. Reptiles outnumbered other creatures two to one. She counted a rat snake, a common garter, a corn snake with brilliant red bands. There were turtles she knew—snappers and cooters—and others she'd never seen. A long, armoured beast that could only be an alligator floated among lily pads in bloom.

One frame held an animal she had no name for. Its skin was luminous, new-apple green, save for patches of golden brown along its back, broad stripes about the whip of its tail. It gripped a branch with slender fingers, yellow claws.

"That's Lucy," Iris Ash said behind her.

Rachel turned to her. "What is she?"

"Was, I'm afraid. Green iguana. She left us last year, poor thing, just lay down and died." She pushed against a panel that revealed itself to be a door. "Mrs. Pryce," she called down the corridor, "we have company." No response. "I'll have to go down to her. She'd never admit it, but she's getting deafer by the day."

Rachel nodded, her eye drawn to a painting on the far side of the hall. Still in her bonnet and cloak, she crossed to the foot of the stairs. The portrait dominated the landing. Its subject was a tall man around Papa's age—his hair touched with grey at the temples, his pointed beard still black. Spectacles softened his dark-eyed stare. His cheekbones marked him as a man of narrow build, but it was impossible to be sure: the shell of an enormous turtle obscured everything from his collar to his trouser knees.

Iris Ash came to stand beside her. "And that's my Mr. Ash." She laughed. "He was carrying that shell the first time I laid eyes on him, lugging it home from the docks."

"How else could I catch your eye?"

The portrait's living echo stood above them at the head of the stairs, somewhat less imposing in waistcoat and shirtsleeves. Rachel glanced at Iris Ash to find her gazing up at her husband, her mouth soft.

"I'm afraid Mrs. Pryce has ventured out with her basket." Mr. Ash removed his spectacles and rubbed at them. "Something about a nice piece of shad."

"Never mind. Come and meet Miss Weaver, Walter." Iris Ash slipped her arm through Rachel's. "Come and meet our new friend."

Rachel starts at a sound. A step on the front stairs? No, only someone passing in the street. She glances at the hall clock: half past nine. Shouldn't he be here by now?

Paul Ash. No, she corrects herself, *Paul.* She must accustom herself to using his Christian name only, a particular wish of Iris's. Rachel has only a vague idea how far he has to travel from Harvard to Philadelphia—far enough that he visits no more than two or three times a year. Walter put it down to success, his son taken up with his studies, his work at the Museum of Comparative Zoology. Neither of which can claim precedence now. Rachel's been doing her utmost, but Iris needs family about her, and Walter's son is the nearest thing she has to blood.

He's nothing like his father. Scarcely taller than Rachel herself, Paul Ash must take after his mother's people. Strange for a body so solid to move with such grace, as though he were part bulldog, part deer. He has a deer's colouring, too, autumn-brown even in the dead of winter. A deer's dark, watchful eyes. Perhaps it's a blessing he resembles Walter through expression alone—no spitting-image visitation for the widow to bear. And for Rachel, nothing worse than his customary formality, a coolness she's come to expect.

2

arver's Taproom is quiet—only three tables, including the one Paul occupies by himself. It isn't the first such establishment he's visited, though it's one of very few. On those rare occasions when he finds himself asked along to the Fresh Pond Hotel, he tends to slip away after the boating and before the bar.

One night, having forced himself to linger for the duration of two pints, he set off back to the boarding house alone. He knew the glades and copses of Mount Auburn Cemetery well; it was good collecting ground. Telling himself he might happen upon a spotted salamander about its nocturnal rounds, he took the long route home.

His sense of purpose faded amid the moonlit graves. To begin with he only passed among the headstones, occasionally pausing to pat a carved lion or stroke the stone feathers on an eagle's back. Soon, though, he was stooping to make out the names.

Many were too dark, but some, angled just so, caught the moon's cool beams. *Almira Dewson. Katherine Wright Williams. Benecia Benson Crowell.* On an older stone set into a slope, he came upon one with the right initials. *Zelda Arnot.* A line of verse threaded through his mind: *Whoever is not in his coffin and the dark grave, let him know he has enough.* The book was one of those that lived on his bedside table, as opposed to the narrow shelves by his desk—though with a title like *Leaves of Grass*, it might have passed for a natural history text. *Let him know he has enough.* Zelda Arnot, Zuleica Ash. Even by moonlight, he couldn't fool himself into reading it wrong.

Carver's house ale is pleasantly bitter. Paul downs the dregs of his second and catches the barman's eye for a third. Until tonight, two pints has been his record, enough to send him in search of a grave he knew to be located in a different country, a different hemisphere. No chance of his father's final resting place playing tricks the way his mother's does. Paul will be there tomorrow, standing witness as they fill it in.

He nods as his empty glass gives way to a full one. Tipping his head back to drink, he suffers an unnerving sensation of the floor opening up behind him. He must take care. Keep his movements controlled or risk going over, falling who knows how far.

⌒

This time Rachel barely taps on the bedchamber door, in the hope that Iris has cried herself to sleep.

"Who is it?"

"It's Rachel, Iris. Won't thee open the door?"

The bed boards give a creak. Footsteps. Iris slides back the bolt but leaves the door shut. At the sound of her padded retreat, Rachel lets herself in.

"I thought we were finished with all that." Iris climbs back into the mess she's made of her covers.

"Finished with what?"

"*Thee, thy, thine*—you sound like a little church mouse."

Rachel sets her lamp down carefully on the washstand. Iris's loose hair gleams in the light of her bedside candle. Her eyes are smaller, darker than Rachel has known them.

"I see you're dressed in mourning," Iris adds. "Or is that just your usual grey?"

Rachel looks down at her charcoal silk.

"Tell me, what happens if a pretty little Quaker wears a yellow dress? Does she burst into flames?"

Two years Rachel has abided in the Ash household—the fullest years of her life—and Iris has never spoken to her thus. "It's only—"

"Only what?"

"It's only what I know. What I'm used to."

Iris stares at her. It hurts to hold her gaze, but Rachel does. She holds it until Iris crumbles, burying her face in her hands.

The walk has gone some way to clearing Paul's head; he has only a moment's difficulty fitting his key to the lock. It's his home too—Iris has said so from the beginning—but that doesn't stop him feeling like a tradesman slipping in by the wrong door.

No sign of life. He sets down his case, removes his hat and places it on the stand. The ale has left him feeling hollow. He could use something to eat, but Mrs. Pryce will be in her bed by now. He can't think how they manage with only an aged cook-housekeeper and whatever day help the old woman sees fit to hire. As far as Paul can tell, Miss Weaver's duties don't run to the domestic.

He moves into the front hall, stepping softly as though he

would pass unheard. The portrait hangs where it always has, yet somehow it catches him off guard. He steadies himself with a hand at the banister.

Few would take them for father and son. Walter had a good four inches on Paul, but only a handful of pounds; Paul came into the world with broad shoulders and muscular legs. His father wasn't always that pale. Summer collecting trips had the power to turn Walter bronze, though never copper like his son. Black hair they shared, even if Paul has none of his father's wave. At twenty-one, he's given up trying to grow a beard.

The turtle shell was Iris's idea, and it turned out her instincts were right. Another man might appear ridiculous in such a pose, but Walter Ash looks like the brave, brilliant man he was. Perhaps a touch braver and more brilliant—a loving bias in the artist's eye.

Funny to think the two of them might never have met. His father was hawk-eyed when it came to detecting a dorsal stripe among leaf litter, but as a rule he took scant notice of his human surrounds. In any case, on the day in question he was taken up with the business at hand. The first mate of the *Arara* knew of Walter's weakness for specimens of Brazilian origin; he'd folded his arms to show he was sticking to his price. For his part, Walter was making a thorough inspection of the turtle shell, now and then muttering a query in his rusty Portuguese. Which left Paul free to observe the lady on the nearby pier.

She would have caught his eye under any circumstances—he was a healthy sixteen-year-old—but her beauty was just the beginning. Everything about her was fine, yet she perched on an old crate like a dock urchin, glancing up at intervals from the sketchbook in her lap. Not three paces from where she sat, a shark hung head-down—a sand tiger, perhaps eight feet in length. A trio of fishermen stood at a little distance, pleased by the attention, not entirely at ease.

Paul drifted from his father's side. Hands in his pockets, he strolled out onto the pier. The sand tiger wasn't the most elegant representative of its class; drawing near, he saw how accurately she'd rendered the slight hump, the snaggle-toothed maw.

She felt his gaze and looked round.

"I beg your pardon," he began, but she was already staring past him. Paul turned to see what had captured her attention. Walter had succeeded in acquiring the shell. He was advancing on them happily, brandishing it like a shield.

"Mr. Ash. Mr. . . . Paul?"

He looks up. Miss Weaver stands at the head of the stairs, still as an unstruck bell in her iron-grey dress.

"Have you been here long?"

He blinks. "No, not long."

She descends with a girlish ease unexpected in one so grave. One small hand skims the banister. She's at home here, he realizes with a pang. It's something he's never quite managed—not during that first year of Walter's second marriage, and not on any visit since.

Miss Weaver comes to stand before him, the strain of the past days evident on her face. "I'm so sorry about your father."

"Yes." He looks down. Until now he's had only formal condolences to bear: his dry-eyed landlady, a handful of his colleagues at the museum. Miss Weaver knows his father. Knew him.

"Iris is asleep," she says.

"Yes, well, I'll speak with her in the morning."

"Oh, no, she's been asking for you. She only sleeps in patches. We could go up in half an hour."

He nods, suddenly aware of his breath, the malty taint of ale.

"I wonder," she says, "if you'd care to see the atrium."

The atrium? Any other woman would have suggested the parlour and perhaps something to eat or drink. Her grey eyes rest on him.

"Very well."

She turns without a word and leads the way down the central corridor. The north wall supports a long display case. Paul pauses to consider its central specimen: *Shell of Podocnemis expansa, the Giant Amazonian River Turtle.* It's a dull, grey thing, nicked in several spots around its edge. For a moment he imagines it moves.

Miss Weaver awaits him at the end of the hall. The first time he passed through those double doors—five years ago now—they led to a private courtyard open to the sky. He and his father had been asked to luncheon. It was a meal unlike any Paul had known: tender chicken sandwiches among the rose bushes, his first bright mouthful of wine. Walter had as much cause as his son did to feel out of place, yet he betrayed no symptom of unease—perhaps because he sat so close to the mistress of the house.

Miss Weaver draws open the doors, releasing a gust of earthy air. Stepping onto the dark flagstones, Paul looks up at the stars. During his last visit, the welders were still erecting the fretwork; now the courtyard boasts a vault of glass.

As Miss Weaver lights the wall lamps, ragged shadows reveal themselves to be clumps of immature tropical trees. Set among the growth, three large, dry ponds lie ringed with fieldstones.

But surely, Father, those species are aquatic.

Not to worry, Paulo. We'll provide them with all they require.

Easier said than done. Walter's letters were full of setbacks: *Next week we sink the ponds. After the trouble with the ventilation pipes I hold out hope for no further delays, though I am informed concrete can have a mind of its own . . .*

Never any mention of the cost. Looking about him, Paul can't help wondering just how much money his stepmother has. Like him, she's an only child, but the similarity ends there. In its heyday, her late father's brewery dwarfed its neighbouring concerns.

"This one was to be for the turtles," Miss Weaver says, indicating the nearest pond. "Walter said they were the most sympathetic, so people should see them first."

"Yes." Paul hears the irritation in his voice. Is it her familiarity—his father's Christian name on her lips—or her ease with referring to him in the past tense?

She gestures to the second depression. "Caiman here. Anaconda saved for last." A look of wonder crosses her face. "Forty feet they grow to, can you imagine? Of course, we could never have managed one that big."

Paul says nothing. *We?*

She crouches down, her dress pooling darkly. "You can see where they've marked out the partitions. Walter wanted stone to separate the enclosures, and glass between the animals and the crowd." She stands. "It was tricky, though, with the fretwork. He hated anything that looked like bars."

Does she imagine he knows nothing of his own father's philosophy? *Prisons inspire pity, Paul, and from pity it's only a small step to disgust.*

"That's where he planned to glass in the arboretum." She points to a tangle of vegetation in the northwest corner. "He had hopes of securing another iguana, maybe an Amazon tree boa."

Paul doubts whether she would know a tree boa if it wound around her little waist. Unless Walter had been tutoring her. It hasn't occurred to Paul until this moment, but if his father was foolish enough to include his patroness-wife in the planned expedition, why not her companion too?

He'd been after Paul to commit to the trip for months. *Is it a matter of Mr. Agassiz not wishing to spare you?* How could Paul tell his father he doubted whether the great man knew him by name—or, worse, that Paul had yet to obtain a leave of absence from the museum because he had yet to ask? What if Walter had been hedging his bets, considering Miss Weaver as a less qualified but more willing third? Well, what if he had. They're none of them going now.

"That door leads through to the supply room," Miss Weaver informs him. "Cleaning equipment and so forth, cages for the rabbits and rats. Walter had a boy, Jim Sweeney—he was going to look after all that."

"Yes, I know." He pivots away from her, crossing to a bank of rectangular recesses set into the northern wall.

She comes to stand beside him. "Terraria for the smaller species."

There's something disquieting in her tone, a gentleness edged with grief. Paul looks down. The spot where he stands is discoloured, as if light has bleached the stone. Suddenly the hothouse air feels unhealthy. He turns and makes for the doors.

The eastern wall draws him up short. The mural reaches from floor to ceiling—understorey, canopy, a lone emergent species extending into imagined realms. *The scene is to be in no way fanciful. It is vital that we present the creature in context—in this we are entirely of one mind.* Iris has roughed it all in, but the detail work remains to be done, doubtless slated for completion upon their return. The result is a dream jungle, all shadow and haze—an echo to the one Paul has carried with him since birth.

"He wanted people to see them in their element," Miss Weaver says behind him.

He keeps his back to her. "Believe it or not, Miss Weaver, my father and I did correspond."

"Yes, of course. I didn't mean—"

He proceeds to the doors, holding one open for her to hurry through. Closing it behind him, he feels calmer, more in control. "I should like to see my stepmother now."

"Of course."

This time Paul leads the way, striding purposefully down the corridor, launching himself up the stairs. He can hear her working to keep pace with him, the whispering of her skirts.

She catches up at the bedchamber door. "She may still be sleeping."

"Indeed she may." He closes a hand on the doorknob. "Has she taken any supper?"

"Very little."

Her concern is palpable. He hardens himself to it. "Then perhaps you'd be good enough to fetch us both something to eat."

3

No sense waking Mrs. Pryce. Rachel will make up a plate of sandwiches herself—just not quite yet.

Her feet carry her back to the atrium. One by one, she turns out the hissing wall lamps. She waits while her eyes adjust, then crosses the glassed-in space by starlight. The stain is pale now rather than dark; Mrs. Pryce had the day girl scrub until she lightened the flagstones. Rachel gathers her skirts and kneels. It's been months, perhaps as long as a year, since she quieted herself in search of the Inner Light. She closes her eyes, finding blackness. In her mind she returns to the open courtyard that was, the three of them seated at the ironwork table, taking tea.

"I'll miss the roses," Iris said, setting down her cup.

Rachel looked around at that year's bloom. "Miss them?"

"Time, I think," said Walter, "that we apprised your young assistant of our plans."

Iris smiled. "High time."

"All this," he said, gesturing to the garden, "it's all coming out. A sacrifice, I know, but in a noble cause. You are seated in what is to become the Ash *Domum Reptilium*."

Rachel glanced from him to Iris. "You're building a dome?"

Iris laughed. "No, dearest. *Domum* is Latin. It's just a more . . ."

"Scientific," Walter prompted.

"Yes, a more scientific way of saying *house*."

"Domum Reptilium," Rachel said carefully.

"You may have noted my husband's predilection for reptiles." Iris patted Walter's knee. "One might even say mania."

"I can't deny a special interest." He laid a hand briefly over his wife's. "But there's more to it than that. You're familiar, are you not, Rachel, with Mr. Darwin's ideas?"

"Only what you . . . what I've learned."

As a rule she worked alongside Iris in the upstairs library, where Walter was often moved to read aloud. *Ah, now, this is perfectly put: "It may be said that natural selection is daily and hourly scrutinizing, throughout the world, every variation, even the slightest; rejecting that which is bad, preserving and adding up all that is good . . ."*

"You appreciate, though," Walter continued, "the principle of adaptation over time."

Rachel nodded, ignoring a twist of guilt. The theory was so elegant she couldn't help but appreciate it—in spite of the heresies it contained. If all species must adapt or die out, what of the fifth and sixth days, when God created every living creature and saw that it was good? Not to mention the generations such adaptation required. If Mr. Darwin was right, the world was far, far older than Rachel had been led to believe. She understood now the Friends' mistrust of the written word. *Natural selection*—a tidy phrase to overturn the world.

"Well, then," said Walter, "I put it to you that nowhere is this most fundamental of principles more evident than in the reptilian scale. Just consider, a single structure adapting to form an alligator's armour, an iguana's spines, a turtle's shell." He leaned in over the tea tray. "Consider the snake's perceptive belly, alive to every aspect of the jungle floor."

The guilt was a thin shadow to the creature that wound through her mind. She'd never been to the jungle, but Walter had. Whenever he spoke of it, something inside her turned quiet, alert.

"The serpent in the garden." Walter rapped his knuckles on the tray. "That's what you were taught, isn't it, what we were all taught. *The serpent more subtle than any beast?*"

Again, Rachel had to nod.

"But don't you see, it's that very subtlety that proves the point. Once we're rid of these preposterous conceits, these *fables*, we're free to marvel at nature itself. Never mind the serpent in the garden, it's time we took a good look at the serpent in the jungle—the anaconda shaped by the river, the tree boa designed by the tree." Walter sat back, folding his arms. "The creature in context, that's what we'll give them. That's what they need to see."

Rachel's knees are beginning to ache. Opening her eyes, she tilts forward, distributing her weight to all fours. The flagstones are hard, unforgiving beneath her palms.

There was nothing anyone could have done. She's told Iris a dozen times, she tells herself again now. Even if the two of them had been home. Even if Mrs. Pryce had heard the crash and come hobbling, her ears miraculously made young.

Iris and Rachel had been up and down Market Street; it seemed the coming expedition required no end of supplies. They arrived home shortly before lunch. Rachel set down her armload of parcels and removed her bonnet while Iris leafed through the post.

"Here's one from Brazil." Iris held a letter up to the light. "Walter," she called. "He's probably in the atrium. Run and check, will you, Rachel?"

Rachel can see herself now, walking briskly across the front hall and down the corridor. Entering the sunlit expanse.

It was plain enough what had occurred. He'd been carrying a pane of glass—a large one, destined for the bank of terraria along the northern wall. He must have stumbled, shattering the pane as he sprawled.

Rachel's childhood on the farm had shaped her for that moment—the hot, happy mess of calving, the necessity of the slaughter block and chain. When Iris came up behind her, she whirled to bar her way. When her mistress screamed and tried to shove her aside, Rachel shoved harder. She drove Iris backwards through the double doors and tackled her. Lay across her while she thrashed and howled.

Iris hasn't stirred. Paul has carried the dressing table chair to her bedside; he's close enough to hear her breathe.

In five years he's never seen her look less than radiant—until tonight. Even asleep, she's clearly worn out, her hair damp about her face. But what hair. It's a shock seeing it laid out like that, seeing it loose. It was tidied away beneath a bonnet the first time Paul saw her, but an escaped curl gave the colour away.

He'll never forget the eagerness with which she rose to meet his father. *Iris Grafton. Walter Ash.* It took Walter a few seconds to remember Paul was there too.

"Miss Grafton, my son."

She betrayed a moment's confusion, but none of the usual disdain. Her hand milk-white in his. "Delighted to make your acquaintance."

While Walter admired her studies of the shark, Miss Grafton stooped to examine the shell. "What is it?"

"*Podocnemis expansa*. Amazonian river turtle." Walter cleared his throat. "I've seen them in the wild."

Miss Grafton straightened. "How marvellous."

"I was fortunate enough to visit a nesting beach in season. An island, actually, Ilha das Tartarugas. They come there by the thousands."

Paul stared at his father. It was rare to hear him speak of that fabled trip in private, yet here he was conjuring up a turtle-covered beach to a woman he'd only just met. *Ilha das Tartarugas.* Paul filed the name away.

"I take it you're a naturalist, Mr. Ash," Miss Grafton said.

"I am."

"I should love to see your collection."

"Oh . . ." For a moment Walter appeared genuinely at a loss. "That is, yes, whenever you like."

She tapped lightly on the shell. "I imagine you'll be taking this monster straight home."

"I will."

"And is it far?"

"Not far, no. Just over on Race Street."

"Well, then, it's settled."

Paul shrank inwardly at the thought of her setting foot in their shabby rooms. The coins Walter pressed into his hand were damp with sweat. "Run to Fitzgerald's and get a tin of tea." Did he have to put it that way, as though Paul was still a boy in knee breeches?

"Oh, don't go to any trouble on my account." Miss Grafton took up her satchel and stood smiling.

"It's no trouble." Walter adjusted his grip on the shell. "See if Mrs. Cosburn will let you have a drop of milk," he added quietly, and when Paul opened his mouth to protest, "Go on."

It took Paul an age to secure the tea. The woman who stepped in ahead of him at Fitzgerald's counter had a list of some dozen items, each of which came with the tale of its intended use. He ran the few blocks from there to home, only to stand waiting again in the dried-brush atmosphere of Cosburn Brooms while the landlady fetched him a grudging measure of milk.

The staircase felt narrower than usual, scarcely wide enough to permit passage of a lady's skirts. Paul paused at the landing to collect himself. The door to their rooms might have been cut from sailcloth; he could hear every word.

"I prefer sketching from the living creature," Miss Grafton said. "Or at least one that's not long dead. It's not always possible, of course. I often make do with the specimen cabinets at the Academy of Natural Sciences."

"I wonder that I've never seen you there."

"Oh, are you a member?"

"Not a member, no. I have . . . business there from time to time."

Paul winced at the note of injury in his father's tone. In his haste to interrupt, he opened the door with undue force. He caught a glimpse of the congenial scene: Walter leaning against his desk, Miss Grafton in the green armchair, Lucy the iguana posing obligingly on the ottoman stool—before the door hit the bookshelf, startling the yard-long lizard from her perch.

In a flash, Lucy shot across the carpet and grappled up Miss Grafton's skirts. While Paul stood helpless, his father sprang. Walter was on his knees before their guest in an instant, one hand firm about Lucy's belly, the other plucking a clawed forefoot from the velvet detail at Miss Grafton's knee.

"Don't be alarmed," he said evenly.

But the expression on her face was only a cousin to alarm. Miss Grafton was plainly, unmistakably, thrilled.

Paul has been silent, sunk in memory, yet Iris starts awake. Seeing him, she reaches both arms out and begins to cry. He's embraced her before—greetings, partings—but never for so long. Her smell has changed; he can detect only a trace of the usual spice and violets. He holds her until she pushes him away.

"I've been indulging myself," she says, wiping savagely at her eyes. "Rachel will tell you, I've been locked away up here howling like a madwoman."

Paul says the only thing in his head. "You loved him."

She stares at him, trembling. "I ought to be comforting you."

Nonsense, he wants to say, but all he can manage is a sound. Curling forward, he feels her hand come to rest on the back of his head. She strokes his hair until he's done crying, then delivers the lightest of smacks to his skull.

"You smell like a brewery."

He sits up, wiping his nose, smiling sheepishly. "You ought to know."

She laughs, a single, sharp note.

He searches for something, anything, to say. "Miss Weaver—"

"*Miss Weaver*. Each of you is as bad as the other."

"Very well, then, *Rachel* tells me you haven't been eating."

"You've seen her?"

He nods.

"I was cruel to her earlier."

"Well, she seems . . . she seems fine. In fact, she gave me a tour."

It's the wrong thing to say. "Oh, God, Paul," Iris says softly, "I can't bear it. The thought of it all down there—and the trip, Paul, all our plans . . ."

"I know," he says, closing his eyes. His head is ringing. There must be something he can do.

~

Rachel carries the sandwiches up by the back stairs, direct from the basement kitchen to the second floor. Emerging into the south corridor, she's transported to a winter's night some six months gone. Mrs. Pryce had sent her up with cups of cocoa. She opened the stairwell door to the sound of Iris's voice.

"Walter, I'm freezing. You can kiss me in the library by the fire."

Rachel should have retreated, quiet as a cat's shadow on the servants' stairs. Some part of her she was little acquainted with chose not to. She put an eye to the crack of the door.

Walter—spare, studious Walter—backed his wife up against the wall. For the duration of the kiss, Rachel hovered outside herself, in danger of letting the cocoa crash to the floor. Walter drew back and studied Iris's face. Then he led her, flushed and obedient, to their bedchamber door.

The very door Rachel approaches now. Balancing the tray on her hip, she knocks.

"Come in," Iris calls.

She's sitting up against her pillows, a strange, almost febrile light in her eyes. "Oh, Rachel," she cries, "you'll never guess!"

Paul has his back to the door, his chair pulled up tight against the bed. When he looks round, his eyes too are brilliant—with fear.

4

Rachel lies on her back, adrift in her oversized bed. It took Iris a while to settle. She'd eaten half a sandwich at Paul's insistence, but only on condition that they talk the expedition through. Rachel did her best to join in, calling up Walter's jungle without him, telling herself Paul's commitment was real. Anything to see Iris smile.

She turns on her side, a memory stirring. *Locker's Dining Rooms, home of Philadelphia's finest oyster stew.* She'd been a year under the Ashes' roof, and was used to her role—a shifting hybrid of assistant, companion and friend. Still, the invitation surprised her. She stood uncomfortably behind Iris, the pair of them framed in the vanity mirror.

"But wouldn't you and Mr. Ash prefer—"

"How many times? *Walter.*" Iris met her reflected gaze. "And no, we wouldn't." Taking up a glinting earring, she leaned in close to the glass. "I'm thirty-four today, Rachel. *Thirty-four.* Thank God, Walter is older—only eight years, but I'll always be his young wife."

Rachel said nothing. Was it possible even a woman like Iris could find fault with her reflection? She considered her own slight image: a sprig of greenery sticking up behind a startling bloom.

Iris turned in her chair. "The point is, it's my birthday and I want to go to Locker's." She caught hold of Rachel's hand. "And I want you to come along."

As promised, the stew was very fine—once Rachel surrendered to its slippery richness. Walter ordered glasses of ale for himself and his wife, and for the first time ever Rachel joined shyly in a toast, raising her lemonade to drink Iris's health. She could see no harm in it. It might have been different if the Ashes were given to excess in their drinking, but their customary glass or two with dinner never produced anything worse than a broadening of Walter's smile, a touch of colour in Iris's cheeks.

On the walk home, Iris linked arms with them both. They were crossing Walnut Street, intent on stargazing in Washington Square, when a gentleman of small stature hailed them from across the way. Rachel felt Iris stiffen beside her. Glancing at Walter, she found his easy smile gone.

"*Ash.*" The man's hat gleamed in the gaslight as he approached. It brought him almost equal to Walter in height. "Well, well, Walter Ash."

"Ingleby." Walter withdrew his arm from Iris's. "I believe you know my wife."

"I do indeed." Mr. Ingleby grasped Iris's fingers.

"And may I present Miss Weaver."

Mr. Ingleby gave Rachel a nod. "I've just come from a meeting of the Philosophical Society. Davis read a fascinating letter from a Mr. Butler, British fellow, just back from Van Diemen's Land—well, Tasmania now."

"Indeed?" said Walter.

"We never see you about the place these days. Nor at the Academy, now that I think on it."

"No."

"Pity. Difficult to find a decent field man. These young fellows load up with any old shot. Boy brought in a screech owl the other day, looked as though a dog had been at it."

"Mr. Ingleby," Iris said, "my husband no longer supplies collectors."

Walter nodded. "I'm very much taken up with my plans."

"Ah, yes. An attraction of some sort, I believe."

"No mere attraction, I assure you. The *Domum Reptilium* is to be an institution devoted to scientific inquiry and instruction."

"*Domum Reptilium*, is it?" Mr. Ingleby's eyes danced. "Well, I imagine Grafton Mansion—or does one refer to it as Ash Mansion now? In any case, I imagine it could house a goodly number of skulls and skins, not to mention a host of charming studies by your charming wife."

"We won't be limiting ourselves to skulls and skins." Walter's voice was beginning to betray him. "We'll be mounting an expedition to the Rio Negro—"

"An expedition?" Mr. Ingleby turned to Iris. "Forgive me, Mrs. Ash, but why risk one's inheritance when one might just as soon stock a menagerie here at home? Only last week there was talk of a stevedore doing tricks with a constrictor down at the Black Bull. *Python reticulatus,* I believe."

Iris touched a hand to her collar. "I wonder you did not seek to purchase the creature yourself, Mr. Ingleby."

"I, Mrs. Ash?"

"Certainly, for the Zoological Gardens. It is a decade or more since the committee formed, is it not? Surely the time has come . . ."

"My dear lady, the war—"

"My dear sir, the war was won a year ago. Wouldn't you hold that those of us engaged in scientific pursuits should look to the future, rather than the divisive past?"

———

Rachel opens her eyes in the dark. She tries to halt the memory there—Iris with her golden eyes flashing, Mr. Ingleby shrinking under her gaze—but there was more. The little man made his excuses and turned to go, but not before landing a final shot. It echoes in the blackness of Rachel's bedchamber. *Rio Negro, you say. Carry home a piece of the jungle, eh, Ash? And not for the first time.*

Walter's desk is a mess. Paul stands for a time with his hand on the back of the chair, then gives up and crosses to the salmon-coloured wingback, the seat in the library he knows best. It's more comfortable than it looks. He might even spend the night here, dozing upright.

Wherever he sleeps, the coming day will dawn. He can just about imagine the wake, even the interment—but after that? He shakes his head. Scarcely a month until they board the *Kittiwake*, bound for the Brazilian port of Pará. It troubles him that a city should go by a nickname, the inhabitants preferring Pará—the river, the vast jungle state—to the official designation of Belém. As though the namesake of Bethlehem, with its Old World connotations of peaceful beasts and starlit reverence, is too civilized by half.

He tells himself it's what Iris needs—and, more to the point, what Walter wanted. *I'd be only too glad to write Agassiz myself and apprise him of our plans. Surely your august employer cannot fail to see the merit of such an expedition, having lately returned from the region himself* . . . Paul shuts his eyes. Sleep is nowhere near; in its stead, a memory, vivid as any dream.

His father's visitor was late. Paul was reading by the last of the day's light when they heard Mrs. Cosburn let someone in downstairs. He closed his book reluctantly; Uncas, last of the full-blood Mohicans, had finally appeared, startling the scout Hawk-eye with his voice. *Uncas is here! Who wishes Uncas?*

Paul lit the lamp as his father rose to open the door. A gentleman with moustaches like a tern's grey wings stood on the landing, panting from the climb.

"Quint," said Walter.

"Ash." Mr. Quint consulted his pocket watch, as though Walter and not he was responsible for the lateness of the hour. He made no pretense of acknowledging Paul, treatment Paul had come to expect from the better class of his father's clients. "I believe you have something to show me."

Walter wasn't without a sense of theatre. Having waited to unlock the tallboy doors, he did so with Quint breathing heavily at his side. Paul cleared a path, shifting the footstool, the low table with its tower of books. He stood wordlessly to one side as his father lifted down his treasure and knelt.

Like a monk with a manuscript, Walter unrolled the skin. First came the head—the eyeholes with their oblique black bars—then the parade of dark diamonds on amber ground. Foot after foot of it, nine and a half in all. Milk-white belly scales formed a fringe along either edge. The thorny tail bent up against the bookcase. Was there a room so narrow anywhere in Quint's house? Perhaps an attic chamber where the parlour-maid slept.

Quint too got down on his knees. "Anaconda?"

Paul caught his father's eye. Never mind the markings—reminiscent of forest floor rather than dappled shallows—the width was a dead giveaway. Anacondas were fat-bodied beasts, the heaviest serpents in the world. The skin laid out across their dusty carpet was that of a slender killer, one that favoured flesh-melting venom over brute, convoluted force.

Walter had to be careful; a humiliated collector was less likely to buy. "The length would suggest a constrictor, yes. What we have here, though, is *Lachesis mutus*, the bushmaster. Largest pit viper known to man." He trailed a finger down the skin's central ridge. "The prominent dorsal keel is distinctive—" he began, but Quint wasn't listening.

"Venomous?"

"Extremely. One this size could subdue an adult tapir in minutes. The fangs hinge forward—" Walter demonstrated with an index and pinky, a quick jab of his hand.

"And a man?"

"A man would have to suffer a little longer."

Quint's eyes glittered. "How'd you come by it?"

"Fellow I deal with regularly." Walter stood up. "He got it from a trader in Pará who had it off a Mura Indian."

That was a lie. Not that Paul knew the real story; when it came to the most exciting chapter of his life, his father was select-ive about which passages he shared. The bushmaster might have struck at Walter's trouser leg in the dark, or it might have come to him already lifeless, slung over the shoulder of some bright-eyed hunter in a breechcloth. Paul knew only that the skin had been with them since the beginning. It was as old as he was— older, like as not. Walter hadn't managed much collecting once he was burdened with an infant son.

Quint struggled to his feet. Nudging the white fringe of the skin with the toe of his shoe, he gave Walter the nod.

"Fetch me some brown paper, son," Walter said, "and a length of string."

While Quint stood over them, Paul helped his father roll and wrap the skin. Parcelled up like that, it might have been a joint from the butcher—something to grace Quint's table instead of his library wall. The men exchanged goods for cash and shook hands. Walter followed Quint out onto the landing.

"You'll let me know if you come across anything noteworthy," Paul heard Quint say.

"I will indeed." Walter stepped back in and closed the door, leaving his guest to make his own way down the pokey stairs. "Greedy fool."

"What's that, Father?"

"The skin of a bushmaster under his arm—a *bushmaster*, for pity's sake—and he wants to know what's next." Walter crossed to his desk and unearthed the money box from beneath a slide of scribbled notes. Snapping up the lid, he thrust Quint's bills in on top of what little they had left.

"That's what passes for the brains of the operation." He looked up, his gaze burning. "It doesn't matter how much you know. If you learned it in the field—if you actually left off polishing your cabinet glass long enough to meet a specimen in the wild—well, then, at best you're a servant, and at worst . . . at worst, you're some kind of bush-mad mercenary."

Paul nodded. He'd learned to hold his tongue when his father got going on the old grievance.

"Quint and his ilk hold the keys to every membership, every publication. You think they'd let a field man get his hands on a museum job?" He rapped on the desk. "Education, Paul. Credentials. It's the only way."

Paul felt the familiar response forming in his mouth. He was used to the unwholesome taste of it, to neither swallowing it entirely nor spitting it out. *But Father,* he didn't say, *there's more to it when it comes to you and me.* It was one thing to disappear into the jungle in the spirit of scientific endeavour, quite another to emerge from that rank wilderness with a half-breed son in your arms.

Walter let out a sigh. Crossing to the armchair, he took up his battered edition of Harlan's *Fauna Americana* and sat. It was a familiar sight, his father folded into the moss-green chair, head bent over the solace of a book. Paul experienced a sudden surge of misery—an urge to throw wide the door, take the stairs three by three and hit the cobbles at a run. He could follow his soles to the bottom of Race Street, push through the crowd of dark-eyed dray horses and pound along the echoing dock. He was a strong swimmer; Walter had seen to that. It was anyone's guess how far he'd get.

5

achel is surprised to see how much food Mrs. Pryce and her help have laid out. In the two years she's passed at Grafton Mansion, only a handful of visitors have come to call, and most of them had a skin or some other relic to sell. As ever, the housekeeper knows best. Come one o'clock, the mourners begin to arrive.

Rachel counts only three women among their number: two young ladies in floating muslin and feathered hats, and Bessie Marten in her good brown poplin—too hot for the weather and smelling faintly of her father's dockside shop. Rachel has visited the cramped establishment with her employers on more than one occasion. Old Joss Marten specializes in parrots and other popular birds, but now and then he gets his hands on something interesting with scales.

Of the men in attendance, roughly half have made their way up to Fourth Street from the docks. Not one of them takes a drink or a bite of food. They gather about the casket, hats gripped in their hands, while the diminutive Mr. Ingleby and his colleagues help themselves.

Rachel is on her way to fetch a cup of punch for Iris when she spots a man belonging to neither group. Clad in his broadbrim hat and collarless coat, her father stands still as a heron in the doorway's arch. Rachel's throat tightens. Somehow he's heard.

He scarcely knew Walter—their only meeting a formal discussion of terms—yet he's come to pay his respects.

She makes her way to him. "Papa."

"Rachel." His embrace is brief. "The woman at the door spoke of a bereavement."

She looks at him, confused. "Yes, Walter . . . Walter Ash. There was an accident."

"I didn't realize . . ." He looks past her. "May the Lord keep him."

Glancing round, she sees the wake through his eyes. Afternoon light picks out the decanters on the sideboard, the glasses in the gentlemen's hands. Even more damning is the glint of Iris's hair. Rachel has dressed it simply, in keeping with the occasion, but there's no disguising its glory.

Her father shakes his head. "I sometimes wonder if I have been derelict in allowing thee to live here."

Allowing me? She hasn't the heart to speak it. She can see her stepmother now, heavy with child, blocking the farmhouse doorway as she lifted her hand in farewell. Rachel kept her eyes forward as the cart pulled out of the yard, but Papa couldn't resist craning round for another look.

She takes a breath. "Won't thee come in?"

"I won't, no. What I have to say won't take long."

It seems natural to lead him back to the vestibule, sit beside him on the bench, but only a child would do such a thing. "Shall we go into the parlour?"

Again he shakes his head. "Rachel, this journey thee writes of, this *expedition*, I think it most ill-advised. Indeed, I came to tell thee I forbid it." He pauses. "Though I see now the matter has been taken from my hands."

"What do y—" She catches herself. "What does thee mean?"

"Thy employer. The Lord has put an end to his plans."

Behind her, quiet comes over the room. She turns to see Paul standing by the casket, Iris beside him in a high-backed chair. "Forgive me, Papa." She rises on her toes to kiss his cheek, then hurries to Iris's side.

"My father was a man of science," Paul begins, a murmur of approval rippling through the crowd. He looks around the room. "Those of you who knew Walter Ash will know the value he placed on research conducted in the field. Indeed, many of you have benefited from the knowledge he amassed during those researches—not to say the specimens themselves.

"You may have heard of the journey he made up the Amazon and Negro rivers in his youth. You may also be aware that, after an absence of two decades, he was planning to return." Paul clears his throat. "His friends will no doubt be gratified to learn that those plans were not in vain. The expedition will go ahead."

A second murmur travels the room—this one louder, and not nearly so benevolent in tone. Rachel places a hand on Iris's shoulder. Looking behind her, she finds what she expects: the doorway empty of her father's form.

The workingmen are first to take their leave, each one touching the flat of a palm to the casket before shaking Paul's hand, and Iris's, and even Rachel's, in farewell. One young fellow in sailor's slops presses what appears to be a bone toggle into Rachel's hand. "Nile crocodile," he says softly. "You pass it on to his missus." She nods her thanks, closing her fingers around the two-inch tooth.

Next comes Jim Sweeney, the boy Walter had hired. He

stands before Iris with reddened eyes, his coat pockets bulging with bread rolls.

"We'll be in sore need of your assistance when we return, Jim," Iris tells him. "In the meantime, why don't you come see me tomorrow about some work that needs doing in the atrium."

The boy brightens a little. "Yes, ma'am."

"Good lad. Now off you go."

The gentlemen take forever to leave. Rachel finds herself longing for the controlled formality of the funerals she attended as a child: a pair of designated elders to keep ostentation and idle chatter to a minimum, the body removed to the burial ground after no more than an hour.

Mr. Ingleby is among the last to depart, timing his leave-taking to a moment when Paul is drawn away from Iris's side. He flashes a tight smile at Rachel as he approaches, her proximity to the widow making it impossible for him to ignore her outright.

"My dear Mrs. Ash," he says, taking Iris's hand. "A terrible loss."

"Thank you, Mr. Ingleby."

"You will forgive the impertinence, I hope, of my speaking plainly."

Iris withdraws her hand. "Certainly."

"I fear that in your grief you fail to see things clearly."

"What can you mean?"

"Don't misunderstand me. It is most commendable that you should wish to fulfill your husband's plans, but to venture into the jungle alone—"

"I won't be alone."

"Yes, well, I'm sure the younger Mr. Ash brings a certain . . . native understanding to the endeavour—"

"The younger Mr. Ash is a graduate of Harvard University. Indeed, he is currently employed at their Museum of Comparative Zoology."

"Quite so, and yet I fear—"

"And that fear is unfounded." Rachel hears the tremor in her mistress's voice, a moment's weakness quelled. "I assure you, we will be among friends in the Amazon. My husband's friends."

PARÁ, BRAZIL

21ST OF AUGUST, 1867

6

Pará rests in a sheltered bay, some seventy miles upriver from the Atlantic coast. Its whitewashed houses may be capped with Mediterranean tile, but the surrounding jungle makes its presence known. Every ledge, every crevice is sprouting, every wall furred with moss. Riverfront buildings wear dark fringes—rows of birds that reveal themselves to be swallows when they rise. Above them, above Pará's many domes and spires, the looping vultures glide.

Paul can scarcely believe he's here, first one down the gangplank after the deckhands who made the ship fast. Standing on the pier, he feels the sea still rolling in his bones. All around him, men labour—sailors, stevedores of every build from slight to frightening, every shade from gold to bluest black. To a one, they pause in their work to watch Iris descend the plank.

Paul's heart beats in his throat as he reaches up to hand her down. An arm's-length deep in that muddy flow and a body would be lost to sight. What if he were to let his father's wife—father's widow—slip away?

Iris places her neat, slippered feet with care, keeping hold of the guide rope until she can take his hand. Above them, Captain Trent stands flanked by his officers on the quarterdeck, the wax in his white moustaches no longer holding the tips aloft. The *Kittiwake*'s crew have lined up along the bulwarks for one last look; three weeks at sea with Iris and they still haven't filled their eyes. Mourning becomes her, though her dress must be a burden in this heat. Paul leads her to the shade of the ship's hull.

Rachel is halfway down the gangplank by the time he returns. Sure-footed as a cat, she tucks her hand into his out of politeness. "Any sign of Senhor Felisberto?"

Paul shakes his head. He sent word ahead with the customs agent who came aboard as they lay at anchor; surely the news of their arrival must have reached his father's friend by now.

"You stay with Iris while they disembark the trunks," he tells Rachel. "I'll see what I can find out."

He hasn't gone far when he spots a middle-aged man in a cream linen suit hurrying down the pier. Paul feels his heart lift, then sink as the man turns abruptly and boards a long, dual-masted canoe. What now? Venture to the head of the pier? Beyond?

He makes it to the turmoil of the riverfront road. Bare-chested men shoulder burdens. Women with hair braided or swaying down their backs carry babies on their hips. A cart drawn by a gaunt, long-horned bullock rumbles past, its elderly driver yelping; an open buggy displays a pair of yellow-skinned beauties dressed for evening, one in violet, the other in cream. Everywhere—in the gaps between traffic, in ragged teams along the dusty verge—there are children. Dogs run and sit and lounge among them. One small, naked boy drapes his arm about a nanny goat's neck.

It's nothing like the village Paul imagined. They passed a few of them on their way upriver, dark-limbed figures walking on white beaches, clusters of huts that were charming from a distance, doubtless less so to those who called them home. It's been years since Paul and his father lived above the broom shop, but he hasn't forgotten the sound of rat-scuttle in the walls.

"Senhor Ash?"

Not a man's voice but a boy's. The child before him is perhaps eight years old, clad in loose white trousers and nothing else. His hair stands up like a crown of black feathers. His skin is only slightly darker than Paul's.

"Senhor Ash?"

"Sim," says Paul, "Senhor Ash."

The boy grins and produces a letter from his waistband. "Uma mensagem do Senhor Felisberto."

"Thank you. Obrigado." The paper is heavy, damp with the boy's sweat. Paul unfolds it to find the message is indeed addressed to himself and Iris—and is, of course, written in Portuguese. For a moment he's overcome with chagrin. Walter had done his best to pass on his outsider's grasp of the language; why had Paul taken so little of it in? *Sim, não, obrigado, bom dia, boa noite.* He might at least have followed Rachel's example and studied during the voyage here.

He looks at the boy. "English? Do you speak—"

"Não."

Paul nods. Nothing for it but to deliver up the note. "Come." He beckons to the boy. "Come along."

"Oh, Paul," Iris calls out as he approaches, "the mosquitoes have found me." She sits fanning herself on one of the trunks while Rachel draws a length of grey netting from the carpet bag. "The long gloves too, dearest."

Paul smiles at her. "Sweet blood."

She blinks and forces a smile in return. He must learn to think before he speaks; it's what his father would've said—what he did say on every picnic and collecting jaunt, when the inevitable bloodsuckers sought her out.

Rachel fixes the veil to Iris's hat.

"Who's this?" Iris asks from inside the gauzy shadow.

Paul realizes the boy has pressed in close beside him. "A messenger from Senhor Felisberto." He hands the note to Rachel, but instead of opening it, she addresses the boy.

"Bom dia."

He smiles. "Bom dia, senhorita."

"Meu nome é Senhorita Weaver." She presents Iris and Paul. "Senhora Ash e seu . . . seu filho, Senhor Ash."

The boy gives a little bow. "Muito prazer. Eu sou Benedito."

Rachel holds out her hand. "Muito prazer, Benedito."

Iris claps. "Rachel, how marvellous."

Rachel's accent is appalling—even Paul can tell as much—but she's making herself understood. "Indeed," he says. "Now perhaps you might turn your attention to the note."

"Yes, of course." She puzzles over the message for a long moment before stooping again to the carpet bag. Paul smiles to himself when she produces his father's Portuguese grammar. *Not quite bilingual yet.*

He gazes past her toward the bay, crowded with trading vessels and steamboats at anchor, canoes large and small. One great dugout, long enough to seat twenty men but paddled by three, appears little altered from the trunk that gave it form.

Beyond, a string of islands serves to create a sense of the river's opposite bank—an illusion for which Paul finds himself grateful. The breadth of the Rio Pará makes his head swim: thirty-six miles across at its mouth, twenty where he now stands. As often as not since they entered its stream, the far shore was nowhere to be seen. Best get used to it. The steamer will wind through the narrows of the Pará estuary to begin, but thereafter they'll be a week on the Amazon proper, the largest river in the world.

"It would seem Senhor Felisberto has been called away."

"What?"

Rachel looks up from the note. "There's a problem at his fazenda—his ranch. He's gone to the island of Marajó."

Paul feels a knot form in his stomach. "You must be mistaken."

"No." She shows him the line. "See, 'minha fazenda na Ilha de Marajó.'"

Benedito nods. "Está certo, Ilha de Marajó."

"I don't believe it." Paul looks to Iris, but his stepmother says nothing, her expression obscured by the veil. "What kind of a man promises to meet a party of guests who've never set foot in his country and sends an eight-year-old boy in his place?"

"You have," says Iris.

"What?"

"You've set foot."

"Iris, I was an infant. I hardly think—"

"It says here everything is in order," says Rachel. "Benedito will escort us back to the rocinha—"

"Where we're to do what, wander the place in search of our bedrooms? Find ourselves something to eat?"

"Oh, do be quiet." Iris stands. "Rachel just said the arrangements have been made. It's only two nights, Paul, don't fuss."

He stares at her, but it's impossible to tell if she meets his eye. He looks away, just as a two-man canoe passes close beneath the *Kittiwake*'s bowsprit. The paddler is a muscular young man of mixed blood. The girl in the bow looks too young to be a mother, yet she supports a baby astride one thigh. They watch him, three dark, unyielding gazes, until he finds he must lower his own.

"Benedito," Rachel says, "homens para ajudar e um—" She flips through the grammar. "—e uma carruagem."

"Sim, senhorita." Benedito spins on a bare heel and flies.

"Wait," Paul cries, "stop him!" He grabs Rachel by the wrist. "Tell him we need help . . . porters, we need some kind of cart—"

"It's all right." She smiles at him. "I just have."

7

Senhor Felisberto's rocinha is strangely welcoming, given how many of the home comforts it lacks. As far as Rachel can see, the large, single-storey dwelling contains neither carpets nor couches. Instead, it houses air. Thick white walls and high ceilings, windows open to the garden's hum. Benedito shows them down a wide corridor to their quarters, their steps echoing on the bare board floor. He opens the door to each bedchamber with a flourish—Paul's, then Iris's, then her own.

Left alone to change for dinner, Rachel sets her case down and surveys her room. The bed is conspicuous by its absence; in its stead, a white cotton hammock describes a curve between two brass hooks. What little furniture there is looks to be mahogany: a simple washstand, a desk and chair. Hanging over what must be the head of the hammock, a sleepy-eyed Madonna in oils.

The only other ornament sits on the window's deep sill. Rachel crosses for a closer look. The little clay beast is weighty, surprisingly cool in her hand. It could be the offspring of a hog and an elephant, its drooping nose a stunted trunk. She's seen one before in drawings; categorizing Iris's old sketchbooks was one of her first duties, starting with the record of her mistress's days spent haunting the Zoological Gardens during her London tour. Of course, Walter had encountered tapirs in the wild. His primary interest lay in their role as a prey species for both caiman and anaconda, yet he wrote of them with an admiration bordering on affection. The silent feet, the tender, shoot-seeking snout. Rachel tilts the figurine in the waning light before setting it back on the sill.

The garden she grew up with did little to prepare her for the one she looks out on now. Even at the height of harvest, Papa's vegetable plot showed the impress of his plans; the rocinha's grounds appear barely tamed, let alone tended. Shrubs and creepers vie for space beneath the trees. She recognizes the banana by its sheltering leaves, the orange by its fruit—though these are twice the size of any she's known. Several species have the look of figs. Others, squat with broad, glossy leaves, could be coffee. The vines are mighty, the atrium's hothouse varieties mere house cats to these muscular cousins with their split-leaved paws. The garden's scent, too, is part animal, an earthy, bewildering funk.

Only the sand path marks the territory as human—that and the great liana-draped wall of jungle it leads down to, a reminder of what the true wild can do. Palm trees tower at the verge. Beyond, in the forest proper, the odd monster stands. Emergent species, Walter called them—those few that are strong enough to break cover in the struggle for light.

It's tempting to gather her skirts, climb up alongside the little tapir and leap out into the green. She could be in the jungle in minutes, lay a hand to the great blade of a buttress root, perhaps even reach for a liana and climb. A foolish idea. She's meant to be getting ready for dinner.

By the time she's bathed her face and changed into her one dress not stiffened by sea spray, night is coming down. She returns to the window. The tropical twilight will take some getting used to. Evenings lasted along the Neshaminy back home—plenty of time to steal down to the creek and witness the changing of the animal guard. Often Papa came with her, content to sit for as long as she wanted, nodding at each creature she brought to his attention, occasionally pointing one out himself.

The signs were there, if only she'd allowed herself to see. Between chores—when he might have whistled for Patch and come to seek his daughter along the bank—he took to changing his milk-sour smock for his town coat and walking off down the lane. Time and again Rachel returned from the creek to find the unhappy spaniel tethered to the gate. Once, she was in time to see her father disappear around the bend in the road. There was something unfamiliar in his gait, a youthful spring that made her question for a moment whether it was really him.

She was sitting on the bank one afternoon when the sound of his step made her look round. "Papa," she said.

"Rachel."

No hand on her shoulder, no *What has thee to show me, my sprite?* She might have told him of the sleek young muskrat that had passed only minutes before. Instead, she returned her gaze to the water, the June light skipping off its back.

"Rachel," he said again, "thee knows how much thy mother did for us."

Rachel flashed on her mother's hands, small but powerful, rarely still. "I do."

"Eight years she's been gone."

"I know it."

"Thee does." It wasn't like him to circle a point. "I believe thee is acquainted with Annie Coffin—"

She looked up sharply.

"I need someone about the farm, Rachel."

"Thee has me about the farm."

He lowered his eyes. "I need a wife."

Rachel found handholds in the grass. She'd known eight years under her mother's watchful eye—not a moment free from work or worship—followed by eight years of peace. And now Annie Coffin, youngest of only three recorded female ministers in the Monthly Meeting, and as firm in her convictions as any Friend. Not so unlike the late Isobel Weaver, Rachel saw suddenly. Annie was black-eyed, black-haired, where Rachel's mother had been fair, but the two of them shared an unnerving straight-backed stance.

When had Papa recognized it? How long had he been watching Annie mount the stairs to the Meeting House, contriving to cross paths with her in town? The answer was clear: for as long as Rachel had been missing him. Stuffing cast-off feathers into her apron pocket with nobody to show.

Papa was waiting. As Rachel thought of what she might say to him, a shiver in the grass caught her eye—the muskrat slipping back along its path. She kept its presence to herself, saying nothing of the initial appearance, nothing of the return.

The knock makes her jump. Crossing to the door, she opens it to find Iris and Paul waiting with Benedito, bathed in the glow of his lamp. She follows the little party out to the verandah, where a candlelit table stands crowded with platters and bowls.

"Isn't this lovely?" Iris settles into the chair Paul has drawn out for her. He nods and skirts round to the far end, leaving Rachel to slip in along the wall.

It's a curious feast. The roast is an odd, angular shape, as though it was freed from the bone with an axe. Instead of potatoes, it comes with fragrant, reddish rice and a dish of what appears to be sawdust. Farinha, Rachel realizes—her first encounter with the Amazonian staple. Bananas she's seen before, though rarely; tonight's come in fried medallions. Other, less familiar fruits are served fresh.

"Where's Benedito?" Paul asks.

Iris looks round. "He was here a moment ago."

"Will he be back, do you imagine, or are we meant to begin?"

As if in answer, a woman steps through the doorway bearing a plate of oranges, some whole, others cut into wedges and wheels. Her long, softly kinked hair is streaked with grey, gathered in a girl's loose tail. Her colourless shift reveals a neck and slender arms that might be carved from some dark heartwood.

"Boa noite, senhora," Rachel says, eliciting a smile.

"Boa noite." She sets the plate down between Rachel and Iris, nudging it into the last free space. "Bom apetite."

"Obrigado," Iris says.

"Obrigada," Paul corrects her, and again the woman smiles, this time revealing a gold eye tooth. She takes a step back, turns and is gone.

"Well, that's a relief," Iris says after a moment. "I was beginning to think poor Benedito had to cook for us along with everything else."

"God forbid." Paul rises to carve. "I presume this is beef." He saws a chunk from one puckered, well-done end and lays it on a plate. Rachel passes the portion along to Iris.

"That's far too much."

Rachel looks at her. "Iris, you need to keep up your strength."

Paul lays a slab on Rachel's plate. "I suppose she's keeping the good cuts back for the master, whenever he should see fit to return."

Iris's fork clatters against her plate rim. "Will you stop going on about it."

"I'm not," Paul says stiffly, resuming his seat.

Rachel tucks a serving spoon into the rice. "Rice, Iris?"

Iris ignores her. "We've been looked after, haven't we?"

"After a fashion."

"No, not *after a fashion*," Iris says as Rachel spoons rice onto her plate, "perfectly well. That's enough, Rachel, I'm not a longshoreman." She reaches for the wine. "Do you plan to carp about the food on the steamer too? And what about when we're on the Rio Negro?"

"Yes, well, hopefully Senhor da Silva takes his commitments seriously."

"Of course he will. You know your father held him in high regard."

Paul stuffs a chunk of meat into his mouth. Rachel says nothing, forking two slices of fried banana onto her plate before slipping one onto Iris's.

"In any case," Iris adds, "he's family."

Paul stops chewing. The quiet that follows is anything but, alive with the night's whirr.

"My first taste of farinha," Rachel says, sprinkling the toasted manioc flour over her rice. "I was half hoping for salt pirarucu, Walter wrote about it so often—"

The look on Paul's face silences her. "You've read the notebook, then."

"Of course she's read it," says Iris. "She's the one who thought to bring it along."

"I see. Well, that explains why I couldn't find it."

"I'm sorry," says Rachel. "Iris asked me to pack any books that might prove useful. Shall I fetch it for you?"

"Don't be silly, Rachel, he can get it later." Selecting a fat orange from the plate, Iris cradles it in both hands. "Remember what he said when Mrs. Pryce brought home those oranges? Poor dear, she thought he'd be so pleased."

Rachel knows the answer, but it's plain the question isn't meant for her. She watches Paul out of the corner of her eye.

"You call that an orange?" he says finally.

Iris nods. "One day, I'll show you the real thing."

8

Nothing stands between Paul and the garden. Beyond his unglazed window, pale moths ride the darkness like scraps of ash, fireflies like cinders from the same unseen blaze. At the foot of the yard, grades of shadow abut the jungle's black. Palm trees mark the border, grey trunks touched with starlight, mops of jagged fronds.

The night is far from still. Walter wasn't exaggerating when he spoke of the racket frogs can make—quack and clatter, hoot and boom. Now a three-note avian cry. Now a distinctly mammalian scream. Paul can't possibly sleep with the window open, yet the thought of closing the shutters calls up a panicky stricture in his chest. He closes them all the same.

Easing out of his shoes, he finds his socks are wet through. He removes his waistcoat, shirt and breeches, folding their damp weight over the back of a chair. The hammock is alien to him. After a moment's consideration, he moves the lamp from the washstand to the bedside chest, then turns and lowers himself into the soft sling. Lying back, he swings his legs up with a little push.

Iris is right, he must cease longing for the familiar. The known world fell away the moment the *Kittiwake* set sail: every night, the stars grew stranger; as they neared the equator, light began to rise from the depths. Iris too was changed. He'd anticipated some measure of melancholy on her part—had gone so far as to dread it—but she was rarely still for long enough to appear grieved. Only Rachel remained constant. She was never far from Iris's side, swishing paintbrushes in a jar, looking up from the grammar and mouthing a foreign phrase.

The hammock holds him gently, soothing the last of the ocean-upset in his blood. He must admit the house is pleasant. He feels vaguely foolish, recalling the sense of apprehension that all but overwhelmed him on the ride here. The buggies had bucked like a pair of young goats, causing Iris to jostle against him. He kept an eye on the lead vehicle, the luggage lashed to its rack; with every jolt, he pictured the collection jars shattering, preservative spirits soaking the straw.

His doubts only doubled once they left the populous streets and tree-lined avenues behind. At its outskirts, Pará bore a closer resemblance to the village he'd imagined: families crowded beneath tilting porch roofs, gardens run riot over fences let fall. Livestock roamed the red sand road. At one point the driver hauled back on the reins, sparing the herd of pigs he'd flushed from the roadside scrub. For a time a mottled dog ran alongside them, something rat-sized and wriggling in its jaws.

At length the shantytown gave way to rocinhas, some of which presented a well-tended aspect, while others showed no more than a glimpse of roof tiles among the green. Paul felt a wave of relief wash over him when they drew up in front of the long, embowered verandah of Senhor Felisberto's country home.

Benedito makes no sound with the door latch. "Senhor?"

Paul starts. "Yes? What is it?"

The boy comes to stand by his hammock. Dark-eyed, smiling, he holds out Walter's notebook. Paul accepts it with a nod, the yellow calfskin familiar to his fingers. He sets it aside on the chest.

Benedito glances up at the wall. "Osga."

Following his gaze, Paul sees nothing but a patch of rough plaster—until his eyes adjust. The gecko is small, scarcely a hand's breadth from nose to tail. Its skin is ghostly.

The boy holds up a small bottle stopped with a cork. "Para sua rede, senhor."

Rede—that's hammock, a word Paul didn't realize he knew. Benedito uncorks the bottle and tips it against his palm. He holds his hand to his nose, then shows it to Paul. The skin is slick with oil, its scent so astringent Paul can feel it in his teeth. The boy grasps the hammock rope and rubs it, a cloud of bitter aroma settling around Paul's head. As he proceeds to coat the far rope, Paul finds the words he needs. "Por que?"

Benedito slips the cork back in the bottle neck, thumbing it tight. He thinks for a moment, then makes a puppet of his hand. It lands on the hammock rope and scuttles down; reaching the section treated with oil, it rears up, finger-forelegs waving in an arachnid display.

Paul swallows. "Aranhas," he says, his father's voice echoing in the back quarter of his skull. He definitely remembers more than he knows.

Benedito lets the hand drop to his side. "Sim, senhor, aranhas, escorpiões, formigas ..."

So, not only spiders. *Escorpiões*—that's clear enough. And *formigas*—members of the family Formicidae, like as not. Paul can recall only common names: fire ants, bullet ants, army ants. Thank heaven for the boy and his bitter oil.

Paul points to the bottle. "Senhora Ash, Senhorita Weaver ...?"

"Certo." Benedito makes for the door. "Boa noite, senhor."

"Boa noite."

As quietly as he came, the boy is gone. Paul reaches for the lamp to blow it out. His hand finds the notebook instead.

He would have packed it himself, given the chance. Or would he? In truth, he made only a cursory search—a quick pass over Walter's bookshelves, a sweep of his untidy desk drawers. He shakes his head, remembering how, as a boy, he'd pored over his father's account, sifting in vain for traces of his mother, the seed of himself. Walter spoke of her rarely and only in the most general of terms. *Your mother was Brazilian. Your mother died when you were small.* Paul was Benedito's age before it occured to him that he might ask for more.

It was an afternoon like any other, the pair of them reading in companionable quiet, when he rose on shaky legs. His stomach crowded up against his heart. "What was her name?"

Walter stared at the book in his hands. "Zuleica."

Paul was hurting him—he could see as much—but he kept on. "How did you meet her?"

"She was . . . her sister was married to a man I knew. They were *ribeirinhos*—river people."

"Indians."

Walter looked at him. "No, they were *mameluco*. Mixed."

"How long were you—"

"Not long. Less than a year." Walter stood up. "Time we were thinking of supper." He looked about himself, as though the meal might be something he had to catch. "Are you hungry?"

Paul weighed his response. "Starving."

"Good."

———

The notebook lies against Paul in the hammock. He takes a breath and stands it up on his breastbone. It opens to a page twenty deep.

September 4th, 1844, Ilha de Marajó
We have been camped ashore for three nights now, one day's paddle from Senhor Felisberto's fazenda up a winding stream. The night monkeys whose territory we have invaded are quite tame, descending to play upon our hammocks once the camp falls still. My own rede has become a favourite, it being fixed to the tree in which the family makes their den.

Neither so large as *Mycetes*, the howling monkey, nor so diminutive as any of the marmosets, this nocturnal species measures up to fourteen inches in the body, a length doubled by its tail. Having observed them by the light of the overnight fire, I can report that they are creatures of charming aspect. The alternate name of owl monkey is well earned, all features being secondary to the yellow saucers of their eyes. Their presence at our little camp is most welcome, for in addition to providing diversion throughout the night, they are possessed of senses keener than our own. At the approach of any significant predator, they oblige us with a chorus of eerie hoots.

Last night they set up such a row as to have us reaching for our guns. On Senhor F.'s orders, our trio of Indian paddlers carried torches down to the beach. They returned to sound the all-clear, but the morning told a different tale. Not ten yards from our canoes, we came upon the fresh pug marks of *Leopardus onça*, the American tiger or jaguar.

The natives call it simply onça, a subtle word spoken with reverence and often a curious note of pride. Since my arrival in this country I have seen skins at market, both spotted and black, as well as teeth and claws, but I have yet to glimpse the creature itself. Would that we might remain here longer in the hopes of such a sighting, but Senhor F.'s business calls him back to Pará. In any case, Senhor Chryostomo will set sail for the interior within the fortnight, and I would be a fool to risk losing my place on board.

Movement catches Paul's eye. The osga has stirred on the wall above him, lifting a forefoot and setting it back down. Closing the notebook, he lays it on the bedside chest.

Imagine, a hammock strung up in the open jungle. His father—a young man, no older than Paul is now—lies back in the firelight. Above him, owl-faced monkeys peer out of their tree hole. The beach isn't far; soon one of them will catch wind of the jet-black onça emerging from the stream.

9

Benedito makes a questionable guide. He threads a path through the busy streets, continually disappearing from view. Hurrying after him, the three of them garner stares—from children at iron balconies, men in doorways, old women on painted chairs. Not an hour past breakfast and already the heat is oppressive. It may have been a mistake leaving the buggy at rua de Mangabeiras; Rachel's grey gingham is damp, but Paul and Iris must really be suffering—he in his dark jacket and waistcoat, she in her bombazine.

All of Pará seems bound for the river. Paul takes Iris's arm, leaving Rachel to fall back in the face of every buggy or bullock-drawn cart. The market has yet to come into view, but she can smell it now: fruit and flowers, river mud and blood and filth. Beneath it all, a twisting undercurrent of fish.

"Benedito!" Paul calls out. "Damn the boy." But the curse is premature. Not twenty paces ahead, their guide pops up above the throng.

Iris gives Rachel a strained smile. "Saved."

Benedito beckons them on, hopping down from his handcart perch as they draw near. "O mercado," he announces.

"Bom," Rachel answers for the party. "Obrigada, Benedito."

"Tell him to slow down, can't you?" says Paul.

She searches her mind. "Mais . . . mais devagar, Benedito. Por favor."

The boy looks at her quizzically, so she walks her fingers quickly across her palm, then again at half the pace.

"Ah, *devagar*," he repeats, softening the *d* to a *j*. "Certo."

Iris slaps at her neck; the riverfront mosquitoes have found her again. While Rachel reaches up to help arrange the veil, Benedito hops from foot to foot.

"Venha, senhorita, venha."

Rachel has imagined a wilder version of the markets she knows—laneways defined by rows of covered stalls—but Benedito has delivered them to the head of a long pier. Laden canoes line its flanks, everything from two-man dugouts to twenty-foot vessels with two and three masts. Those nearest sit high and dry, beached by the receding tide.

Benedito leads with greater attention now, the three of them snaking after him through the jostle and din. All but the poorest of boats support shelters of thatch, shady havens crowded with children, grandparents, dogs. Several of the flimsy roofs double as stages for birds; Rachel spots a duo of jewel-green parrots, a banana-beaked toucan, a stalking macaw. A white heron stands guard over a monkey with a friar's black fringe and beard. The monkey crouches, tied by the neck to a wooden block. When Rachel catches its eye, it whistles fiercely, lashing its tail.

Benedito halts before every display of merit: baskets of clambering, hairy-legged crabs; an electric eel wound like a turban in a tub. Fish are everywhere, some of them familiar from Walter's books. Rachel recognizes a bushy-mouth catfish with tentacled lips, strings of toothy piranha, a five-foot monster that can only be the fabled pirarucu. She expects her mistress to call for her sketchbook, but Iris simply stands gazing at the massive fish. When the youth who guards it raises a blade the length of his forearm, Benedito intervenes. Everything beyond *Senhora* and *peixe* is lost on Rachel, but the exchange appears amicable enough. The young vendor lays down his knife, resuming his seat with a shrug.

"My God," Paul says as they move on, "must they always be waving those machetes?"

"Tresados." Rachel corrects him before she can think better of it.

"Surely you don't expect him to use a fillet knife on a fish like that." Iris stops short before a basket of spiky fruits. "Goodness, what are these?"

While she and Paul pause for a closer look, Benedito skips ahead, leading Rachel on to a dugout some dozen boats along. At first it makes no sense—he's brought her to an old woman whose only wares appear to be lengths of cotton cloth. Then she sees. A narrow plank canoe floats tethered to the dugout's stern. In it, a small Indian boy sits surrounded by turtles of varying sizes, from plate to platter. His backrest is an empty shell, longer by half than the biggest of the living catch.

Rachel points to herself, then to the boy's canoe. "Eu . . . eu vou?"

Benedito nods. After securing the old woman's permission, he hops down lightly into her dugout. Glancing back, Rachel spots the top of Iris's black bonnet, still a good way behind. She takes Benedito's hand and steps down. "Obrigada, senhora."

"De nada." The old woman shuffles to one side on her bench.

The boy grins widely as they board his canoe. He clears a space, stacking turtles like living flagstones. An inch of river water has seeped in through the little boat's seams. Rachel's leather slippers are soaked.

"Bom dia, senhorita."

"Bom dia." She wishes she had the language to continue. *Did you catch all these yourself?*

"Tartaruga," the boy says, patting the nearest one.

Rachel nods. "Tartaruga. Lindo."

"Linda," Benedito says behind her.

"Linda."

In fact, they aren't all that beautiful as turtles go, mud grey and unadorned, apart from the odd butter-coloured facial splotch.

"Tartaruga?" Rachel says again, pointing to the giant shell, and the boy nods vigorously.

"Quer tocar?" he says.

Tocar—that's touch, isn't it? Benedito nudges the back of her arm, so she takes hold of the gunwales and steps over a stray turtle to crouch beside the boy. He smiles shyly as she lays a hand to the shell.

The plates of the carapace are smooth, fused with scarcely a seam. Rachel runs a finger along the gently scalloped edge. *Tartaruga.* She knows the creature by a different name, etched alongside another species beneath the portrait she's come to know. *Homo sapiens, Podocnemis expansa*—Walter and his happy find, the unwieldy specimen that caught his beloved's eye.

Walter had mounted the shell on the library wall, and there it remained until the display case in the main corridor was complete. When it came time to stock the long glassed-in cabinet, he and Iris chose carefully from the collection, selecting those pieces most likely to facilitate a passage between worlds. Carrying *Podocnemis expansa* downstairs, Walter struck a pose beneath the portrait and cleared his throat—one of the few times Rachel saw him play for a laugh.

Once Iris had positioned the shell just so, Walter closed the cabinet lid. "Ilha das Tartarugas," he murmured.

Iris looked at him, something beyond the customary attentiveness in her gaze. Rachel lowered her eyes, watching the pair of them reflected in the glass.

"It's the sand that draws them," Walter said after a moment. "The whole head of the island, nothing but rippled, pristine sand. It burns your feet by day, but by night it's like . . . like walking on moonlight."

Rachel had never heard him speak in such a manner. Taking her cue from Iris, she held her tongue.

"We built a platform," he went on. "A sort of tree house where the beach met the jungle's edge." He shook his head. "You can't imagine. Thousands of them hauling up out of the river and digging, depositing their hundred-some eggs . . ." He trailed off, his eyes fastened on the shell.

"I can't wait to see it," Iris said softly.

"Yes." He turned to her. "Yes, you must."

Rachel has forgotten herself. How long has she been hunkered here, stroking the tartaruga's shell? She rises too quickly, coming close to stepping on a turtle's back.

"I beg your pardon. Desculpa."

"De nada, senhorita." The boy's face falls; clearly he was hoping for a sale. He takes up a shallow shell, dips it into the puddle about his feet and bails.

Rachel turns, stepping carefully along the canoe's centre line. Benedito too appears disappointed, or at least confused. "Não ontem," she says, but this only deepens the furrow in his brow.

"Não hoje?" he offers.

Of course, *ontem* is yesterday. She nods.

Following him back along the old woman's dugout, Rachel reasons with herself. It makes no sense to stockpile specimens that can be had at market when the expedition is barely under way. More to the point, if she were to carry back one of the tartarugas, Iris might take a fancy to visit the boy herself. Which would mean seeing the shell that's a twin to the one she knows.

As Benedito hands Rachel back onto the pier, she catches sight of Iris and Paul standing before a wall of bamboo cages. Rachel can read the fatigue in Iris's shoulders. She presses through the crowd to her side.

"There you are," says Paul.

"Rachel, dear." Iris turns away from the bird vendor, who throws up his hands. Her face is pale; beneath her eyes, the soft shadows Rachel hasn't seen since the *Kittiwake* cast off from Philadelphia's docks.

"You shouldn't wander off like that—"

"Oh, Paul, I'm sure she was perfectly safe." Iris slips her arm through Rachel's.

"I'm afraid we'll have to start back, dearest. I'm a little tired."

"Of course, Iris."

"Did you come across anything of interest?"

Rachel has never lied to her mistress, not once. Looking down on the soaked noses of her slippers, she measures her words. "Nothing we haven't already seen."

10

Paul wakes from his siesta pleasantly surprised; he'd doubted his chances of sleeping in this heat. Summer nights above the broom shop, he would flop and twist in his sweat-drenched drawers while his father snored in the nearby cot. Once, when he'd finally managed to drop off, his body made its way to the outer room on its own. He woke to find himself bunched on the sill of their only window, his hands thrust into the passing breeze.

Planting his palm on the wall beside him, he pushes off, enjoying the hammock's lilt. The osga is tucked away in a high corner, the exact position it held when Paul lay down over an hour ago. It could almost be a shadow, its day-skin grubby grey. Watching it, Paul feels a familiar twinge. If Walter were here, he'd carry a chair to the corner and stand on it for a closer look— or, more likely, reach up with a broom and dislodge the sleeping creature so that he might examine it in hand.

Paul stills the hammock, swings his feet out and stands. At the washstand, he splashes his face, running his fingers through his hair. The mirror returns a face browner than he's seen it in years. As a boy he suffered red-Indian taunts upon his return to school each fall; being his father's helper meant endless hours spent tramping in the summer sun. At Harvard, he devoted more time to his desk. When he did venture into the field, he took care to wear a hat.

The thought has him reaching for his panama. Angling the pale, finely woven brim across his eyes, he admires the maturing effect. Iris might have bought one here for half the Philadelphia price, but she'd insisted he would be glad of it during the voyage. In the end, though, no hat could have stopped the equatorial sun glancing back at him off the sea. The results signify less in this country, where the races have long been marrying across the lines. Still, he wonders how dark he'll get.

Turning away from his reflection, he considers the waistcoat and jacket hanging on the back of the chair. The thought of putting them on again makes his skin crawl. Surely Iris won't mind him going in his shirtsleeves; it's only a ramble down the forest track.

In the corridor, he meets Rachel coming out of Iris's room.

"Is everything all right?"

She sets down her rucksack, drawing the door closed. "Iris isn't coming. She says she's tired."

"Still?"

Rachel says nothing.

"Well, best she get some rest. We're due to leave port early."

"She wants us to go."

"I beg your pardon?"

"Iris. She insists you and I go. I offered to sit with her in the garden, but she said it was time we got out into the jungle." She toes the rucksack, producing a soft clink. Collecting jars. Somehow he's been thinking of this afternoon's walk as simply that—a walk.

"Benedito's waiting on the verandah," Rachel adds.

Paul swallows his disappointment. Iris will be brighter once they board the steamer and get properly under way. "Right." He starts off down the corridor.

"Wait a moment."

He turns to see Rachel hiking the rucksack onto her slim shoulders.

"Here." He walks back. "Let me take that."

"It's all right, it isn't heavy."

Her gaze, grey and steady, registers as a rebuke. He glances away. "Shall we?"

Tasked with leading them away from town, Benedito maintains a mature, unwavering pace. The man apparent in the boy—an effect heightened by the tresado hanging in its scabbard at his side. Paul's knife is more modest, a six-inch hunting blade fixed to his belt. Walter's shotgun rests snugly against his back, bird-shot in one barrel, buckshot in the other, in case they should meet with anything large.

As they pass beyond the garden fence, the road dwindles to a two-man track. Trees tower to either side, the verge an impenetrable mantle of briars and vines. Rachel walks wordlessly beside him, her face hidden by her bonnet's brim. Bird calls fall across the quiet. The path is busy with beetles and ants.

After perhaps a quarter of an hour, the track begins to rise. Here the forest is younger, closer in stature to the ones Paul knows. Shrubs give way to a meadowy margin. Up ahead, Benedito walks softly, his eyes in the grass.

"Quite the little tracker," Paul says.

Rachel nods. "I asked him to keep an eye out."

Just then Benedito freezes, halting the breath in Paul's chest. A second more and the boy pounces—a brief, bewildering scuffle, Benedito on his knees, then his belly, then leaping wildly to his feet. A lizard shoots across the track in a blur of grey and green—a foot and a half long, and most of that tail. It dives into the grass, Benedito plunging after it. Again it breaks cover, this time tearing away down the track.

With Benedito in pursuit and gaining, the lizard takes to its hind legs, suddenly doubling its speed. As the track curves left, carrying hunter and hunted out of sight, Rachel lets out a laugh. It's a startling sound, one Paul can't remember having heard.

"Did you see its colouring?" she says, turning to show him her face. "The head and forelegs just like stone, but the rest of it brilliant green." Her eyes are shining. "Some blue in there too, don't you think?"

Paul nods, though his own impression is hopelessly vague.

"It put me in mind of a racerunner," she says. "Those sketches Iris did on Fenwick Island. Different markings, of course, but—"

"*Cnemidophorus.*"

She nods, expectant, but Paul has nothing to add. He has no idea whether the genus is represented on the southern continent. "Hadn't we better catch up?"

Rounding the bend, they come upon Benedito stooped over a clump of tall, pale green grass. He holds up his empty hands. "Capim navalha."

"What's he saying?" says Paul.

"I'm not sure."

"Desculpa," the boy says as they draw near, addressing himself, as ever, to Rachel.

"It's all right, Benedito, tudo bem." She reaches to part the grass, but Benedito catches her by the wrist.

"Não toque, senhorita." He mimes a slashing motion across her forearm. "Capim navalha." He releases his hold with a lopsided smile.

"I see." She glances at Paul. "I think it's some kind of razor grass."

"So I gathered."

She watches him for a moment before turning back to the boy. "Vamos, Benedito?"

"Vamos. A picada não é longe."

If Rachel understands, she doesn't offer to share. In any case, the boy's meaning soon becomes clear. Some hundred paces on, he draws his tresado and hacks at a fretwork of creepers, revealing a shaded path.

From here they must travel single file. Paul motions for Rachel to go first—what kind of man lets a woman bring up the rear? A loose strap on her rucksack bobs like a friendly tail. As the forest closes in, he fights a ridiculous urge to grab it and hold on.

Before long he becomes conscious of a slight decline. Soon a carpet of wolf's-foot clubmoss cushions their steps, the air cooling as the understorey thins. Now each tree claims a broad footprint for itself and its host of hangers-on—vines and spiked bromeliads, enormous, raggedy ferns. The canopy retreats to a dizzying height. Looking up, Paul catches glimpses of blue-white sky, some of which prove to be butterflies on second glance. He's read about creeping, climbing trees, but no words could have prepared him for the mess of woody cables that meets his gaze. Coils hug branches; lines and spirals describe countless light-seeking paths. It's like the life's work of a mad giant, an obsessive, territorial monster armed with a ball of twine.

Rachel and the boy have moved on. Paul hurries to catch up, stopping short as Benedito once again holds up his hand. A stone's throw from the path, a tree has fallen, carving a slim canyon of light. The site fairly glows with growth, shoots and saplings, a sprawl of flowering vines. Benedito wends his way toward it, ducking under woody snarls. Rachel follows. After a moment, so does Paul.

Leaf litter deadens their footfalls. Every step sends up a breath of vegetable rot. Paul treads on leathery bean pods the length of his arm, snow-white petals drifted down from blooms too high to see. Boyhood lessons crowd his mind: tree roots are favoured hideouts; never step over a log without checking what lies coiled on the far side. How can Benedito stand to go barefoot? Sweltering in his boots, Paul shakes off visions of fangs sinking into his calf.

At the edge of the sunlit alley, the boy stands and points. There, on a dark limb of deadfall, a lick of copper light. The lizard is perhaps eight inches long, black legs and tail, its dorsum the source of that new-penny glow. A species of skink, like as not, given the serpentine body and shimmering skin. And not just one, Paul realizes. There, on a mound of leaves, and there, emerging from a crevice on a sun-washed trunk. He counts a dozen of the glinting creatures gathered to bask.

Benedito takes a step, hands flexing at his sides. Neither Paul nor the target anticipates the spring. This time there's no scuffle, no chase. Benedito rises victorious, wriggling skink in hand.

Rachel shrugs off the rucksack, retrieving a basket with a fitted lid. While she and Benedito secure the prize, Paul runs an eye over the narrow clearing. The other skinks have taken cover—not a flicker to be seen. He can hear them, though, a mouselike, rustling retreat through the litter. They're nowhere near as fast as the racerunner, or whatever it was. Perhaps Paul might catch one of his own.

Years have passed since he last darted after lizards, but he can still remember the rush of fearful pleasure when he got one—and, more common, the wave of shameful relief when he missed. The first—or the first he can recall—was also a skink, striped white and brown, but otherwise similar to Benedito's catch. Six years old and pleased as a retriever to be aiding in the day's work, Paul snatched the dark whip of its tail. In a flash, the skink was free of it, scurrying stump-ended beneath a log.

Walter was surprised to find his son upset. "Never mind, Paulo," he said, crouching down, "you'll get the knack." He took the tail from Paul's fingers. "And he'll grow another one, good as new."

Paul did his best to smile. He hadn't the words to explain the shock of the appendage snapping free, the life still tangible, kicking in his fist.

In the time it takes Paul to remember, Benedito captures a second skink. As he tucks it into the basket, a third specimen emerges from the litter not far from the tip of Paul's boot. Rachel stoops in a flash and grabs it. Silent regarding his own triumphs, Benedito lets out a happy cry.

Again she laughs, and this time the sound grates on Paul's nerves. "I think that'll do," he says, turning back the way they came.

Back on the path, he finds the way forward less definite than he'd supposed. After an uncertain fork, he stands aside to let Benedito and Rachel pass. Falling in line, he can just make out a low scratching coming from the rucksack. He wonders if she can feel them in there, striving against her slender back. He shakes his head. He must be getting hungry. It's difficult to judge in the canopied gloom, but given when they left the rocinha, it can't be long until dinner. Until dark.

The path begins a slow curve, a sign, he hopes, of their return to the main. A slight incline encourages him further, and soon he can almost smell the relative open of the track.

The path has all but healed over at the join. Again the boy draws his blade. Motioning for Rachel and Paul to stand back, he swings rhythmically at the heavy skein. Light spills through a low opening, cut to its creator's height. Rachel ducks and follows, leaving only Paul.

As he stoops beneath the ragged fringe, a vine catches at his hat. Emerging into the light, he reaches up and feels something slip through his fingers. Not vegetable, he understands, *animal*. It slithers across his shoulder, its skin a cool ribbon at his throat.

Rachel whirls at the sound of his scream. Eyes wide, she lunges. He knows a moment of the noose—a second's pure terror—before she flings the snake aside. Benedito tracks its flailing arc; in seconds he's after it, stabbing his thin arm into the grass.

"Careful, Benedito!" Rachel cries as Paul feels the blood leave his head. Squeezing his eyes shut, he bends forward, hands on his knees. Rachel's hand at his shoulder threatens to topple him. "Is thee all right?"

"Yes. Yes, of course."

"Why don't you sit down."

He takes a breath, opens his eyes and straightens. "I'm fine."

The boy joins them, holding up the snake. It's a delicate thing, striped with candy-stick colours: peppermint green and white, butterscotch brown. Benedito grips it expertly behind the head, supporting its rigid length. Its dark mouth gapes in a defensive display.

"Ela não vai te machucar."

"I think he's saying it's harmless." Bending over the ruck-sack, Rachel produces a folded canvas sack. "Is that right, Benedito, é . . . é mal?"

"Não, não é venenosa."

"It's not dangerous." She holds open the sack.

Paul nods as the boy bends the snake and drops it in. He can see now it's nothing but a common vine snake—hunter of small lizards and frogs, its bite no more trouble than the sting of a bee.

Iris has her sketchbooks specially bound—heavy linen paper with no watermark, an easy spread at the spine. Rachel inscribed a fresh one on the flyleaf before she and Paul set out. *Iris Ash, August 22nd, 1867, City of Pará.* She finds it lying on the garden path, not far from the hammock her mistress occupies. Brushing away a thin column of ants, she turns to the first page, the second, the third. Not so much as a mark.

Perhaps Iris is still recovering from the voyage here. Rachel had never seen her so nervy: she laughed too easily and too often with men of every rank—a sudden, brittle trill unfamiliar to Rachel's ears. Like a child, she clapped at every wonder the sea offered up, from the black back of a porpoise to the eerie wave-light of the tropical night. The first time a shower of flying fish arced over the bow, she let out a startled scream.

The shark delighted her no end. It was an impressive speci-men, dragged up thrashing on a heavy line in a bid to divert the loveliest passenger on board. The crew squabbled over who would bait the hook, who would tear it from the creature's jaw. Iris cheered as they clubbed it to stillness, then embarked on a fevered study of its form.

Paul kept his distance, observing the proceedings with his back to the rail, but Rachel hovered close. Once she got over the shark's beauty, she did her best to view it with what Walter had called a naturalist's eye. What she saw was a creature shaped by the hunt—snout like an arrowhead, pectoral fins cut like a cliff swallow's wings. It wore the sea's dual nature of darkness and light: cobalt back to blend with the depths, pearly belly to disappear against the surface gleam.

She expected her mistress to take her time getting those colours right. Instead, Iris bashed off countless studies in pencil, flipping the page every few minutes, shifting her camp stool to begin anew. A half-hearted attempt to render the tail seemed to finish her. She sat deflated for several moments before looking up as though someone had sounded a bell. "Paul," she cried, "fetch your scalpel."

On the surface of it, there was nothing odd about the request. Walter had facilitated Iris's artistic inquiry with countless dissections; now it was his son's turn. Though possessed of sufficient skill, Paul demonstrated none of his father's flare. Iris appeared blind to the grim determination with which he approached the task. She paid no notice when, in spite of a smooth sea, he rose and strode swiftly aft, bending to be sick over the rail.

11

The gangplank is a thin tongue of wood—no guide ropes, no rails. Rachel watches from the pier as Paul leads Iris aboard. He walks backwards up the plank, coaxing his stepmother as though she were a skittish mare—and there is indeed something equine in the figure Iris cuts: the round of her bustle under glossy black silk, her veiled head weighty and dark. Paul hands her onto the *Tatatínga*'s deck beside a wall of firewood. The foredeck is crowded, the aft chaotic, main-deck passengers stringing up their hammocks cheek by jowl. Rachel loses sight of her friends, then spots them again as Paul helps Iris negotiate the ladder stairs.

The wait to embark has been trying. Mosquitoes that ought to have withdrawn for the day rose in droves from beneath the pier; too slow with the veil, Rachel trapped a cloud of them inside the net, sending Iris into fits. Later, while Paul oversaw the loading of their trunks, Iris fixed on a more distant swarm. Vultures by the score rode the high currents. "What are they doing up there?" she demanded. "They can't possibly see anything from that high."

"Perhaps they're resting." Rachel watched her mistress. "Iris, why don't you sit down?"

She looks up herself now, shading her eyes. Still there, still circling.

"Senhorita?"

Benedito holds out a bunch of small, chubby bananas.

"Oh, Benedito. Muito obrigada."

He beams. "De nada."

He's done something to his hair, she realizes, slicked the black crest down with oil or pomade. That, and it's the first time she's seen him in a shirt. It suddenly strikes her that she has a brother of her own—not a little man like Benedito but a weanling, just two years old. George Coffin Weaver. How is it that she's never been home to meet him? Iris would have spared her without complaint; doubtless she would have insisted on hiring a horse and buggy. It can't be right that Rachel feels more sisterly affection for the boy standing before her than she does for her own flesh and blood. Or half-blood. Never having laid eyes on little George, she can't help but picture him with Annie's high forehead and black button eyes.

"A serpente," she reminds Benedito. He's agreed to mind the meagre beginnings of the live collection until they return.

"Certo, senhorita." He's serious now, standing up straight, extending his hand. She takes it in hers.

"Passe bem se Deus quiser," he says.

Passe—go, *Deus*—God.

"Obrigada, Benedito. Ate—" No, not *ate logo*. She won't see him soon; they'll be upriver for at least three months. "Adeus," she says gently.

He nods, takes up the carpet bag and hands it to her. "Adeus."

Having settled Iris and Rachel in cabin number one, Paul stops off at his own quarters just long enough to load his satchel with books. From there, he carries on to the aft ladder stairs.

It's like passing through a picture frame, rising to the upper deck. Other passengers will no doubt follow suit, but for now Paul has the place to himself. The sheltered portion harbours café tables and chairs; hammocks hang doubled from posts. Ignoring both, Paul sets himself up on one of three lockers that run along the back of the captain's quarters. He'll be in the shade here, no matter how the sun slants.

He's selected a few key accounts of the region—the first volume of the Humboldt, the second of the Bates—but there's no question as to where he'll begin. Twisting the satchel's hasp, he hooks his father's notebook out by its spine.

September 14th, 1844, Pará

After endless preparations we are due to set sail with the tide. We lost several days to the laying in of provisions and other goods. I stowed my trunks in the tolda or covered hold, arranging them among Senhor Chryostomo's casks of cachaça rum, and the sacks of farinha and cakes of salt pirarucu that will feed the crew. The cabin lockers that double as our bunks are packed to capacity with ham and salt beef, Brazilian coffee and Portuguese wine, hard biscuits and rice. Cockroaches scatter when we have cause to lift a lid.

These material preparations, however extensive, were slight in comparison with the official arrangements required. No vessel can depart the port of Pará before procuring a bewildering array of documents from the

Custom House; without the proper permits we would never even pass the fort at Gurupá, gateway to the Lower Amazon. Then there are the letters commending one to the care and protection of at least one notable citizen per stop. Here again Senhor Felisberto has been my unerring guide. It was he who secured my passage on Senhor C.'s galliota, the *Sasurána*, bound for its home port of Barra. Indeed, without Senhor F.'s aid, it is doubtful whether Senhor C. would yet have replaced the half-dozen Indian paddlers he had lost to the lure of the port.

Paul glances up. His seat on the locker offers a wide, albeit backwards-facing, view; he's surprised to find the city hidden behind an island, gone.

He closes the notebook, setting it aside. Imagine relying on paddlers, on sails. Walter wrote with affection of the inland trade wind, but it failed the *Sasurána* on more than one occasion, leaving them no alternative but to send Indians ahead in the canoe to fix a line to a tree, whereby all hands would haul the boat along the shore.

By comparison, the present voyage is laughably simple. Just two decades after his father ventured into a largely uncharted world, Brazil's rivers have been declared open to international navigation. More to the point, competing steamboat lines have reduced a voyage of two months to one of a mere eight days. What would Walter have made of such luxury? He'd planned the current trip, yet Paul can't help feeling he would have been disappointed, even dismayed.

Iris is resting, one long violet glove lying empty across her eyes. Rachel unpacks quietly, first her mistress's things, then her own. She's about to close up her own small case when, on impulse, she slips a hand into the satin pocket in its lid. It's a modest bundle, a dozen letters tied with butcher's cord. Rachel sits down where light from the porthole crosses her bunk. After a moment, she pulls the tail on the small white bow.

April 7th, 1865

My daughter, I trust this letter finds thee in good health and keeping counsel with the Inner Light. I cannot help but wonder how life in the city suits thee. The Delaware and the Schuylkill are fine rivers to be sure yet neither is our own Neshaminy Creek.

Rachel wept the first time she read those words, holding the page at arm's length, careful to preserve the ink. Reading them now, she feels something akin to calm.

I write to thee in the hopes that the country will soon be free of war, and in the faith that no matter how Mankind errs, the blessings of the Lord are many and manifest. Thee will not have forgotten the nests and dens to be found along the creek this time of year. The farm too is graced with new life, three heifers in the last fortnight and more to come. And of course Annie will be delivered of thy brother or sister before long. She continues in good health and spirits. I fold up her greetings with mine.

Which is where Annie's greetings remain. More than once Rachel has been tempted to separate Papa's letters from those of his wife, but something always stops her hand. It's what he chose, this folding together of lives. In any case, it's nothing Rachel can undo.

Annie's letter is longer than her husband's, penned in a tidy hand that puts his looping script to shame. Rachel's eye catches partway down the page.

> . . . I mind thee makes no mention of the Arch Street Meeting in thy last. Rachel, I pray thee is not living out-side the preserving influence of thy fellow Friends. Surrounded by worldly diversions thee might well come to wonder what harm could lie in a lace collar or a ribbon for thy hair. And piece by piece vanity builds, blinding thee to the light of Christ in the soul of man . . .

There's more of it, lines and lines, but Rachel sets the letter aside. The voice on the page has woken a memory, the one that rises most often in association with her father's wife.

"Rachel, thee hasn't gone bare-headed again."

Rachel was caught off guard to find Annie idle, seated at the kitchen table in the afternoon. Touching a hand to her bonnet, she felt the telltale leaf sticking out from beneath its brim. "Just down by the creek. There was nobody about."

"We are never alone, Rachel." Annie spread her hands on the table. "Sit down."

"I should be getting the cows in."

"So thee should. I won't keep thee long."

Rachel pushed the leaf into her apron pocket and sat.

"Thy father and I have been married some months now."

Three months, Rachel thought, only three. Annie made a sound in her throat, and then, in language as plain as any spoken between two women, she moved both hands to her belly and lowered her eyes. Rachel's heart gave a kick. *Already?*

"What age has thee now, Rachel?"

Rachel hesitated, confused. "Sixteen years. Nearly seventeen."

"Seventeen." Annie gave a tight little smile. "And is there no Friend who's caught thine eye?"

Rachel's heart sent a second report. Surely there was room enough in her father's house for two children, even if one of them was mostly grown.

Annie held her gaze. "What about the Sewells' eldest boy?"

Rachel felt her cheeks grow warm. Annie didn't miss much; Peter Sewell had made his interest known at the village picnic, opening his hands to show Rachel the toad he'd captured, hoping to raise a scream. She'd taken the frightened creature from him without a word, walked off into the poplars and set it down among the mouldering leaves.

"No," she said, "not Peter Sewell."

Just then Papa backed in through the door with a bushel basket of marrows. Rachel rose to help him, but Annie was quicker.

"What's this about the Sewell boy?" He delivered his line formally, as though addressing the Monthly Meeting on a point of concern. "Women's talk, is it, not fit for a father's ears?"

Rachel saw the look that passed between her father and his wife. Saw him refuse to hand her the heavy basket with a boyish smile.

12

P aul wakes from his siesta slick with sweat. Folding up to
sit at the edge of his bunk, he finds the midday meal is
still with him: rice and red beans, wedges of fried fish.
Even the fruit was rich—pink, perfumed slices that coated his
tongue as though they were marbled with fat.

It was an oddly staid affair. The dining room doors and windows stood open, yet the air was stagnant, hung with the heat of
bodies and food. Captain Faria, a barrel-chested man in late
middle age, rose to greet Paul and Rachel when they arrived.

"Senhor Ash, Senhorita Weaver."

"Boa tarde, Capitão," Rachel replied. "Senhora Ash diz desculpa," she went on, making Iris's excuses. "Ela está . . . ela está
cansada."

The captain betrayed a moment's disappointment before
waving the apology away. "De nada, senhorita."

He fell quiet upon discovering that Rachel spoke only scraps
of the language, and that Paul, whose looks might suggest otherwise, knew even less. As the meal wore on, the company at table
divided further along linguistic lines. A pair of flaxen-haired
brothers introduced as the Senhores Drescher exchanged clipped
greetings with those gathered before retreating into an intense
discussion in their native German. A well-dressed Peruvian
named Piscoya murmured assiduously to his young wife. A trio

of nuns ate in silence. Paul did his best to answer Rachel's questions about the region, but she would keep asking him things he didn't know.

Planting his bare feet, Paul rises from his bunk. His porthole is a dull sun set into the wall. The ceiling looms close; elbows bent, he flattens his hands to its painted boards. It's like standing in the damp chamber of a heart, the *Tatatínga*'s pulse chugging through him, palms to soles. Letting his arms drop, he takes up a pair of drawers from his case and pats himself dry. Dresses hastily, eager for the open air.

It's not much of a breeze, though it freshens as he follows the promenade forward past cabin doors. Outside number one, he hesitates. Perhaps it's better to leave Iris be. She'll show herself when she's ready—in time for dinner, if not before. After which he'll take her for a stroll in the evening air.

Turning back, he climbs to the upper deck, emerging into untempered sun. Again he makes his way forward, halting where the door of the bridge stands open, hooked back against the cladding. After a moment he steps into the pilot's line of view. "Boa tarde."

The pilot takes him in at a glance. "Boa tarde, senhor." He stands easy at the helm, a handsome man of perhaps forty. His reddish, tightly curled hair betrays a faint cast of negro blood. "O Pará para aqui."

Pará-Pará? Paul shakes his head. "Desculpa, não falo Português."

His eyes forward, the pilot nods. "Você é Americano?"

Not entirely, Paul would tell him if he could. "Sim," he says, "Americano."

They've arrived at what appears to be a lagoon—a vast,

shallow expanse Paul understands to be the head of the Rio Pará only as they leave it behind for the channel of the Breves. Forested banks close in. It's the end of open waters for a time; from here they'll wind their way through a watery maze en route to the river sea.

"Licença, senhor." The hand on his back makes Paul jump. The mate flashes a smile as he squeezes past.

"Oi, Marcellino," the older man says.

"Olá, Pai."

Pai—of course. The mate has the same amber skin and glinting curls. How strange to resemble one's father so closely, to stand in the world like portraits of a man painted two decades apart.

Paul comprehends nothing more of their easy exchange. When the pilot laughs and rests a hand on his son's shoulder, Paul eases out of the door frame without a word.

⸻

Iris's hair has changed. The jungle air seems to have doubled its weight; its scent too is heavy, rising with every stroke of the brush.

"Something quick," she says, meeting Rachel's gaze in the mirror. "Just so long as it's up off my neck."

Rachel gathers a handful, revealing a section of nape scratched raw. She's seen her mistress come up in welts before, but never anything like this. The bite near Iris's left eye has swollen it partly shut.

She twists the hank and pins it in place. At least the colour is still true. In the low, still light of the cabin, it's not far from Rachel's own light brown—though Rachel's has nothing like the shine. If they were sisters, Iris would be the first-born girl who drinks up all the beauty, leaving the dregs for the quiet child to come.

It pleases Rachel to imagine them sharing a childhood, perhaps even a room—a pair of beds, and Iris sitting at the dressing table in her chemise, just as she does now. They wouldn't have been playmates, but an indulgent older sister might have taken her hand and walked with her down to the creek.

"You must take more care to keep out of the sun," Iris says.

Rachel glances at herself in the glass. Her freckles have multiplied since she first set foot on the *Kittiwake*'s deck. "I may be a lost cause."

Iris smiles, raising a hand to a bite on her cheek.

"Don't scratch."

"I'm not."

"They'll turn septic."

"I'm *not*." Iris reaches for her scent bottle, removes the stopper and sniffs, sets it back down. "Oh, hurry up, can't you."

"I'm nearly done." Rachel fixes the last strands. "There."

"Sorry, dearest, it's just, I'm just so . . ."

"It's all right." Moving to the shallow wardrobe, Rachel takes down the black silk.

"I don't know why we're bothering with my hair." Iris twists round on her stool. "I look as though I've been in a brawl."

"You do exaggerate." Rachel lays the dress out on Iris's bunk. "It'll be better once we're on the Rio Negro, not nearly so many insects."

"Have we any more hartshorn? These bites are agony."

"We do, but you really ought to be getting dressed. The first bell's already gone."

Iris eyes the dark dress, a flash of something like panic crossing her face.

"Here." Rachel holds up Iris's stays. After a moment, Iris stands and raises her arms. Rachel laces her in gently, a good inch looser than usual.

Iris turns. "Thank you."

"You're no good to anyone if you can't breathe."

"No." Iris steps into the mass of pearl-grey petticoats Rachel holds open at her feet. Taking hold of the waistband, she turns again. "I'm not even hungry."

"It's the heat," Rachel says, slipping hooks into their eyes. "You'll get used to it."

"Will I?"

"Of course you will."

As Rachel gathers up the dress, Iris whirls and falls forward, taking its place on the bunk. "I can't. Not tonight."

"Are you ill?"

"Not ill," Iris says into the linens, "just . . . tired." She rolls over, laying the back of her hand across her eyes. A bite on her forearm oozes blood. "The two of you go on without me."

The two of us. Rachel flashes on Paul's face, the way it fell when she told him Iris wouldn't be coming on their first-ever jungle walk.

"You can bring me something back," Iris adds. "Something cool."

Rachel opens her mouth to protest just as the second dinner bell sounds.

Iris lifts her hand and glares at her. *"Go."*

⌐⌐

Paul sits alone on his locker, the other cabin-class passengers still lingering over drinks or strolling the promenade below. Night has come down. A trio of lanterns dangle overhead.

Another meal without Iris, he and Rachel intent on their plates as the conversation passed them by. Nothing new there; as a rule, Paul contributes sparingly to the staged discussions his landlady conducts. He was desperate to join one of the smaller club tables in his freshman year, but looking back, he's just as glad the invitation never came. Nothing in his upbringing had shaped him for boisterous debate. He and Walter had formed a reflective school of two. Even after they joined Iris at her fine table, Paul never had to fight to be heard.

The lanterns swing softly, unequal to the wider night. Paul knows the jungle flanks them on either side, but his eyes deliver only blackness. His ears tell another story. The rumble of life is distinct from that of the boat's engines by dint of its high notes—a range of hoots and spine-chilling shrieks.

The lower deck is quietening down. A lone guitar lulls the last of the wailing babies; intermittent swells of laughter surmount the splashing of the wheels. Mosquitoes gather in soft, humming clouds. *Carapanãs*—he smiles to find the word rising of its own accord. The odd blood-hungry female lands, but for the most part they leave him be. If Iris's blood is sweet, his own must be unusually sour.

The lantern light is sufficient to read by. Taking up his father's notebook, Paul suffers an undeniable sensation of the night drawing close. In moments he's surrounded by a leaden echo: the guitar's low song doubles and becomes muddied; a shout from bow to bridge resounds. Suddenly, Paul knows exactly where he is. It takes him a minute to locate the corresponding page.

September 22nd, 1844, Jaburú Channel

Upon entering the channel, I was struck by the sudden alteration in sound. Our nine Indians might have been ninety, so numerous were the echoes of their paddles. One of them cried out to hear his voice returned, then another, and we were assailed by ghostly replies, the effect of which was troubling to the soul. To cheer the company I cupped my hands to my mouth and added my voice. "Viva, senhores," I called out in my best local accent. "Viva!" I was rewarded by the rare note of Senhor C.'s laugh.

It was the straightest watercourse we had travelled thus far, the channel measured in yards—perhaps a hundred at its widest point—rather than miles. The depth appeared considerable, even as close as we dared venture along the banks. We were travelling in what felt like a bottomless cut, the sides of which extended skywards in two great ramparts of green. The canopy proper attained a height of some eighty feet, the domes of silk-cotton trees and other emergent species reaching higher still.

Palms made up a goodly portion of the mass. Ubussu were abundant, their pale green crowns a welcome relief in that solemn scene. The smooth-trunked miriti grew singly, whereas the slim, feather-topped assai formed graceful groups. Jupati palms reached their ragged, fifty-foot leaves out over the stream. The water's edge supported species of a more ornamental scale—representatives of *Geonoma* and *Bactris* interspersed among varieties the names of which I have yet to learn.

Paul looks up from the notebook. "*Geonoma*," he says quietly. "*Bactris*." He's grateful for the darkness; it allows him to focus on the names alone, without attempting to match them to their trees.

At Paul's age, Walter hadn't set foot in the humblest of colleges. How in God's name had he come to know so much? Paul can tell a palm from a pale-barked cecropia, but even that he had to learn more than once. Why must the knowledge that flowed into his father's mind be ferried inside his own thick skull load by unwieldy load? It's not as though he lacks the capacity. In school, he was always the first to have a verse by heart. *Old Yew, which graspest at the stones / That name the under-lying dead, / Thy fibres net the dreamless head, / Thy roots are wrapt about the bones . . .*

Paul shakes his head, forcing his gaze back to the page. His father's handwriting is even, assured. *Ubussu, miriti, assai, jupati.* He shuts his eyes. "Ubussu, miriti, assai . . . damn!"

13

The upper deck is quiet. A handful of passengers play at cards, but most doze in hammocks and chairs. Paul reads his father's well-thumbed volume of Humboldt's *Personal Narrative of Travels to the Equinoctial Regions of America*. Now and then he glances up to confront the stupefying green. If not for his slow progress through the text, he might imagine himself to be trapped in an unending moment, the *Tatatínga* treading water in time.

The *Personal Narrative* was a favourite of both father and son—though Walter occasionally expressed frustration at Humboldt's tendency to digress. *Must we have so much of this man Lozano?* he said once, referring to a passage Paul loved. When the villager Lozano's wife became ill, he comforted their infant son at his breast; imagine his surprise when the child's suckling drew forth a steady supply of milk! And Lozano wasn't alone. Apparently there were other recorded cases of lactating fathers— one in Syria and another in Ireland—not to mention the milk-yielding billy goats of Corsica.

Another of the great man's digressions occupied Paul more darkly. In a cavern off the Orinoco River, Indian guides led Humboldt and his companion Bonpland to the graves of an extinct race. The explorers were thrilled to discover hundreds of intact skeletons packed neatly into baskets and urns. Ignoring their guides' protests, they helped themselves. They lied their way through every subsequent village, claiming their baskets held the remains of alligators and manatees. The Indians weren't fooled. They could smell the sacred resin on their ancestors' bones.

It was a cheat of sorts, Paul's habit of seeking the veins of pure narrative in the bedrock of a scientific work. Walter never dictated what his son should or shouldn't read; he tended instead to gaze in puzzlement at any unsuitable choice. At times he was clumsier, reading aloud from some more edifying text, but even this gentle interference ceased once they abandoned their own small home for that of Walter's new wife.

It was different reading in a room that was all your own; a book could swallow you whole. Not long after they moved in, Paul was lost in medieval England when there came a knock at his chamber door.

"Come in."

"Here you are." Miss Grafton stood at the threshold. No, that was wrong: she was Iris now, his stepmother. "Goodness, it's frigid in here." She looked to the grate. "Why haven't you lit the fire?"

Before there was snow on the ground? It hadn't occurred to him. "I'm all right," he said. "Thank you."

"Nonsense, come join us in the library. I'm working on your father's portrait."

Paul hesitated. It was lonely in his room, but at least there he could be certain of not being in the way.

"Come along. My father's old wingback is the best reading chair in the house." She stood holding the door open until he closed his book and rose.

"Ah, Paul." His father turned from the window as they entered the library. "You've come to liberate me."

"No," Iris answered, "he's come to thaw out. His chamber was like a tomb." She crossed to her easel. "Back to work, Mr. Ash."

Walter took up the turtle shell. "Yes, Mrs. Ash." Not so much as a glance at the book in his son's hand. Paul might have been reading the Bible for all his father cared.

"Chin up," said Iris. "Turn to the light a little. There. Don't move."

For a moment Paul too stood immobile, watching the newly-weds in their shaft of November light. Between them, the air danced with particles, just as it had that first day on the pier.

Paul turned, made his way to the wingback chair and sat. He tugged at the ribbon that marked his page. Rebecca, the beautiful Jewess, sat where he'd left her, awaiting immolation as a witch. The stranger come to ride as her champion spoke: *"My name,"* said the Knight, raising his helmet, *"is better known, my lineage more pure, Malvoisin, than thine own. I am Wilfred of Ivanhoe."*

It was the moment Paul had been waiting for, yet it proved unequal to the scene playing out in the window's light.

"What a brow you have, Walter," Iris said.

Paul looked up, catching the tail end of his father's smile. "A gift from my mother's side of the family. People were always saying I was the spit of my uncle Walter. I have a daguerreotype somewhere."

A daguerreotype? Any picture Paul had formed of his relations was the product of imagination alone.

"You must dig it out," Iris said.

"Perhaps." Then, "He was no great proponent of my work. He took it hard when I sold the business, saw it as a betrayal."

"You were meant to carry on your father's line."

Walter nodded. "Though how any of them ever imagined I would. I was forever slipping off with my collecting bag when I was meant to be helping in the saddlery. I did my best with the place after my father died, but only until my mother joined him."

Iris stood back, peering at the canvas with a critical eye. "My father was the same, shipping me back to London so his sister could marry me off."

"Oh, yes? And when was this?"

"The year I turned eighteen."

And when exactly was that? Paul would've liked to ask. Just how many years between Walter and his bride?

"I imagine you were beset by suitors."

Paul caught the note of false lightness in his father's voice.

"I was, as it happens."

"And have you a gallery of their portraits hidden away somewhere?"

Walter didn't mean it to wound. Paul could see as much, the pain flaring in his father's eyes the moment it showed in his wife's.

"No," she said quietly. "Before you, I never . . . there were none."

"Oh, my love."

"Walter, you mustn't move."

But he ignored her, setting the shell down against the wainscotting and stepping close. As Iris turned her mouth up to be kissed, Paul made himself lower his gaze. On the page, Ivanhoe and Bois-Guilbert dropped their visors, took up their lances and charged.

He's been staring at the same paragraph for miles. Corralling his thoughts, Paul touches a fingertip to the line where he left off. Humboldt may have been a man of science, but he was clearly no stranger to the workings of the human heart: "Separated from the objects of our dearest affections, we are forced to fall back on our own thoughts, and we feel within ourselves a dreariness we have never known before."

Rachel draws the cabin door shut quietly behind her. If only she could leave it ajar, let the slim breeze in to where Iris lies twisted in the sheets. The promenade is deserted for the siesta hour. She steps to the rail, her gaze stretching to the far shore. An island slips into and out of view. She could go aloft with a book, but the notion holds little appeal. What she wants, what she longs for, is a walk.

Cabin-class passengers don't descend to the main deck. It's not a rule, but it's understood. Before she can think better of it, Rachel walks swiftly to the forward stairs, turns and backs her way down.

Heat rises up her skirts. Touching a slippered foot to the deck, she realizes the rumbling room before her must house the engine for the starboard paddlewheel. If it's this hot out here, what must it be like inside? She's making up her mind to see for herself when one of the firemen steps out of the engine room door. He starts at the sight of her, recovers and touches a hand to his soot-streaked brow. "Viva, senhorita."

She nods. "Boa tarde, senhor."

As he crosses to the wall of firewood, Rachel quells an urge to help. Papa used to stand by the woodpile with his arms extended while she loaded on piece after piece—surprising strength in a man so thin. What would the fireman make of her? Doubtless he'd be polite, even kind, thinking her touched in the head.

She feigns interest in the view, waiting until he disappears back through the low doorway before making her way aft. Beyond the engine room, the deck stands open on both sides. The corners are crowded with baskets and sacks, the odd curled form of a dog. Two long tables sit empty amid dozens of hammocks slung low. The nearest—a fringed, sea-green rede—holds a girl not much younger than herself. Her face is soft in sleep, sheltered in the dark nest of her hair.

Following the narrow aisle between rows, Rachel does her best to keep her eyes to herself. It's impossible, though, to avoid seeing the feet. Pair after pair jut up out of the cloth cocoons, broad and slender, old and young. All those glossy toenails and hardened, dust-dark soles. Damp inside their slippers, Rachel's own extremities feel trapped.

The sensation stirs a memory: Papa kneeling beside her in the barred light of the barn. It was a large litter, Patch's first. Having whelped and nuzzled three, the young bitch succumbed to exhaustion with the fourth still wedged in the canal. Papa's face was serious as he slipped a thumb and finger in to prise out the pup. Sliding the sac free, he set the blind, unmoving creature in Rachel's hands. When she looked at him, frightened, he smiled. *Give him a rub.* And she did, Patch watching through hooded eyes as she urged the pup's blood to the surface, chivvying it back to life.

The farm is always with her. Times like this, remembrance threatens to overwhelm the present—the human scent of all those sleeping bodies overlaid with an ammoniac tang of chickens. Her mind isn't playing tricks. Beyond the last hammock, a stack of slat crates forms a sizable coop. She approaches on tiptoe, careful not to raise a squawk. They're long-necked, mottled things. Plenty of meat on them, though, judging by the thigh on her plate last night.

Nearby, an open platform juts out over the stern. Its planks are stained with blood—and not just fish or fowl. In the shade of a loose curtain, a white bullock dozes on its feet, tethered too close to lie down. Rachel hums in her throat, laying a hand to its heavy neck. Its reply is the softest of groans.

~

It's early evening by the time they pass Gurupá. Paul leaves his locker seat to stand at the rail, raising his hand alongside the others in answer to shouted greetings from shore. A waft of what he's come to recognize as toasted farinha winds up from the deck below. Not long till dinner, and again Iris has yet to appear. He caught sight of Rachel perhaps an hour ago on his way past the dining room. The grammar open in her hand, she appeared intent upon communicating something to the steward. The young man stood closer than was strictly necessary. Paul watched the pair of them through the open window for a moment before carrying on.

As the town falls away behind them, he nods to the elder of the two Drescher brothers and turns from the rail. Walter's notebook lies where he left it, on top of the pile.

October 2nd, 1844, mouth of the Rio Xingu
I despair of our Indians. Only Caetano has shown any real inclination to assist with my collections, and even he joined in on the feast they made of the iguana I had captured near Breves. It was a fine specimen, four feet three inches in length, with an impressive crest of spines.

Caetano stood apart from his fellow oarsmen when Senhor C. took them to task, but I caught the shine of grease about his mouth.

Doubtless he was in on this recent mischief as well. It was exhausting work skinning the black caiman, its armour so heavy that at times I was forced to employ an axe. *Jacaré nigra* is the largest crocodilian found in the region, similar in size and appearance to our own alligator. It took hours of boiling to clean the massive, foul-smelling head.

This morning while shifting crates in search of my half-gallon jars, I took it in mind to unwrap and admire the skull. Imagine my distress upon finding half its teeth were gone. Our mulatto pilot Romão, on break from his post at the helm, lay close by atop a roll of canvas. He lifted his head long enough to offer a comment concerning Índios and feitiços, by which I understood him to mean that my caiman's teeth had been knocked from their sockets for use as Indian charms. He soon made a show of sleep, but I doubt whether he was wholly without blame.

Notwithstanding such losses, I continue to amass an impressive collection, a portion of which is destined for sale. I could fund my researches indefinitely if I were to bend my days to the market's shape, hunting birds and butterflies by morning and plucking up beetles of an afternoon. Lord spare us the demands of the curiosity cabinet—a laughable term, for what could be more deadening to the mind than those ordered and bloodless displays? "I have one in green already," the jewellery-box collector declares. "Have you nothing new?" Fieldwork blunts such vanity. In a country where a man might spy out an unknown species from the comfort of his hammock every afternoon, the hungriest discoverer begins to feel a fool.

Even the so-called men of science, taken up with naming cratefuls of type specimens delivered to their doors, risk passing from the world no wiser than they came into it. The work of classification has its place, but if we confine ourselves to such acts of listing, do we not create a necrology rather than a study of life?

In truth, the naming of a beast is but the beginning. We have long been familiar with *Eunectes murinus*, the fearful anaconda known to the natives as the sucuruju, yet a man might easily spend a lifetime in the study of this powerful predator. By what mechanism, for instance, does it remain so long submerged? To what unseen lair does it retreat when not hunting or sunning its massive, mud-green coils?

Come to that, how can a man hope to know *Jacaré nigra* by a mere examination of its skull? Such an artifact relates nothing of the male's great bellow delivered at dusk, the female's fierce attendance upon her nest.

"Mamãe!" A girl's voice from below. Paul looks up to see that the jungle has given way to open acres. At their heart, a well-constructed house. He blurs his gaze. If it wasn't for the shade-making bananas, it might almost be a riverbank farm back home.

"Mamãe!" the girl calls again. "Jacaré, Mamãe!"

One then another passenger rises, crossing to the rail. Setting the notebook aside, Paul joins them. Two decks down, an Indian girl perhaps six years old leans out over the rail, pointing to shore. Paul follows the line of her finger with his eye. *Jacaré.* There it lies, as though conjured by his father's pen. A sizable beast, it hangs in the shallows like a black, half-sunken log.

Beneath him, the sounds of chaotic mustering. The girl's braided head disappears as men crowd along the bottom rail. Glinting barrels rise, and now the sudden, ragged thunder of guns. The water dances with lead.

Not a sharpshooter among them. As the caiman sinks away to safety, Paul feels a corresponding lift in his chest. At least he won't be called down to the lower deck, expected as the man of science on board to get up to his elbows in blood.

The mess of the blue shark is still with him. Iris's excitement carried him far; he was deep into the necropsy before the old trouble arose. His stepmother was too busy with her inventory of the shark's organs to notice, but Rachel didn't miss a trick—he could tell by the way she averted her eyes when he made his way back from the rail. A weak stomach is a handicap, but it's nothing he can't work around. He can hold his own with small specimens, having learned on so many fence lizards and snakes. It's the larger bodies that get to him.

The harbour seal was his first, and he knew he was in trouble the moment he caught sight of its whiskered face. The opening incision fell to the boldest in the class, a cheerful plug of a fellow best known as third oar on the heavyweight rowing crew. Paul watched with a dozen others as the rower parted the silky, speckled coat. He could just about breathe his way through dermis, blubber and blood, but when the tutor reached in to tease out the intestines, Paul turned on his heel. He made it out the side door to a stand of young maples, where he vomited as efficiently as he could.

The tutor caught his eye when he returned but carried on. As instructed, the rower severed a flipper neatly at the joint. Despite the size of his callused hands, he proceeded to lay open the appendage with enviable skill, revealing bones like so many bright hairpins set in velvety flesh. Paul looked on in misery. There was something the rower had that he lacked. Curiosity, perhaps. Desire.

14

Paul waits for a long moment outside cabin number one. He's about to knock again when Iris opens the door, her face hidden beneath the veil. It's been so long since he's seen her in anything but black. Her blouse is the soft off-white of an oyster shell, its buttons lustrous. Her skirt—yards of it belling out from the narrow circle of her waist—is a delicate shade of green.

"You think I shouldn't?"

"What? Oh, no—"

"Honestly, Paul, the bombazine was torture. Rachel said no one could fault me in this heat."

"No. I mean, yes, quite right." He looks past her shoulder. "Where is Rachel?"

"Probably gone down to visit the livestock again. She's a farm girl, you know. I stole her away to the city."

He did know—not that he'd given the matter much thought.

"Did you want her?"

"Not especially. I was hoping for a turn about the deck with you." He catches the faint flash of her smile. "I shouldn't think you'll need the veil, though. No carapanãs about this time of day—certainly not this far from shore."

"That's as may be, but you're forgetting the damage already done." She steps out over the raised threshold. "I'm a sight."

"I'm sure you're not."

"And I'm sure I am."

"Very well." He's left his jacket behind on his bunk, even gone so far as to roll up his sleeves. She takes his arm, her hand in its pale blue glove resting on his skin. Together they walk the promenade, circling from full sun on the portside to starboard shade. Even with her face covered, Iris attracts all eyes. Fellow passengers turn from the rail to offer greetings; a pair of deck-hands stand to attention as they pass. *Bom dia, senhora, bom dia.* Paul nods and smiles and steers her on.

On the fourth lap, he guides her to an unclaimed stretch of rail. He can't think why he's so tongue-tied; he's been banking observations, all of which seem to have left his head. Looking out over the river, he has a sudden, unfounded impression of Rachel standing beneath them, her grey eyes trained on the same view. He doubts whether she could hear him over the paddlewheel. Still, he continues dumb.

He's never been wholly at ease with Iris's companion, not since he arrived for a visit to find her installed in his father's home. It was hard enough to know how to behave with the true servants, let alone one who sat down with the family to dine. His father showed no such discomfort, launching into his customary inquiries as Mrs. Pryce moved from place to place, ladling out the soup.

"Well, Paul, what news from the front? Is our Mr. Gray still keeping that fool Agassiz in check?"

Our Mr. Gray? Paul's irritation turned to shame when he met his father's eye. Walter had followed Professor Gray's defence of Mr. Darwin in the *American Journal of Science* with zeal. Unlike Paul, he'd never had the opportunity to hear Asa Gray—or Louis

Agassiz, for that matter—speak. He'd longed to travel to Boston and attend the public debates, but at the time they hadn't the fare.

"I believe so," Paul said. "Though at present the talk is of Professor Agassiz's imminent departure for South America."

Walter shook his head. "Imagine mounting an expedition to Brazil, *Brazil* of all places, in the hopes of disproving the mutability of species."

"Thank you, Mrs. Pryce," Iris said, but the housekeeper was already heading for the back stairs with the tureen hugged to her chest.

"One needn't travel nearly so far to encounter evidence of transmutation," Walter went on. "Rachel, your father keeps cows, does he not?"

"He does."

"And when it comes time to breed them, does he use his own bull, or—"

"Father," said Paul, "I hardly think Miss Weaver—"

"Oh, Rachel's all right," said Iris, "aren't you, dearest. No escaping these matters on the farm."

Dearest? All eyes on the newcomer now, including Paul's.

"We used to keep a bull," Rachel said after a moment, "but my father found the herd kept in better health when he had more choice."

"There you have it," said Walter. "Sexual selection, accelerated by the hand of Man."

Paul felt himself flush. His stepmother's pet, on the other hand, seemed unperturbed.

"Like Mr. Darwin's pigeons," Rachel said.

"Precisely." Walter beamed. "You see?"

———

"I have to keep reminding myself it's a river."

Iris's voice startles Paul, calling him back to the *Tatatínga*, the starboard rail. He looks at her. "I'm surprised you can see anything through all that."

"Yes, all right." A note of admonishment in her voice—the closest she comes to mothering him. She points toward the bow. "Look."

The tree is a monster, torn or toppled from its bank, now rafting slowly downstream. Its crown is full, still overwhelmingly green. Passing them—rather narrowly, Paul can't help but feel—it measures double the steamer's length. Its buttress roots describe a massive semicircle, a crude, compelling sculpture of a rising sun.

"Imagine," he says, "all those years come crashing down."

"Not to mention the creatures that called it home."

"All drowned, I suppose. Or crushed." He hears himself. "The ones that didn't fly off in time."

"Or swim."

He nods. "Or swim."

"And some are undoubtedly still living among the branches."

"Parrots, sloths . . . an entire troop of spider monkeys."

"Riding to the river's mouth."

He grins at her. "And beyond."

"Passing galleons . . ."

"Passing whales . . ."

"Pitching up on African shores."

"My brother monkeys"—Paul hunches, tucking his fingers into his armpits—"I bring greetings from the New World."

Her laugh is musical. He's thinking how best to prolong it when he spots a large fly with curious black and white wings. It winks in the light at the hem of Iris's veil, just where it rests against the collar of her blouse. And now another, alighting by her temple, adhering to the gauze like a burr.

"Hold still."

"What? What is it?"

He swats the second fly away, but the first is more diligent, burrowing up under the veil. Iris shrinks as he grabs for it and dashes it between his palms. His father's spirit inhabits the gesture, forever vigilant when it came to protecting his wife's flesh.

"Did you get it?"

"Yes." He pulls out his handkerchief to wipe the mess away.

She reaches up to secure the veil, feeling along the brim of her hat then down about her throat. Bare skin shows between her glove and the cuff of her sleeve. The surviving fly—or perhaps another one altogether—has discovered it. It lifts away before Paul can get it. At the site of its feeding, a trickle of blood.

"What was it?" Iris says as he presses a clean corner of his hanky to the spot.

"Nothing sinister." He can feel the welt begin to swell against his finger. "Something like a horsefly."

"But I thought you killed it."

"I did. There were . . . It's all right, they're gone."

"But where did they come from?" Her laughter has a shaky edge. "My God, are they riding out on trees to find me?"

He wishes he could see her face; he'd know then whether he should joke along. He settles for offering her his arm. "Let's walk."

She allows him to lead, but only so far as her cabin door. "I think I'll go in."

"But you've only—" he begins, just as Rachel draws open the door.

"Iris, what is it? What's wrong?"

How does she know without a word, without so much as a glimpse of her mistress's face?

"I'm fine." Iris breaks from Paul's side and steps past Rachel into the gloom. "Really, I'm just a little tired."

It's late—one o'clock in the morning? Two? Rachel would be lucky to find the pocket watch on Iris's bedside table, let alone make out its golden hands. A body can lie staring into blackness for only so long. She listens for a moment longer to Iris's steady breathing, then sits up and feels for her dress.

Outside, the breeze is sweet. No need to dampen a finger, she can feel its easterly origin all down her right side. It will be even cooler up top. Her eyes open to the darkness, she makes her way to the aft ladder stairs.

The upper deck is deserted, its lanterns extinguished for the night. She unhooks a hammock and carries it down to the far end. Fixing it between two posts, she nudges her feet free of their slippers and lies back. The breeze laps at her ankles. Reaching down with her bare toes, she pushes at the planks and swings out from beneath the overhang, glimpsing the southern sky.

The heavens are crowded with countless stars, a closer, brighter moon. The firmament itself is a dark, deepwater blue, a shade she can characterize as neither warm nor cool. Iris would call it up in a single wash, touch in the moon and stars with gouache, or else mask the surface to begin with, preserving its original white. If only Rachel could whet her mistress's appetite for her work. Walter would know what to do; he and Iris always worked so well together—or nearly always.

The memory is a vivid one, perhaps because Rachel witnessed so few instances of discord between them. Iris sat painting where the light was best, several sketches arrayed on the table before her, along with a box turtle's shell. Walter pushed back from his papers and came to observe.

"Tricky pattern," he said after a moment.

Iris nodded. "Mm."

He pointed to the watercolour. "See here, along the anterior costal scute? Looks as though you've given way to a decorative impulse."

Iris said nothing.

"You'll be faced with countless species you've never seen when we're in Brazil. If you were to take such liberties with the colouring of a coral snake, the results could be deadly."

She laid down her brush. "Rather an extreme example."

"Extreme but illustrative."

Iris stood abruptly. Skirting the table, she crossed the Persia rug.

"Iris, my love—"

She silenced him with the slam of the door.

Rachel watched from her corner, her heart racing; she'd never in her life seen a couple fight. For a moment Walter stood frozen. When he moved, it was as though Iris had pulled him after her, as though a line that ran between them had stretched taut.

15

Not yet dawn. Sound enters through the open porthole: the steamer's plash and hum overlapped by a distant, wavering roar. The territorial song of *Mycetes seniculus*, the howling monkey. Paul gives up trying to sleep and lights the lamp.

October 8th, 1844, Santarém

We started at daybreak, setting the sails to catch the light land breeze. Before long, the mud-yellow main current began to give way to the clear green waters of the Tapajos. The shoreline too presented a pleasant change—since crossing the Xingu's mouth, we had passed untold miles of swampy, impenetrable growth.

Two hours' paddling brought us to Santarém. The town itself presents an orderly face, set on a slope that leads down to a bright stretch of beach. Senhor C. informs me that it is home to some four thousand souls, including those inhabitants of the Indian village and the fort. We are to stay at the home of Senhor Innocencio Almeida, a venerable trader who counted Senhor F.'s late father among his closest friends. I doubt whether Senhor C. will be content to remain here much more than a week; labour is hard to come by in these parts and he would be nervous of losing his crew. I will commence my explorations this afternoon. Given the predominance of open campo, I am hopeful of running down a representative of the genus *Teius*—the largest of the region's predatory terrestrial lizards.

After taking lunch with Senhor Almeida, Senhor C. and I made our way along the grassy streets to present our documents at the office of the town. I was surprised to learn that among those letters being held for Senhor C. there lay one addressed to myself. I had not thought to hear from my uncle after our last meeting. His message was not overly long. I copy the meat of it here:

> My boy, if you have kept yourself out of harm's way long enough to read these words, I urge you again to quit that heathen land and abandon this dangerous scheme. You have gone against the wishes of your father and my poor sister, lost to us not a year after his death. Can you continue to defy your uncle too? The saddlery is gone, no undoing that. I have been to see Thompson and he will not hear of selling it back at any price. Still, you might invest what remains of the proceeds and make a start in some business or trade. Walter, you are all the family I have. I beg of you to see sense and come home.

Paul shuts the notebook, spreading a hand across its calfskin back. Leaning his head back against the wall, he takes the hum of the ship's engines into his skull. He never met his great-uncle; it was only after reading of the old man's death in the *Ledger* that Walter consented to visit his house. Two storeys of quarried stone at the city's verge—Paul's heart sang at the sight of it. Thirteen was old enough to know about inheritance, and according to the obituary, the deceased had no children of his own.

"Can we go in?"

"No key." Walter kept his eyes fixed on the house. "Besides, we'd be trespassing. The old fool left it to the Church."

It took Paul a moment to comprehend. *Then why did you show me?* he wanted to say, but his father was already on the move. Together they skirted the property, following a soft slope to the back fieldstone fence. Walter led him to a tumbledown corner where a clump of forsythia stood in stark bloom.

"I used to come down here looking for snakes. My uncle would give us tea in the parlour, or out under the plum tree if it was fine, but I'd be off the instant I finished my cake."

Paul said nothing, imagining tea in the parlour, a plum tree of your very own.

"This whole end was full of eastern garters." Walter grinned. "I remember finding a big one and carrying it back. My mother screamed herself hoarse." He peered among the stones. "Looks as though the colony's still active."

Paul glanced away, his eye lighting on something in the grass. It might have been a root mass—if roots could move. A second more and Paul knew what he was looking at: perhaps a dozen male garter snakes had mobbed a single female, forming a mating ball.

"Oh-ho," Walter said beside him, "it's our lucky day." The house forgotten, he crouched over the writhing knot, his eyes lit up like a boy's.

Rachel wakes to a soft tap on the cabin door. She rolls over, surprised to see Iris sitting up in her bunk.

"Cheeky boy," Iris says, "knocking this early."

The tap sounds again, and Rachel rises, reaching for her shawl. When she draws open the door, Paul raises his hat briefly, looking past her.

"Iris, you must come up on deck."

"Must we?"

"Yes, both of you, of course. It's a fine morning and there's nobody about." He pauses. "The breeze is considerable."

Iris brightens. "Truly?"

"One might even call it fresh."

The three of them sit at a table in the overhang's shade. Iris appears relaxed; she's even gone so far as to tuck her veil up about her hat. "It's a pity they don't serve breakfast up here," she says.

Paul nods. "Or coffee at least."

"I'll see about getting some," Rachel says, rising.

"No, no." Iris lays a hand over hers. "They'll ring the bell soon enough. You sit down."

Rachel resumes her seat.

"Somehow I didn't imagine so many islands," Iris says after a moment. "They're lovely, aren't they? Rather like creatures themselves."

"Shall I bring you your sketchbook?" Rachel asks.

Iris fixes her with a look. "You needn't always be fetching and carrying."

Rachel looks down at her hands. For a time no one speaks—until Iris sits up suddenly in her chair. "What's that?"

"Where?" says Paul.

Iris stands, pointing. "There." She crosses to the rail, Paul and Rachel at her heels. A pale flash in the muddy flood, then another. Iris turns to Paul. "Did you see?"

"Dolphins." He grins. "Botos."

Botos vermelhos. Rachel manages not to say it out loud. Red dolphins—only they're actually pink, a raw, infant shade. Some show grey patches, like true dolphins with their skins half worn away. Rachel counts seven of them, each glimpse no more than a wedge of fluke, the disappearing ridge of a back.

She wonders if the species ever possessed dorsal fins. Walter made mention of the missing appendage in his notebook—that and the boto's lateral flexibility, a trait more serpentine than cetacean, ideal for threading through flooded forests, hunting among the trees. It's one of Rachel's favourite entries. The *Sasurána* had anchored for the night in a calm, moonlit bay. Long after Senhor Chryostomo and the crew retired, Walter lay atop the cabin, watching a score of the rosy creatures plunge and roll. He fell asleep to the sound of them blowing, a chorus of sudden sighs.

"Come on," Iris calls down to the pod, "keep up!" But the dolphins are falling behind, even as the *Tatatínga* begins to slow, angling toward shore. "What's going on?" Iris says. "They're bringing us in awfully close."

"We must be stopping for fuel." Paul points to a clearing where a pair of thatched shacks stand amid head-high piles of wood. Half a dozen men toil among the stacks; three more stand at the ready on the makeshift dock.

Iris rolls down her veil. Simple vanity, Rachel wonders, or anticipation of the swarms that haunt the shore? She spots a tremor in Iris's hand. "Perhaps we should be making our way to the dining room." She helps fix the veil's hem. "Breakfast can't be long."

"I'm not hungry," Iris says flatly.

"Iris," says Paul, "you really must—"

"Must I, Paul? *You must come up on deck, Iris, you must eat your breakfast, Iris.* Tell me, is there anything else I must do?" She turns on her heel, headed for the ladder stairs.

Paul hurries after her. "Iris, wait. Let me go down first—"

"I'm perfectly capable!" Grabbing the mass of her skirts in one hand and the rail in the other, Iris backs recklessly down the rungs. "Leave me be," she cries, disappearing. "Both of you, just leave me alone!"

Rachel halts at the edge of the overhang. Iris is gone, and Paul is staring after her, like a man who's lost something down a well.

⌒

Paul is alone at the rail when he catches sight of the fin— gunmetal grey, perhaps twenty yards from the *Tatatinga*'s hull. It must be a bull shark. In this country, where even nature flouts its own laws, they're known to follow their hunger thousands of miles inland. It's the kind of detail he might share with Iris, if only she would emerge.

When the fin drops away as suddenly as it surfaced, he knows a moment of sheer vertigo. He forces himself to look at the horizon. Opaque water, opaque wall of green.

Returning to the locker, he passes one of the nuns swaying gently in a hammock. A fold of her habit drags its black point over the deck.

October 21st, 1844, Óbidos

Having arrived by dark, we woke to behold the town perched atop cliffs of pink and yellow clay—a welcome vision after two days of nothing but cacao plantations. The morning's jungle chorus included a familiar cry, that of *Homo sapiens*, the female of the species. We lay at anchor some distance from shore, yet half a dozen Indian girls had swum out to school about the *Sasurána* like dolphins greeting sailors becalmed at sea. Indeed, they seemed shaped to purpose by an aquatic life, a certain streamlined athleticism evident in their limbs.

Romão and the Indians made ready to join them, but Senhor Chryostomo, ever mindful of misplacing his crew, barked the order to remain aboard. The girls graced us with their presence for perhaps a quarter of an hour, bobbing and laughing, occasionally calling out some pleasantry in Língua Geral, the fluttering common tongue. One, a slender girl with lively eyes, surprised us by diving down at the *Sasurána*'s stern and reappearing in moments off her bow.

Paul lifts his gaze. He remembers the first time he read about the pretty swimmers—followed by turning the page to find Walter had moved on to the next phenomenon of note. It shouldn't have come as a surprise. For the most part, women made fleeting appearances in his father's account: a ribeirinho mother hurrying her daughters out of sight, a proud mulatta sporting a tray of sweets like an oversized crown.

In his mind, Paul gave the swimming girls more play. As a boy, he pictured them in mythical terms: brown-backed, leaping creatures with subtle fins, they wrestled anacondas in the murk. The older he got, the more human they became—*a certain streamlined athleticism*. Eventually they spawned a series of feverish poems. He came upon several examples while packing for the move to Iris's—mortifying scribbles he tore into fragments before dropping them into the stove.

The girls were never really his. It was his father, not he, who'd woken to their rousing cries. It was Walter who'd stood witness as the one with the flashing eyes upended herself and dove.

16

They've been hugging the southern shore all afternoon. To Rachel's surprise, Paul has convinced Iris to join them for dinner—their final one on board.

He's leading them to the dining room when Iris cries out and begins pawing at herself like a woman possessed. They bundle her back to the cabin, Rachel lifting away her hat while Paul lights the lamp. Minute, pale-winged flies cling to Iris's forearms, her bosom, her face. She whimpers at the sight of them, her eyes filling with tears.

"It's all right, Iris." Rachel hands the water jug to Paul. "Perhaps you could bring us some cool water."

"Yes, of course." He hesitates, his hand on the doorknob. "You have to press out the blood."

Rachel nods.

"Each and every—"

"Bite, yes." She too has read Walter's accounts of the infamous pium—the infernal itching occasioned by the sudden, vaporous swarm.

When he's gone, she helps a trembling Iris undress. "Hold still now." Slowly, methodically, she sets about plucking and crushing the pium. Turning Iris round in the lamplight, she kneels to get at the ones on her ankles and calves. At the sound of the knock, she wraps her mistress in a shawl and opens the door, just wide enough to receive the jug.

"Is she all right?"

"She's fine." Rachel sees her own doubt reflected in Paul's expression. "You go on without us. I'll find you when I can."

"You're very good to me," Iris says quietly.

They're sitting close, Iris propped against her pillows, Rachel perched on the edge of the bunk. "And you to me."

"I feel like such a fool. Did anyone notice?"

"I don't know. I don't think so."

Rachel has made her way to the last of the bites, a dark, raised dot behind Iris's ear. The blood bubbles up as she presses to either side of it with her fingertips. She wipes the red bead away. "There. Now you lie back."

Iris complies. "I keep thinking . . ."

"About what?"

"Just . . . well, just how easy it would be to get lost."

Rachel swishes her cloth in the basin. "You mean in the jungle?"

"In the jungle, yes." Iris hesitates. "Only it happened when I was in London too. I used to have these visions of disappearing down the back of my seat at the theatre, or even between the paving stones in my aunt's garden." She gives a short laugh. "So many *very old families* with room for an American brewery heiress. Thank God for the Zoological Gardens. It was one of those eligible bachelors who first took me there—a Lord Waterton, or Waterson? Whoever he was, he must have regretted his choice. I set up my camp stool in front of the quagga's enclosure and promptly forgot he was there."

"I remember the quagga." It was a favourite from Iris's early sketchbooks: the rare equine standing alone in its pen, part exotic zebra, part familiar mare. Rachel had smudged the poor creature's outline, touching her finger to its mane—an error she didn't repeat.

Iris sighs. "Not my best work."

"I thought it was beautiful."

"I was still learning."

"Even so."

Iris is quiet. A bite in the soft crease of her elbow trickles blood. Rachel dabs at it.

"It was the only time I felt like myself over there," Iris says. "When I was drawing."

Rachel nods.

"It seemed as good a life as any, working on my own . . ." Her face twists, the sorrow sudden, acute.

Laying the cloth aside, Rachel takes hold of her mistress's hand. "Rio Negro tomorrow," she says firmly. "Not a bloodsucking pest to be seen."

Iris nods and draws a shaky breath. "Black water."

"That's right, black water. And we're nearly there."

Paul wakes to a glow, the lamp still burning from when he drifted off. The porthole is dark, the promenade quiet. The notebook has fallen closed on his hand.

Rachel never did come find him. As the dining room emptied, he sought the steward and made himself understood. Balancing a stack of covered bowls, he knocked at the cabin door with his foot. Rachel answered with a finger held to her lips, accepted the food and withdrew.

He won't sleep now. Better to read than to lie here worrying, wondering if they were right to come.

November 24th, 1844, Senhor Aracú's plantação, mouth of the Rio Madeira

Last night having been the occasion of my twenty-second birthday, our host made free with his stores of cachaça rum and Lisbon wine. Sore head notwithstanding, I rose at dawn with a view to making the most of our final day here. Caetano was not in his hammock. Having sought him among the negroes' huts where the women were already at their fires, I descended to the beach in the hopes of finding him asleep in one of the dugouts. Instead, I chanced to observe two Indians about their morning bathe.

These men had the look of brothers, or perhaps father and son, generations being difficult to gauge among these races so strangely untouched by age. Only yards from where they strode into the stream, a woman squatted on her heels gutting a paca—this being a rodent similar in size and colouring to a fawn. She stood to fling the entrails into the river, and almost instantly the water's surface began to dance. I thought to alert the men to the presence of piranha, then saw by the glance of one and the nod of the other that both were well aware. They went about their ablutions, secure in the knowledge that the school was being fed.

With Caetano nowhere to be found, I determined to set out on my own. Senhor Aracú's jungle track forms a loop of several hours' duration beyond his furthest cacao field. The forest thereabouts is well established, with a high, dense canopy that casts a greenish gloom. The understorey supports little growth, the ground blanketed with layers of vegetation in varying states of decay.

It was quiet, or relatively so, the birds and other warm-blooded species having taken refuge from the midday heat. I too was in need of rest. I had seated myself on a log and was unscrewing the cap from my water flask when I heard a sound like a gust of wind. I looked to the boughs above me, but their leaves hung motionless. Moments later the source of the sound became clear. While I sat dumbstruck, a snake of astounding proportions flowed past not ten paces from my boots—*Boa constrictor*, some dozen feet in length.

Had it not been for the shush and crackle of its great weight, the creature might have passed unremarked, so precisely did its pattern answer its surrounds. It seemed more fluid than flesh—a brook turned swift and deliberate as it ploughs through a narrow cut. Snatching up my gun, I made chase, but at the sound of my crashing pursuit the snake simply doubled its speed. Where I surged and stumbled, it rippled over fallen branches with ease. I was already lagging hopelessly when it disappeared beneath a dense curtain of vines. I considered dropping to my belly and continuing the chase, but a moment's sober reflection had me turn and retrace my steps.

Paul shakes his head, laying the notebook beside him on the bunk. He sees himself seated beside his father in the jungle. Like Walter, he watches the great serpent come gliding with awe.

Where the father follows, however, the son leaps to his feet and flees.

Paul eyes the open porthole. After a moment he gets up and reaches for his shirt.

He's climbing the aft ladder stairs when a voice comes winding over the waves. *Come, feel with me his blood applied* . . . a rough tenor carried who knows how far. Paul halts, the upper deck level with his chest. He doesn't spot Rachel until she moves, springing from her hammock to cross to the moonlit rail. For a moment she appears to listen. Then, to his amazement, she sings.

"My Lord, my Love, is crucified."

He stands suspended. It's not that her voice is the sweetest he's heard, only that it's so strong, so unerringly clear.

"Paul?"

He sees himself as she must, poorly lit, emerging from a hole. "Sorry, did I startle you?" He climbs the last few steps, coming to stand beside her.

"No, it's all right."

Nothing more from the distant tenor; they must have passed out of his hearing. Either that or he prefers to sing alone.

"Did you hear him?" Rachel asks.

He nods. "Him and you. I thought Quakers didn't sing."

"We don't," she says. "They don't." Then, after a moment, "Creaturely pursuits."

"I beg your pardon?"

"Singing, dancing. Music plays havoc with a body's peace."

"Hm." He surveys the river's blackness. "'I am satisfied . . . I see, dance, laugh, sing . . .'"

"What's that?"

"A poem. Well, part of one."

"Say more."

As God comes a loving bedfellow . . . Paul shakes his head. "I don't remember."

"Another, then. Say another."

Holding on to the rail, he leans back, looking up. The lines come spiralling. "'Up goes my Boat among the stars, Through many a breathless field of light, Through many a long blue field of ether, Leaving ten thousand stars beneath her: Up goes my little Boat so bright.'"

Just as he's beginning to feel a fool, she says quietly, "How do you know that?"

He looks at her.

"How do you know that hymn?"

"It's one of Mrs. Pryce's."

"Ah. Well, the poem is one of Mr. Wordsworth's."

The moonlight has altered her eyes. Once, during a geology tutorial, he held a lozenge of hematite—that weighty silver-grey. He says the only thing he can think of. "How's Iris?"

Rachel lets go of the rail. "She's fine."

"Good."

She steps away from him. "Best be getting back."

17

It's crowded on the upper deck, every chair and hammock full. Still no sign of Iris or Rachel. Paul lays the satchel down beside him on the locker, saving room.

November 30th, 1844, Mouth of the Rio Negro
It was with no small measure of relief that we departed the pest-ridden southern shore. Sailing northwest, we seemed to leave one land for another. Behind us stood torn-away banks topped with a chaos of brilliant green trees; before us lay a scene of receding hills clothed in dark, uniform forest and aprons of ribbed white beach.

The Amazon and Negro rivers meet but do not immediately mix, running ochre alongside black for a distance of some three or four miles. Fish congregate along this churning seam, and with them a long string of canoes. Nor is Man alone in answering the call. We heard the familiar blowing of botos and caught sight of many a rose-coloured dorsal ridge. Eagle-eyed Romão spotted the lone fin of *Carcharius leucas*, the bull shark, knifing along the line as though it would sever the paired currents in twain.

Were it not for the marked distinction between waters, one might easily mistake the tributary for a continuation of the main. While the alto or upper Amazon narrows and curves away to the southwest, the mouth of the mighty Rio Negro gapes dead ahead. We departed the familiar yellow current littered with uprooted trees for what appeared to be a vast lake of ink. The river's true colour—akin to that of strong, clear tea— became apparent as we drew closer to shore. Here the white sand bottom showed bronze to a depth of three fathoms or more.

It is this very sand that is the author of the water's darkness, for those plants that thrive in such poor soil tend to be rich in tannins. Lessons learned at my father's knee: the selfsame poisons that preserve leather from rot render the country hereabouts less hospitable to insect life.

In anticipation of our arrival at Barra, Senhor C. suggested we tie up in a cove and bathe. Here the shallows took on a cast of gold. While not so silky as that of the silt-laden main, the water was refreshing to both body and eye. Upon climbing back aboard, Senhor C. and I took the time to shave and trim our hair before donning our cleanest attire.

I will be sorry to part ways. Senhor Chryostomo has been a generous and steady companion to me these eleven weeks, though a less reserved man might have done more to advance my Portuguese. Perhaps Senhor da Silva will prove more forthcoming. At any rate, Senhor C. assures me that, while da Silva is a canny trader, he is without doubt an homem honrado—an honourable man.

Paul knows this is the end. He turns the page anyway, staring down at the foxed endpaper of his father's notebook as though willing the next entry to arise. Walter never penned another word about the Rio Negro. Not a single observation or collection note; nothing about the honourable trader who became his friend and then his brother-in-law. No matter. Soon Paul will see the inky depths and golden inlets for himself. Soon he will shake the hand of the uncle he's never known.

"Senhoras e senhores." Paul glances up to see the mate standing by the rail. "Senhoras e senhores, estamos nós aproximando do encontro das águas."

Paul recognizes the word *águas*, and the reaction of his fellow passengers supports his guess as to the rest. To a one, they rise and hurry forward. Tucking the notebook into his satchel, he falls in behind.

He could crowd up alongside the bridge with the others, but chances are the view is just as good from the promenade. He's been careful on the ladder stairs until now—easing down backwards, gripping the rail—but this time he descends face-forward like a member of the crew. Passing through the opening in the deck, he grabs hold of the frame and swings down over the last few steps. No time to waste if he's going to collect Iris and Rachel. They'll want to be there when the two great rivers meet.

18

Barra presents a gentle aspect. The open river sparkles darkly with the breeze, but the bay lies black and glassy, cradled between two points of land. As they steam toward the busy docks, Paul spots the remnants of the old fort, now a riverbank ruin. Stretching up from a shoreline of slopes and cutaway cliffs, the settlement shows the Mediterranean colours of Pará. Forest clothes the rolling surrounds, drapes and gathers about the town.

When it comes time to disembark, Paul finds himself scanning the crowd. He gives way without protest when Captain Faria steps forward to hand Iris ashore. In spite of the many blemishes that mark her face and throat, she's forsaken the grey veil for a lighter one in ivory. It floats like a pale mist about her head.

The dock swarms with passengers and crew. Paul ushers the two women to one side, barricading a space around them with the party's smaller cases. He's getting better at this—beginning to feel, if not at home, then not entirely at sea.

"Paulo!"

It's his name and it isn't; his father used it rarely and only when the two of them were alone. Paul turns as the crowd eases apart to allow a man through. He's built like a bull, taller than those around him, a single lick of silver in his close-cropped hair.

"Paulo." Before Paul can stop him, the man who can only be Senhor da Silva closes him in an embrace.

"Senhor—"

"Senhor?" He keeps hold of Paul by the shoulders. His face too is a bull's—broad across the nose and brow, the gaze unsettlingly direct. "You call me Tio, Tio Paulo." His voice wavers, his eyes filling suddenly, incredibly, with tears. "My condolences on the death of your father, nephew."

Paul nods, caught off guard by the man's command of English as much as his emotional display. Walter never shared his brother-in-law's infrequent letters; Paul assumed they'd corresponded in Portuguese. "Thank you," he says. "Thank you, Tio."

Da Silva releases him. "And you are Walter's wife," he says, shifting his attention, "you are his Íris." *Eer-is*—this too da Silva alters, making it his own.

Iris stands terribly still. Then her smile, her hand in its fawn-coloured glove. "Senhor da Silva."

"Senhora, allow me to offer my—"

"And this is my companion," she says brightly, "Miss Weaver."

Da Silva reaches for Rachel's hand. Paul can't help but remark the fresh crop of freckles. When did she give up wearing gloves?

"Muito prazer, senhor," Rachel says.

Da Silva smiles. "Muito prazer, Senhorita Weaver." He turns back to Iris. "My condolences, senhora." Again the tremor threatens in his voice. "He was a brother to me."

Paul senses a crack forming in Iris's composure, a corresponding fissure in his own. "Perhaps we should see to the trunks," he says.

"Not to worry, my men will deal with them." Da Silva takes up the heaviest of the cases as though it's a child's basket. "Come."

"Whereabouts are you moored?"

Da Silva dismisses Paul's question with a wave. "My brother insists we take dinner with him. We will spend the night there also, to make an early start." He holds his arm out to Iris. "Are you hungry, senhora?"

"Do you know, Senhor da Silva, I believe I am."

Paul stands bewildered as the pair of them turn to depart. It takes him a moment to realize Rachel is waiting, carpet bag in hand. "Right," he says, bending for the remaining cases. "Let's go."

In his brother's house, Senhor da Silva turns formal. "Senhora Ash, Senhor Paulo Ash, Senhorita Weaver, may I present my brother, Senhor Honório da Silva, and his wife."

Senhor Honório offers his condolences with a stiff little bow. Clearly the younger of the two brothers, he effects a paternal, even proprietary air. His wife dwarfs him by a good eight inches, though half of that is hair—a mass of plaits and bundles studded with deep pink blooms.

"Seu pobre rosto," the senhora says to Iris. "Como é terrível para você."

Rachel catches only *rosto*—face—and something that sounds like "terrible."

"My wife—" For a moment Senhor Honório is at a loss. "My wife hopes you have not been too troubled with the pium."

"Oh. Thank you," says Iris. "Obrigada, senhora."

Rachel's hand twitches in sympathy with the one her mistress raises to her cheek. Having relinquished her hat and veil to the whip-thin Indian girl who answered the door, Iris can only pat self-consciously at her hair.

The meal is daunting: the smells of a dozen unfamiliar dishes, a conversation that founders more often than it floats. Taking her cue from Senhor da Silva on her right, Rachel makes a small mound of salt and hot peppers on her plate and douses it with a spoonful of gravy. The resulting pool is spicy but not unpleasant. She dabs at it with a morsel of meat.

"You will take some wine, Senhora Ash?" Senhor Honório asks.

"Thank you, senhor."

Down the far end, his wife speaks up. He smiles. "My wife wishes you to know this wine comes from her home country, from Lisboa."

"Home country?" Senhor da Silva reaches across Rachel for the decanter. "She was born in Óbidos." He turns to his sister-in-law. "Isn't that right, Dona Eliana? Você nasceu em Óbidos?"

She snaps a reply, two spots of colour blooming on her cheeks.

Senhor Honório's smile becomes fixed. "I should say my wife's *people* are from Lisboa. Her parents came to this country in 1832."

"Both of them, you understand," the elder brother adds. "Dona Eliana is pure European stock."

The senhora looks to her husband for a translation, but he says nothing. Seated to their hostess's left, Paul wears a trapped, miserable look. Rachel wishes she had Iris's gift for distracting him; it's trying enough to spend time with such a family without having to make sense of them being your own.

"Not so many of her kind in Barra," Senhor da Silva continues. "Our own dear mother came from Ireland, but she had the good sense to marry a ribeirinho."

Senhor Honório clears his throat. "Our father was a merchant."

"O que quer dizer, 'merchant'?" Senhor da Silva laughs. "You might be a merchant, Honório, but our father was a trader, just like me."

Senhor Honório is quiet for a moment. Then, "You remind me, we have had word from Senhor Brandão. He has received more salsaparrilha than he can store."

"What of it?"

"I only wondered if Senhora Ash would mind—"

"Honório," Senhor da Silva says darkly, "a lancha está indisponível."

Iris looks from one man to the other. "Is there some difficulty?"

"No difficulty."

"If the fee my husband negotiated is insufficient—"

Senhor da Silva holds up a hand. "Believe me, senhora, there is no difficulty. We have other boats." He glares at Senhor Honório.

Rachel catches Paul's eye before he fastens his gaze to his plate. In the ensuing silence, the senhora pipes up again, something familiar in her glittering gaze. Rachel flashes on Annie Coffin standing to address the Women's Meeting.

Senhor Honório nods, turning his attention back to Iris. "My wife and I hope you will be comfortable here, senhora."

"I'm sure we shall."

"You will find the accommodation at my brother's sitio a little more . . . primitive."

"Honório, basta." Senhor da Silva shakes his head. "You must forgive my brother, senhora, he is Brazilian but not, as we say, Amazônico."

Iris takes a sip of her wine. "You say your mother was Irish, senhor?"

His expression softens. "She was, senhora. She was born in a town called Drogheda."

"And how did she make her way to this part of the world?"

"She came with an English family. She was the lady's maid." He smiles. "She was just a girl, but strong, you know? She was—" He searches for the term. "Resourceful."

"I should imagine so. I wonder, did she—"

"Senhor Paulo," the senhora says suddenly. *"Senhor Paulo."*

Paul looks startled.

"Você não fala Português?"

"I regret not, senhora. I am learning. Eu . . . aprendo."

Undeterred, she questions him further. He looks to Rachel for help. The grammar is in the carpet bag, but she's caught enough of the meaning to try. "I believe Senhora da Silva—"

"My wife asks if you find Barra much changed," says Senhor Honório.

"I, senhora?" Paul hesitates. "I'm afraid I was not yet one year of age when we departed. I recall nothing of the region."

Senhor Honório passes this on to his wife, who replies with energy. He nods. "We are much built up in that time."

"Muitos Índios." The senhora purses her lips at the thought of the city's native population. "E agora eles querem o nome da cidade—"

"And why shouldn't they?" Senhor da Silva mutters.

"Last year they changed the city's name," Senhor Honório explains. "Manaus is an Indian name—"

"Manaus," Senhor da Silva says loudly, "is the true name. The name before Cidade da Barra do Rio Negro."

"O que ele disse?" the senhora demands. "Honório, o que ele disse?"

What did he say? Rachel is surprised how much she understands.

Senhor Honório shakes his head. "Nada de importante, meu amor."

⌒

The morning is rich with light. As their little party winds through the laneways of Barra, Paul can't help but notice the return of his uncle's bonhomie. Clearly he too is relieved to leave Senhor Honório and his wife behind.

En route to the docks, they pass through the market's sprawl. Once again Paul brings up the rear. He stumbles on the rough cross-hatching of boards, his feet made dull by a poor night's sleep. The room overlooking the scented courtyard might have been comfortable if he'd had it to himself. His uncle had ignored the second bed; throwing open the shutters, he'd strung his woven rede up across the window's eye. *Boa noite, Paulo.* In minutes the older man began to snore. Paul drifted in and out of the steady soughing, vaguely sickened by the garlic and turtle oil repeating in his throat. At the breakfast table he stuck to fruit, until the senhora insisted on loading his plate.

Now, as they file past a chorus line of roasted ham hocks, he feels an unpleasant flutter in his gut. The joints are smaller than the ones he knows; they must be peccary, little wild hogs known to be both dangerous and tasty. The heat among the open grills is intense. Skewers of what look to be elaborate knots turn out to be songbirds, threaded ten to a stick. Paul comes close to stepping on a small, chestnut-coloured dog. Swollen with pups or hunger, it laps intently at a pool of grease.

It's marginally cooler among the fish vendors, but the stench is almost more than Paul can bear. The ground is slippery, winking with scales. It goes on for what feels like a mile: catfish in black armour beside what look to be salmon with fangs; fish like cudgels, like blades. Everywhere, great reeking slabs of pirarucu.

Up ahead, da Silva pauses before a well-stocked stall. "See here, senhora, tambaqui. We had him last night, remember, the sweet fish you liked."

"Oh, yes," says Iris, "*tambaqui*."

"He likes it best in the igapó—the flooded forest," da Silva adds. "He finds a seringueira—the rubber tree, you know—or sometimes a palmeira, and he waits for the seeds to fall."

"How lovely." Iris reaches out as though she would stroke the black and gold fish, her hand hovering over its gills.

"And here, tucunaré." Da Silva pats a tiger-striped monster with a peacock tail spot and a ruby eye. "Look, Senhorita Weaver." He hooks in a finger to draw down its jaw. "This one could swallow you."

Paul's surprised when she flashes a boyish grin his uncle's way.

When they finally move on to roots and leaves, the smell of earth comes as a visceral relief. Paul lingers by a stall piled high with some feathery herb, enjoying the shade of its narrow roof—until a corner of that shade unfolds. The mulatta vendor smiles to see him jump. Her spider monkey watches him for a long moment before swinging out from beneath the eaves. Dragging its leash to the limit, it skitters across the roof. Paul's heart hammers. In the past he's wondered about the creature's common name—perhaps some dietary predilection? No longer. It's clear in the monkey's scuttle, its black, segmented limbs.

He hurries after the others, catching up where his uncle squats before an array of fruits. Passing a hand over what looks like a mound of empty green gloves, da Silva selects a fat yellow fruit with a blush at its plumper end. He rises, holding it out for Iris to smell.

"Oh, how marvellous."

"Senhor da Silva," Rachel says, taking up an egg-shaped fruit with a leathery skin, "is this an alligator pear?"

"Alligator pear, yes. We say abacate." Da Silva takes the fruit from her hand. "This one is finished." Replacing it on the pile, he presses a thumb to several others before making his choice. "Here. You can share with Angelo."

"Angelo?"

"You will meet him soon. Abacate is his special favourite." Da Silva signals to an old man in an apron, indicating both the alligator pear and the fruit with the appealing scent.

Paul draws a handful of copper money from his pocket, but before he can make sense of it, his uncle has already paid.

The name of the launch comes as a surprise: *Bridie Mac*, spelled out along the hull in glossy green script. She's smaller than Paul imagined, perhaps thirty feet long with a beam of seven or eight feet. The cabin clearly sleeps no more than two. He'll be relegated to a hammock under the canopy, crowded in with the boiler, the engine and the crew.

"Oi, Capitão!" A light-skinned negro ducks out from beneath the canopy as they approach. His hair is grizzled, his beard touched white about the mouth, yet he springs from deck to dock like a youth.

"Viva, Deolindo." Da Silva slaps the older man on the shoulder, and another round of introductions begins.

"Senhora, senhorita, senhor." Deolindo drops a series of small bows.

"Muito prazer, Deolindo." Iris turns to da Silva. "And are we to call you Capitão as well?"

"If you wish, senhora." He smiles. "It is the usual thing."

Paul clears his throat. "Pardon me, Tio, but where is your crew?"

"My crew?" Da Silva points to himself. "Here is your capitão. Here is my mate, Deolindo, and our deckhand . . . Oi, Deolindo, onde está Tuí?"

"Buscando uma corda."

"Our deckhand has gone to get a rope."

Paul can't help himself. "Three of you? That's all?"

His uncle grins, translating Paul's question to his mate.

"Certamente que não," Deolindo says, winking. "Há também Angelo."

"Angelo," da Silva barks, "you lazy beggar, show yourself."

No question Angelo knows his master's voice. He squeezes out from between two crates on the *Bridie Mac*'s deck—a cat the size of a beagle, the colour of freshly cut straw.

19

The river is placid, vast. They've been under way for an hour, and Iris has yet to retreat to her bunk. Seated beside Paul under the canopy, she appears almost content.

Rachel too should seek shelter from the sun, but that would mean abandoning her seat at the head of the starboard bench. The *Bridie Mac* plies the current neatly, a sweet and steady launch. Her engine is surprisingly quiet. Deolindo tends it with practised ease, occasionally calling for Tuí to help.

The deckhand appears equal to any task. His build is no heavier than Rachel's, yet he'd arrived at the dock bearing a coil of rope that would have buckled many a grown man's knees. His age is difficult to guess—thirteen? fifteen?—his face dominated by the tattoo around his mouth. A perfect circle of black. The effect is in no way sinister, only strange. "Pure-blood Juri," Capitão da Silva had informed them. "From the Rio Solimões, the upper Amazon. Boca-pretos we call them—black-mouths."

Tuí. Rachel has known other Indians by name: Caleb and John, the pair of Delawares Papa hired to help get in the corn; Little Hannah, who cleaned and carried at Parsons' Dry Goods, herself a convinced Friend. Never an Indian like this, though. Never a hunter who, when nothing is required of him, hunkers unmoving, his eyes alight.

She really should join the others in the shade. Her hands and forearms are already as freckled as they ever were in childhood. Her bonnet offers some protection, but the heat itself will sap her vitality—even if it does feel good.

Her hand finds the abacate, warm in her pocket, the sun having reached it through the folds of her skirt. She draws it out.

"Você quer prová-lo?"

She hasn't heard Deolindo approach. He squats down beside her, holding out his hand. She gives him the heavy fruit. Drawing his tresado from its sheath, he turns the abacate against the blade and twists the two halves apart, revealing a sphere of polished wood set in pale green flesh.

He sets aside the hollowed half. Cupping the other portion in his palm, he drops the blade in a controlled chop, lodging it in the stone. With a delicate twist, he lifts the pretty sphere from the fruit. Knocks it free against the gunwale to float away.

"Nós comemos com açúcar e vinho."

Sugar and wine. Yet he seems to be offering her the fruit as is, straight from the skin.

"Prova," he urges.

She presses a fingertip to the slick green pulp. Scooping out a gobbet, she hesitates before slipping it between her lips. The taste makes her close her eyes: first butter, fresh and slippery from the churn, then . . . green. She can think only of cucumbers, Papa straightening to offer her one fresh from the vine.

"É bom?"

She opens her eyes. "É—" She wants to say "creamy," but "cream" will have to do. "—é crème."

He grins and hands her both halves, shaking his head when she gestures for him to keep one.

"Muito obrigada." As she digs out a second fingerful, something butts at the small of her back.

"Oh-ho," Deolindo laughs, "aqui vem Angelo."

The ship's cat winds around Rachel's hip as though he's known her for years. Here in the bow, with sunlight bouncing off the spray, Angelo shimmers like gold. He looks up at her with longing, and she finds herself nodding a ridiculous assent. It's so easy with some creatures. The first lick does the job, but he follows it up with a thorough, raspy lapping, scraping her finger clean.

⁓

Iris looks well by the firelight; already her welts are healing. For the first time in what feels like forever, Paul has his stepmother to himself. His uncle is busy with his axe at the jungle's margin, Tuí jogging armloads of wood down to the dugout. The *Bridie Mac* bobs at anchor with Angelo sitting guard. Apparently nothing—not even the prospect of fresh fish guts—can tempt the ship's cat ashore.

At the water's edge, Deolindo cleans the evening's catch. For some reason, Rachel has taken it upon herself to act as his helper. She kneels beside him, whittling. From time to time he hands her a rough fillet, which she fixes to a forked stick.

"Hidden talents, our Rachel," Iris says.

"Indeed."

"You're all right, you two, aren't you? I'd hate for you not to get along."

Paul adds a twist of wood to the blaze. "We're fine, Iris. We get along fine."

"Good." She shifts on her camp stool.

"Are you comfortable?"

"As comfortable as a body can be in all this. I do envy you your breeches."

He laughs.

"It is a relief, though," she adds, "getting shut of that veil."

He nods. A relief to him too—no longer making do with the memory of her face. *Lean on me,* the line comes to him, *hide thine eyes: / Only ourselves, earth and skies, / Are present here: be wise.* A chill travels his backbone, just as it did when he first happened upon those words. Shut up in his boarding house room, he lost many a night to his illustrated volume of Miss Rossetti's poems.

"Jaguar sun," Iris says absently.

"Hm?"

She points over his shoulder. "Jaguar sun. Our eyes grow feeble just as theirs come into their own."

He turns to see the sun dull red and dying, caught among the trees. It will be dark before long, the night so definite here, so certain of its share. "Yes," he says, returning his gaze to the flames, "I remember something about that."

From the trees a shrilling of crickets, the bleat and chuckle of frogs. As always, the question that enters Paul's mind is the wrong one—not *What species?* but *What are they trying to say?* He's considering whether to share this with Iris when another sound wipes his mind clean. The grunt-hoot is loud. He scans the treetops: not a single silhouette. A second hoot, this one sustained. Paul meets Iris's eye. A glint of mischief there—or is it unease?

The third call opens out into a chorus, every monkey in the troop giving voice. Paul's eyes close of their own accord. For a time—the duration of several heartbeats—he's with his father. The pair of them lie side by side in their bedrolls, encircled by a lasso. The rope is coarse enough to keep snakes at bay; the campfire persists against all else. Coyote packs have taken up positions to the east and west, dividing the night with their cries. It's a sound to make the heart grow cold, but only until Walter shifts in his sleep, turning his face Paul's way.

"My God," Iris says over the rising din. Nothing ambiguous about her expression now: her eyes are swimming, threatening to spill.

"*Mycetes seniculus,*" Paul hears himself say. "I believe the natives call them guaribas."

She nods miserably.

"It's not an alarm," he assures her. "More of a declaration."

"Of territory," she says.

"Precisely."

Still the troop howls on, and though he searches his mind, Paul finds nothing helpful to add. He's almost thankful to see the others drawing near. Firelight picks out the axe at his uncle's shoulder, the tresado in Deolindo's hand. Tuí brings a load of silvery firewood, but it's Rachel who catches the lion's share of the light. She comes bearing a bouquet of sharpened sticks, her forearms draped with the scaled flanks of fish.

〜

Rachel wakes to the sound of the *Bridie Mac* already under way. The cabin is warm, despite a breeze through the open portholes. Sitting up, she nudges the ceiling planks with her crown. The bunk across from hers lies empty; Iris has risen before her—an unprecedented event. Rachel dresses hurriedly, stooping by the glass to tuck away a stray lock of hair.

No one turns as she ducks out the cabin door. Paul lies reading in his hammock. Across from him, Iris sits sidesaddle on the starboard bench, her skirts flowing down to the deck. Da Silva sits easy at the helm, a thin cigar smouldering in his fingers. Tuí perches beside him on a crate. His hair is wet; he must have slipped over the side before they weighed anchor. As Rachel watches, he reaches for the cigar, draws on it and returns it to the captain's hand.

"Bom dia, senhorita." Deolindo edges up alongside the cabin, en route from stern to engine with an armload of wood.

"Bom dia, Deolindo."

"O dia clareia."

The day is clear—or possibly bright? Either way, Rachel nods and returns his smile.

As she moves forward under the canopy, a padding step alerts her to Angelo's presence overhead. Coming alongside Iris, she feels her heart kick. The sketchbook lies open on her mistress's lap, both pages covered in a tangle of forms.

Iris looks up from beneath her sunbonnet's brim. "Bom dia, dearest."

"Bom dia."

"Capitão da Silva was kind enough to delay our departure while I made some preliminary studies." She indicates a selection of vines laid out before her on the bench. "He had Tuí cut these for reference."

Rachel can see where her mistress has begun to work up the details—veins and tendrils, elastic stems. "It's coming along nicely."

Iris sighs. "Not really."

Rachel steps past the foliage and sits.

"Half the time you can't tell which leaf belongs to which stem," Iris adds.

"I doubt the plants know themselves."

"It's important, though." Iris lays her pencil side-on to the page and begins shading. "You know how Walter . . . how much store he set on accuracy."

Rachel flashes on the pair of them standing before the atrium's bare wall—Iris demonstrating the possible arc of a palm frond, Walter with his head bent over Mr. Kent's *Botany of the Torrid Zone*. "I suppose you must do as you've always done," she says.

"As I've always done. If I only knew."

"You do know, Iris. You look at what's before you, and you set down what you see."

Iris stares at the page, her pencil suspended. Bracing a hand on the gunwale, Rachel turns to take in the view. The shore lies distant across the soft, dark swell. Pendent above the land, a line of flat-bottomed clouds forms a second horizon, a pale echo of the jungle below. Beauty strikes her like a blow. For a moment her eyes fill, causing the scene to blur. "Look," she says. "Iris, look."

—~—

They're passing close by the jungle's edge, easing into a sandy bay, when Paul's uncle glances round from the helm. "We will go ashore here, senhora, take our lunch on the beach."

"Lovely," says Iris. "And after lunch?"

He laughs. "Siesta, of course. Then three, maybe four hours until the sitio, until my home."

Just then Tuí points into the trees. Paul looks up to where a flock of pheasant-like birds have colonized a leafy crown.

Iris raises the field glasses. "Look, Paul," she says, passing them. "Aren't they funny with those crests?"

Recalling his father's technique, Paul fixes his gaze on one of the birds before bringing the heavy brass glasses to his eyes. It's as plump as a chicken, its red eye set in a patch of sky-blue skin. Iris is right, the crest of spiky feathers lends it a clownish air. He hands the glasses back. As Iris passes them on to Rachel, he reaches for the gun. "Ladies," he says, sighting along the top barrel, "I suggest you cover your ears."

The report thunders in his skull. The birds are clumsy in flight, struggling up from the branches as he fires his second barrel into their midst. Not a single one falls.

"Bad luck," says Iris. Beside her, Rachel lowers her gaze.

Paul sets the shotgun down on a trunk. Da Silva gives Deolindo the signal to shut her down—clanking dampers, squealing valves. Gliding quiet now, aside from the retreating echoes of the flock. The launch noses along the trees, Tuí crouched on the forward gunwale, bowline in hand.

"You want birds, Paulo?" his uncle asks. "I thought only snakes and turtles, caimanos."

"Not for the collection, per se. I thought perhaps for our lunch . . ."

"Lunch?" Da Silva grins. "No, no, not cigana."

Deolindo holds his nose. "Catinga."

Cigana—Paul remembers now. Walter learned the lesson two decades ago, when his aim was good enough to bring one of the clambering birds down. *Just because it looks like a pheasant doesn't mean it tastes like one.* Catinga is a specific smell, a fetid blend of musk and manure.

Having lassoed a tree limb and made the *Bridie Mac* fast, Tuí moves aft. When he says something in Língua Geral to Deolindo, raising a chuckle, Paul suffers a wave of humiliated rage.

"Don't worry, Paulo," his uncle says. "Anything you want, you just show Tuí. He's a devil with the gravatana."

"Gravatana?" Iris says, delighted. "He uses a blowgun?"

Da Silva smiles at her. "Of course."

20

There are children on the dock, a boy perhaps four years of age, a girl no older than seven. His cousins, Paul realizes with a jolt.

"Papai!" the boy shouts, and his sister after him, "Papai!"

"Oi, Vitor," da Silva calls back, "Lene!"

"This is it, Paul." Iris tucks her arm through his. "This is where you were born."

He does his best to smile.

The children are on board before the *Bridie Mac* comes to a complete stop. "Olá, meus macaquinhos!" Da Silva presses them to his side, keeping one hand on the wheel. The girl hugs him about the waist, her brother clinging giddily to a leg.

While Tuí and Deolindo make the launch fast, Paul's uncle presents his children to their guests. Vitor turns shy for the introductions, but Lene stands straight-backed at her father's side.

"Pleased to meet you, Senhora Ash, Senhorita Weaver."

"My," says Iris, "such good English."

The girl beams. When Paul extends his hand, she surprises him by turning her face up to be kissed.

"Well?" says da Silva. "Aren't you going to greet your cousin?"

Flustered, Paul drops a hasty peck on the girl's cheek.

"Welcome, Senhor Ash."

"You must call me Paul." He glances at his uncle. "Paulo."

"Paulo," she says. "Like Papai."

He nods, and Vitor takes courage. "Paulo!"

Da Silva laughs, his hand on the boy's shoulder. "Onde está Mamãe?"

Vitor turns, pointing up the bank to where a long thatched-roof house sits overlooking the bay. A lone figure stands on the verandah—yellow shift, black hair drawn back from her face. Paul feels something turn over in his chest.

"Viva, Carolina," da Silva calls up to her, and she raises a hand.

The dock is simple but serviceable, as are the split-log steps set directly into the bank. Paul is the first of their party up the steep incline, the children tugging him by both hands. Forty-four steps—he counts each one, his eyes on his boot tips. At the top, he meets a loose assembly of fruit trees, an overgrown capsicum bush, the peppers cherry-bright. He turns, no longer able to avoid his aunt's gaze.

"Aqui está Paulo, Mamãe," Lene says as she and Vitor lead him onto the verandah. They release him as their mother steps forward to close him in her arms. She is precisely his height. Her scent overwhelms him: woodsmoke and farinha, fruit.

"Meu menino," she says in his ear. "Menino de Zuleica."

At the sound of his mother's name, Paul is helpless. He concentrates on breathing, on willing the strength back into his knees. When he feels able, he breaks gently from his aunt's embrace.

She wipes a knuckle under each eye. "Bem-vindo, Paulo. Eu estive esperando por você."

Welcome—he knows that much. And *esperando*—hoping? Waiting? *Esperando.* A state Paul recognizes only now as his own.

———

149

Swept-earth floor, a smell of dry palm leaves. His uncle's house makes Senhor Felisberto's sparsely appointed rocinha seem cluttered. The furniture consists of hammocks and low stools, a shelf along one wall, a few trunks against the other. In the far corner, the guest quarters are simple stalls constructed of hanging mats. The main door stands open to the verandah; another looks out on a lean-to kitchen and an open shed.

Deolindo and Tuí fill their supper bowls and disappear along the path that follows the top of the bank. The family and their guests dine by lamplight around a cloth laid out on woven mats. Paul's uncle reclines on an elbow; his own bowl finished, he filches morsels from his wife's. Iris sits like a woman at a brookside picnic, her skirts fanned to the side. Beside her, Rachel kneels, sitting back on her feet like a child.

The true children take turns cradling the house's other inhabitant, a tamarin monkey named Flor. She's the first marmoset Paul has seen in the flesh, though he's catalogued countless illustrations, and even handled a golden-maned skin of *Midas leoninus*. Flor's coat isn't nearly so luminous, yet her appearance is by no means dull. Her facial fur is black, save for a set of snow-white, curling moustaches and beard. Her body is perhaps ten inches long and clothed in grey fur, her tail rust-coloured and longer by half. Her movements are delicate, darting—more squirrel than monkey in their effect. For the most part she's well behaved. The children are allowed to slip her slivers of fruit, but when she reaches to help herself, Paul's aunt checks her with a feline hiss.

The fare is simple—some species of boiled fowl served with fruit, farinha and rice—yet Paul finds himself eating long after he's full. At length, his aunt begins gathering up platters and bowls. Lene rises to help, but when Rachel moves to join them, Carolina murmurs over her shoulder.

"Mamãe says no," Lene tells her, taking up one of the lamps. "You are the guest." Mother and daughter carry the dishes out the side door into the night, and there comes the sound of pouring water and low talk.

Flor has been lulled into a state of submission in Vitor's lap. At a small sound she rouses and shoots off into the shadows. Pouncing on some scuttling thing, she jams her hands to her mouth and chews.

"Good girl, Flor," says da Silva. "Three casks of cachaça she cost me, but you see how she earns her fruit."

"Where did you get her?" Paul asks.

"She came with a trader from Iquitos. She was his special pet, but when these two saw her, that was that. And as I say, she is a good hunter—beetles, spiders . . . o que mais?"

"Cricket!" Vitor grins.

Iris claps her hands together. "Clever boy." She murmurs something to Rachel, who rises and crosses to the far corner, disappearing behind a mat partition.

Paul looks at Iris. "What are you up to?"

"Wait and see."

In moments Rachel returns with the sketchbook and pencil box. Iris selects the appropriate lead, turns to a fresh page and commences drawing. Vitor comes to stand beside her and lets out a gasp. Paul resists the urge to join his little cousin, waiting instead for Iris to share her work—which she does in record time.

She's captured the greasy exoskeleton, the high, hinged legs. Lifelike in the extreme, the cricket casts a shadow on the page.

When Iris lays the sketchbook down open on the mat, da Silva nods, chuckling. "Flor." He makes a kissing sound. "Oi, Florzinha, venha aqui."

The tamarin comes scampering. Catching sight of the cricket, she freezes, then leaps on the book. Hearing laughter, Lene appears in the doorway with a stack of bowls. Carolina isn't far behind.

"Mamãe," Vitor cries, "olha Flor!"

Paul's aunt sets her load of dishes down on the shelf and moves closer to watch Flor paw at the drawing. Not even the corner of a smile. After a moment she moves away.

"Come here, girl," da Silva says, scooping Flor up against his belly. Stroking her skull with his thumb, he clamps her busy hands to stillness. "Eh, senhora," he says, grinning, "make a snake."

Iris's eyes light up. "Oh, yes." She reaches for the sketchbook.

"Paulo," Carolina says from her seat in the corner hammock, "basta."

"Relaxe, Carolina."

Paul keeps his seat in the circle but somehow feels himself drawing back from the group. His uncle holds the tamarin close. Rachel is intent upon Iris, who is intent upon her work. The children flank her like carved guardians, watching the life on the page evolve.

"There." Iris lays down the sketchbook, revealing a constrictor made of line and shade. Flor lets out a shriek. Springing free of da Silva's grasp, she scrambles out the verandah door.

As laughter erupts around the circle, Paul glances at his aunt. Her face lost in shadow, she swings slowly, her bare heel braced against the earthen floor. Standing, he finds his foot has gone to sleep. He limps to the doorway. "Flor," he calls. "It's all right, Flor, come back."

"Come," da Silva calls from the verandah. "Everyone, the moon is bright."

Vitor has fallen asleep in a rede with Flor, but Lene is still awake. She leads Iris out by the hand, leaving the rest of them to follow on. Rachel hangs back, unsure whether Senhora da Silva has understood her husband's invitation.

"Carolina," da Silva calls, "venha ver a lua." And the senhora rises from her rede, reaching a hand up to smooth her hair. It's eerie, the resemblance between Paul and his long-lost aunt; she meets Rachel's eyes with a familiar, impenetrable gaze.

The moon is low, doubled in the still, black bay. Lene is the first to sit at the verandah's edge and dangle her legs. One by one the women join her—her mother on one side, Iris on the other, then Rachel. How many years since Rachel last hung her feet over the side of a raft? It's easily fifty feet down to the river, yet some childhood part of her expects it to close about her calves.

The men remain standing, one to either side of the open door. Hearing the scratch and flare of a lucifer match, Rachel turns to watch da Silva light one of his small cigars.

"You want one, Paulo?"

"No, thank you."

"I will," says Iris. "If that's all right."

Da Silva hesitates only briefly. "Certamente, senhora." He stoops to hand her the one from his lips, steps back and fishes in his pocket for another.

"Thank you." She takes a draw. "You needn't look like that, Paul. I'm sure nobody minds."

The sound in Paul's throat is ambiguous. Rachel says nothing; she's seen Iris smoke before, though never more than a puff on Walter's sweet-smelling pipe.

For a time there is only the drone of the jungle, punctuated by the odd whistle or bark. An occasional ribbon of talk reaches back along the bankside path—Deolindo and Tuí, and what sounds like a handful of other men. Da Silva sighs out smoke. Then Iris. Then a third, more forceful breath, a sudden exhalation flung up from the river below.

"Botos," Senhora da Silva says mildly.

"Oh, look, Paul," says Iris, and Rachel feels him come to stand behind them.

"Um, dois," Lene counts, "três, quatro, cinco. Cinco, Mamãe."

"Correto, meu coração."

Rachel makes her own reckoning: five pink dolphins passing close by the end of the dock. Even by moonlight they're more visible than their cousins in the silty main, distinct as they surface, ghostly in the clear brown stream. Movement aboard the *Bridie Mac* catches her eye—Angelo slipping aft to watch them go.

"Adeus, botos," da Silva calls out as the pod makes for the headland.

Lene giggles, raising her hand to wave. "Adeus, botos!"

"Às vezes," Senhora da Silva says after a moment, "boto vem como um homem."

"Ai, Carolina." Da Silva flicks the glowing stub of his cigar past them. "My wife, she likes the old stories."

The senhora gives him a look. "Lene," she says, turning back to the moon, "você dá o Inglês."

"Sim, Mamãe."

"Às vezes, boto vem como um homem," the senhora says again, and her daughter begins to translate.

"Sometimes Boto comes like a man. He comes to women who are alone. Who are . . . lonely." She pauses, listening to her mother. "He comes first in dreaming. Then he comes . . . he finds her on the beach. Always he is wearing white. Sometimes he is a stranger, but sometimes he looks like a husband."

Rachel steals a glance at Iris: no change, at least none she can detect. It's hard to be certain what will touch a nerve.

"Boto gives his woman *presentes*—"

"Presents," says da Silva.

"—presents from the Encante—this is the world at the bottom of the river, where Boto lives. But his love is a secret, his woman cannot tell."

The senhora touches a hand to her chest and continues.

"Mamãe says one woman did wrong. This woman, she showed her presents, and now the shoes Boto gave her, they turn into catfish. And the . . ."

"Necklace," her father says quietly.

"—the necklace turns into a sucuruju."

"A sucu . . . ?" says Iris, and before Rachel can translate, Paul stoops to place his hands on either side of Iris's neck.

"*A-na-con-da,*" he says softly. Rachel feels the hairs stand at her own bare nape. She stares at her lap, her cheeks growing warm.

"Fool." Iris slaps Paul's hands away. "Go on, senhora."

The senhora nods, addressing Iris directly now. Seated between them, Lene stares straight ahead. She says nothing until her mother nudges her.

"Sometimes . . . not so many times, Boto comes like a woman."

"My goodness," says Iris. "And does she wear white as well?"

Lene smiles shyly before delivering her mother's response. "When Boto is a woman, she wears nothing."

As if on cue, a swell of laughter from the huts along the path. It works on da Silva like a summons. "I will leave you now," he says over his shoulder, stepping off the verandah. "I must speak to Deolindo about the boiler." The moonlight is no match for the shadows of the bankside bower. In moments, the shape of him is gone.

21

It was never Paul's intention to spy. He emerged from his sleeping compartment to find Flor chirping at him from the rafters. Voices drew him to the doorway. It was only when he stepped out onto the verandah that he realized the sound was floating up from the beach.

Iris is in up to her waist. She's not far from Paul's aunt, the pair of them scooping water up over their shoulders, their arms. Vitor stands by his sister in the shallows, cupping doubled handfuls over her head. Rachel is farther out, swimming rather than bathing, her strokes surprisingly assured. From where Paul stands, she cuts the figure of a slender frog, her braid a bisecting line down her shirtwaist's grey back.

His aunt has unravelled her braid; her hair hangs black and shimmering down the back of her floating shift. Iris wears hers caught up in a net. Her navy-blue bathing trousers billow beneath the surface. Her dampened shirtwaist clings.

Paul tells himself he should step back from the edge, look out across the wider view.

"Bom dia, Paulo." His uncle steps onto the verandah.

"Oh, bom dia, Tio. I was just—"

"Good fishing this morning." Da Silva sets down his basket. "See what Tuí has caught for us."

"Very impressive."

Da Silva comes to stand beside him, looking down on the scene below. Carolina has taken charge of Vitor; she holds him by the wrist, rubbing handfuls of wet sand across his back. Iris ducks down, fanning her bare arms at her sides.

"Muito bom," da Silva murmurs, and Paul looks at him sharply. "Nothing like a morning dip, Paulo. That's what your father used to say."

The evocation catches Paul off guard. He drops his gaze.

"Don't worry, meu sobrinho. Our turn when the women are done."

When the men descend to the beach, da Silva wastes no time in joining his son. Crouching in the shallows, he returns one walloping splash for every half-dozen of Vitor's. Tuí must have bathed already—perhaps before he set about emptying the bay of fish—but Deolindo joins the party, appearing at the foot of a trail that winds down directly from his hut. He's barefoot, barechested. Striding into the river, he dives and surfaces, rolling over to float on his back.

Standing on the dock alongside the *Bridie Mac*, Paul becomes aware of someone watching him—or, more accurately, some*thing*. Angelo has made his way silently to the cabin roof. He sits gleaming in the morning sun, eyes fixed on the only human who has yet to go in.

Turning his back to the ship's cat, Paul strips off his shirt. The river bottom is visible at a fathom and a half, nothing but ripples of coppery sand. But what of the shadow beneath the dock? Closing his eyes, he confronts a flash of schooling piranha, a sinuous coil the width of his own thigh. Better to keep his eyes open. He squints, scanning the shoreline for questionable logs.

His little cousin comes paddling. "Você não pode nadar, Paulo?"

"He asks if you can swim," da Silva calls.

"Of course I can."

"Claro," his uncle relays.

"Ah." Vitor looks up at him. "Tímido."

It's clear the boy intends no malice; if anything, his tone is tinged with sorrow. *Tímido*. Paul swings his arms up by his ears and dives.

It's better once he's in. He strikes out across the bay, not too deep, keeping the bottom in view. Walter always said he was a natural swimmer. *That's it, Paulo, kick!*—holding Paul up until the buoyant moment then dropping his hands away.

Paul treads water, turning to find he's come farther than he thought. Also, he's the only one still in. Da Silva and the boy are partway up the stairs; Deolindo is nowhere to be seen. Paul is in the water alone.

No one will think it odd if he chooses to walk back along the beach. Chances are no one will even notice. He heads for shore— six strokes and he can touch bottom, a couple more and he can walk. The sand is firm beneath his feet, reassuring. Until it moves.

The pain is like none he's ever known. He screams, buckling at the knees to meet the surface open-mouthed. Water in his throat, the moment slowing as he registers an alien caress. A touch like heavy satin flutters across his ribs. Rolling, choking, he gasps for air. Something flows past him on the river's surface—a mud-ugly, dappled dorsum, a bright, untroubled eye. In the seconds before the pain blinds him, the form of the stingray comes clear.

Senhora da Silva is first out onto the verandah, shouting the name that signifies both husband and sister's-son. Hard on her heels, Lene adds her own thin voice. By the time Rachel and Iris arrive, da Silva is pounding along the beach to where Paul lies writhing on the sand.

"Paul!" Iris screams. *"Paul!"*

"It's all right, Iris," Rachel says stupidly. Below them, da Silva bends over his nephew, lifting him as though he weighs no more than his own small son.

"Vitor!" The senhora runs to the top of the stairs, the others close behind. The boy has frozen where his father left him, halfway up the bank. "Vitor," his mother yells again, "vem para Mamãe!"

Vitor does as he's told, scrambling four-footed up the stairs. He's crying by the time he reaches his mother. She folds him under one arm, gathering Lene beneath the other. For a moment Rachel wishes she too could hide her face against the senhora's sturdy frame.

"He's bleeding!" Iris cries. "Oh, Rachel, his foot!" She starts down the stairs.

"Senhora, não!" Senhora da Silva barks, and Rachel lunges after Iris, catching hold of her hand.

"Iris, please, we must leave the way clear."

"Yes, yes, of course." Iris stumbles back up after her.

Da Silva isn't far behind. "Arraia," he says raggedly, the English an afterthought as he barges past. "Stingray." Paul howls as though the word has injured him anew, his foot passing Rachel at eye level, a bloodied blur.

The senhora pushes her children away. "Lene, traga-me a faca de desossar. Vitor, vai buscar Deolindo."

"What's happening?" says Iris. "What's she saying?"

Rachel shakes her head. Best not to relay the one word she understood: *knife*.

On the verandah, da Silva goes down hard on one knee, laying Paul out on the mat.

"Segura ele," the senhora tells her husband, and he pins their nephew's arms. Turning her back, she straddles Paul's right leg, kneels and takes hold of his injured foot—leaving the other one free to draw back like a fist. Rachel pounces, bringing the left leg down with a slam. Again Paul yells—curse words this time—but Rachel holds firm, hands clamped to his muscular thigh in its sopping trouser leg. Glancing up, she sees Iris slide down the wall and sit heavily.

"Aqui, Mamãe." Lene stands before her mother, holding out the knife. The blade is narrow, gently curved. At the sight of it, Iris hugs her knees.

"Boa menina," Senhora da Silva tells her daughter evenly. "Agora me traz um copo."

A cup? Rachel's head swims. What can Paul's aunt possibly be planning to cut out of him?

In moments the girl is back, crouching to place a clay cup on the mat. "Boa menina," her mother says again, Rachel repeating the phrase inwardly as the leg jumps under her hands. *Boa menina, boa menina*—good girl.

Closing her fingers over Paul's swollen toes, the senhora turns his foot to expose the jagged hole in its arch. Rachel steals a look at his face, the pulse visible in his straining neck. He screams as his aunt touches her knife to the wound. As he struggles to buck free, Rachel has no choice but to kneel on the healthy limb.

When Deolindo appears down the end of the verandah, the senhora barks a series of orders. *Água* and *fogo*: water and, more troubling, fire. Rachel prays God that Paul's treatment won't require his being burned.

Again the senhora probes the wound, and again Paul looses a blood-curdling scream.

"Stop it!" Iris cries. "You're hurting him. She's *hurting* him!"

"Quiet, senhora!" da Silva says sharply. "My wife is right to do this."

Finally, Senhora da Silva lays her knife aside. Maintaining her grip, she tweezes the offending article between thumb- and fingernails, plucking it from the wound. It is the tip, the last envenomed inch, of the arraia's spine. She drops it in the cup.

The leg in Rachel's care slackens. For a blind, unthinking moment she considers freeing a hand and laying it on Paul's belly, quieting the tremble there.

Vitor approaches with the water jug. "Atenção," the senhora tells him, and he sets the jug down with care, giving both knife and cup a wide berth.

Lene returns with the zinc washtub and places it alongside her mother's hip. Deolindo brings the black kettle spilling steam. He empties its contents into the tub, then takes up the jug and pours.

"Pare." The senhora dips a finger into the tub. "Ai! Um pouco mais." She tests it again. "Bom."

Sitting back on her heels, she pivots and climbs off Paul's leg. She lifts the bloodied limb and attempts to bend it at the knee.

"*No!*" Paul shouts.

"It's all right, Paulo," says his uncle. "Give her your foot. Give it to her."

Paul answers with a pitiable howl, holding the leg ramrod stiff. Rachel looks to Iris, but her mistress has buried her face in her hands. Dropping her gaze, she meets Paul's wide-open look.

"Go on, Paul," she tells him. "Go on."

It works. Two harrowing hours of immersion, removal, re-immersion—but eventually Paul can bear his wound. Iris takes up a silent station beside his head, dipping and wringing the cloth, laying it to his brow. Deolindo disposes of the first bowl of vomit, but he's stoking up the wood stove the second time Paul is sick, so Rachel carries the thin mess out to the backhouse and tips it down the hole.

On the senhora's orders, they move the whimpering patient inside to a rede. He quietens once she finishes packing his leg in place. When it seems he'll be able to keep something down, his uncle doses him with cachaça, laughing when Paul holds his cup out for more.

No one has eaten. With the sun high in the sky and her mother rooted to the low stool beside Paul's rede, Lene takes it upon herself to prepare the midday meal. Rachel acts as kitchen maid to her cook, peeling and slicing the fruit Vitor fetches in from the trees. They lay the cloth on the verandah mat so as not to disturb Paul; after three cupfuls of cachaça, he's surrendered to sleep. Rachel carries a plate in to Senhora da Silva, who accepts it with a nod and sets it on the floor. Paul's face is strangely peaceful. His foot is dark red, swollen halfway up the calf. The senhora has fashioned a cloth bandage; a penny-sized blotch of blood shows through.

Back on the verandah, Rachel resumes her place, resting her back against the wall. Iris picks at what little she's taken. Lene continues in her mother's role, batting Flor away when she ventures too close to Vitor's food.

"Where's Tuí?" Rachel thinks to ask, and when no one answers, "Deolindo, onde está Tuí?"

"Ele está caçando."

"Caçando?"

"Hunting," da Silva says, slipping a chunk of fish into his mouth. He looks hollowed out, a decade older than the man who met them on the dock at Barra.

Deolindo leaves them after the meal. Vitor takes himself and Flor for a nap in a nearby rede while Rachel and Lene clear away. Out in the lean-to kitchen, Lene feeds wood into the stove while Rachel fills the kettle and sets it to boil. The zinc tub sits alongside the water barrel, back where it belongs.

Intent on gathering up the last few bowls, Rachel makes her way back toward the verandah, following the outside wall. She stops short of the corner at the sound of Iris's voice.

"But it's not . . . fatal."

"Fatal? No. You see how the poison makes Paulo sick, but it's not so bad. In the chest an arraia can kill you, but not in the foot."

"So we can continue. A few days' rest, perhaps a week—"

"Senhora," da Silva says gently, "he won't walk on that foot for weeks. It will take two, three months for the wound to heal."

"Months?"

"A cut from an arraia isn't like a cut from a knife. It turns the flesh bad. Not the whole foot—not if you rest—but it goes bad in . . . circles, you know?"

"Circles? You mean an ulcer?"

"Ulcer, yes. The scar will be large."

Neither speaks for a time. Rachel is considering whether to show herself when da Silva clears his throat. "We must leave soon to be in time for the tartarugas." When Iris says nothing, he goes on. "He wanted you to see them, senhora. He wrote of this in his letters."

"We can't," says Iris. Then, "How can we?"

"You see how his aunt looks after him."

Rachel wills her mistress to speak. *Yes, but how will he feel if we leave?*

"And who can say," da Silva adds, "he may be well enough to come with us when we return to see the eggs hatch."

"You think so?"

"You never know."

Rachel hears the dull clink of the cachaça jug against a cup, then another; both of them are drinking. She turns and walks slowly back along the wall. Lene squats before the tub, in up to her elbows. Rachel smiles at her before slipping in through the side door.

A second rede hangs alongside Paul's. Drawing close, Rachel sees the senhora is fast asleep. She gazes at the patient. His expression can no longer be called peaceful—at best, it betrays no pain. His bare chest shimmers with sweat. She lowers her eyes, stooping for the senhora's plate.

"*Hnnn.*"

When he reaches out to her, she assumes he wants water, but he waves the cup away. He grasps her hand. The fever must be back; he's mistaken her for Iris, or possibly his aunt.

"Rachel?"

Something tightens in her chest. "Yes?"

"Sit with me?"

Rachel glances over her shoulder. The verandah doorway is a bright landscape, Iris seated outside its frame. She looks back at Paul. His eyes are bloodshot, still faintly wild. "Of course."

22

The air is fragrant, dry. Paul walks with his father among the trees—feathery pitch pines set in hard-packed sand. The afternoon's bag has been good: half a dozen turtles—painted and box—plus a flame-coloured corn snake and an eastern hognose. Only three days into a fortnight's trip, and already they've covered the cost of the ferry to Camden and the horse and buggy hire. *The Pine Barrens.* Paul hadn't liked the sound of the place, but it's turning out to be one of the best collecting trips they've had.

He's nine now, old enough to be of real use. Walter doesn't let him skin the specimens—a slip of the knife would mean a loss of income they could ill afford—but last night Paul cleaned and roasted the cottontail his father had shot. They're easier than reptiles, shucking out of their fur with so little resistance, he can tell himself they don't really mind.

It's thinking about rabbits—in particular the rabbit bridegroom from his illustrated Grimm's—that blinds Paul to the world at his feet. *Come with me, Mary, and sit upon my bushy tail, and go with me to my bushy house . . .* They don't always rattle, Walter taught him. Use your eyes as well as your ears.

The shove to his rucksack brings him down hard on all fours. By the time he looks round, his father has everything under control—the fork of his snake stick pinning the rattler's chin to the ground. Too late, the creature sounds its tail.

"*Crotalus horridus*," Walter says, grinning. Then, as Paul struggles to his feet, "You all right?"

Paul comes to the present through pain. He thinks to call for his father, then remembers his father is no more. Iris? She too has left him. Even Rachel. All of them, gone.

His foot throbs. He'd rather not look at it—puffed up like something rotting, the bandage wrapped around the red socket in its arch—but the hammock holds it up like an offering in his line of view. Beyond, Lene appears in the doorway. In this heat, with his gut still tender, she brings him soup. Steaming scent of fish. Paul shakes his head.

"Mamãe says—"

"Não. Obrigado."

"Não sejá difícil, Paulo." His aunt steps over the threshold, a platter in her hands. Vitor follows with a smaller plate, wearing the pet tamarin like a stole.

Setting the platter down on the mat, Carolina drags the stool beneath her and gestures for Lene to hand her the soup.

"I don't—" Paul begins, but she stills his lips with the bowl. The broth is fatty, ever so slightly sweet. She's thickened it with farinha, added peppers to suit a foreigner's taste.

"It's good," he says as she lowers the bowl. "Bom."

She nods, wiping the corner of his mouth. Behind her, the children eat quietly. Even Flor minds her manners, accepting what Vitor offers without fuss.

Rachel is growing accustomed to bare-chested men. Da Silva seemed to misplace his shirt shortly after leaving Barra, and even Paul wore only pyjama trousers when she saw him last—though that may have been a decision made for him with an invalid's comfort in mind. All the same, she feels herself colour when Tuí makes his way forward from the stern clad in nothing but a narrow breechcloth.

"Goodness," Iris says as he squeezes past them.

Da Silva grins over at them from the helm. "He is better like this in the jungle."

Iris stares after the near-naked youth. "Surely he must wear shoes."

"Shoes?" One hand on the wheel, da Silva hitches a foot up across his knee and slaps his bare sole. "Any thorn meets that, the thorn breaks. Eh, Deolindo? O pé da Amazônia quebra espinhos?"

Deolindo looks up from the crate on his lap. Having removed one end, he's replacing it with a barred wicker door. "Claro, Capitão." He laughs. "Mesmo dente da jararaca."

Tuí's hearing is sharp; at the mention of the deadly viper, he glances back at them, his eyes bright. Rachel lowers her gaze to his heels. Imagine, a foot as hard as a hoof, immune to the serpent's tooth.

"Of course, you ladies must wear your boots," da Silva adds.

"I should think so," says Iris.

"And will Senhora Ash be needing her veil?" Rachel asks.

"No, no. Not so many carapanãs here. Anyway, it would tear. There is a vine, jacitara, it likes to grab."

"A jacitara vai pegar essas saias," Deolindo says, gesturing to Rachel's skirts.

Rachel turns to Iris. "He thinks our skirts may get caught."

"Well, we can scarcely go for a tramp in our bloomers." Iris turns her face to the breeze, seemingly oblivious to any impropriety. Da Silva says nothing, keeping his eyes on course.

As they draw closer to shore, Deolindo sets the crate aside and rises to see to the engine. In the bow, Tuí assumes the pose of a cat at a fish pond. Angelo leaps down from the canopy and hops up to hunch beside him, peering overboard. Having read the river bottom, Tuí signals a good spot to cast anchor.

The passage ashore in the montaria is brief, four of them crossing the shallows in a single weighted load while Deolindo waves them off from the *Bridie Mac*'s deck. Tuí paddles hard, getting a good run at the beach and hopping out before the dugout grinds to stillness against the sand. Rachel follows as best she can, given the encumbrance of her skirts. Meantime, da Silva steps directly from the stern into the water and hands Iris along to the prow.

The praia is steep, more of a bank than a beach. Climbing it, Rachel trails her fingers over shelves of fine white sand. At the top, the jungle stands unbroken except for a solitary gap. This must be the track da Silva spoke of, the dry creek bed they will follow inland.

She turns as Iris and da Silva crest the bank. Below them, Tuí drags the montaria up high and dry. About his neck, a woven quiver; at his thigh, the tresado in its sheath. The blowpipe lies beside him on the sand, a dark line twice his body's length. He stoops to take it up as she watches, balancing it in his shoulder's notch.

Half an hour in, they meet the grabbing vines. First in line after Tuí, Iris becomes well and truly snared. Rachel works to unhook the curved thorns, but her mistress loses patience and tears free, sacrificing a large swatch of her overskirt.

Now Rachel follows Tuí's lead, the gravatana preventing her from walking too close. Here among the trees, his bare back appears clothed in the smoothest of bark. What must it be like to walk through the forest in your skin? Once, Rachel opened her shirtwaist while swimming in the Neshaminy alone. She would have been nine, her first summer with no mother keeping watch. In up to her neck, she let the creek press its current to her flesh. It was no more than a minute's transgression, but she's never forgotten the feel.

They have yet to encounter a reptile. They've seen and heard countless insects and birds—though not, now that Rachel thinks of it, a single sign of the dead. How is it possible? As a girl, she was forever coming upon lifeless sparrows, stag beetles, mice. Once, a mole with a velvety grey coat. Once, at the heart of the woodlot, a half-eaten doe. The jungle must be hungrier than the forests she knows—no time to let a body lie.

The ground beneath her boots softens, the litter suddenly overlaid with a drift of fat petals, purple and bronze. Scooping up a handful, she turns to show Iris, who rewards her with a delighted smile. Together, they gaze up into the canopy: no sign of any blooms still on the branch. Instead, Rachel catches sight of a bird.

The macaw sits silent, head cocked, peering at them from on high. Tuí has carried on ahead, and now da Silva gives a low whistle that brings him padding back. Plucking a dart from his quiver, Tuí twists a pinch of floss about its tail and slips it inside the gravatana's mouthpiece. He hoists the ten-foot tube as though it's weightless, somehow balancing it at his lips. Breath rounds out his cheeks. *Hhwwwwt.*

The squawk is violent. Rachel expects a sudden, dramatic death, but the macaw fights the poison, shuffling on its branch, humping its wings out like a brilliant cape. She wonders what Papa would make of Tuí's method. Would he consider the gravatana to be a cousin of the abhorred shotgun, or would he somehow class it with the acceptable snare?

The bird tips forward and falls. A rush of colour, a bounce among the petals, and Iris claps, setting off a series of disturbances in the trees. Face down on the forest floor, the macaw shows its rainbow back.

"Bravo, Tuí." Da Silva steps forward. "Here is our supper."

"Really?" says Iris.

"Certamente, senhora. The meat is good."

Tuí stoops to retrieve his dart. At a word from da Silva, he lets the quarry lie. Rachel crouches for a closer look. The red she knows from cardinals, though only the males display so bold a shade. She can't judge the sex of the bird before her; the breeding pairs she's seen flying wing to wing exhibit none of the dimorphism common to birds.

She touches a secondary flight feather, goldfinch-yellow against the blue-jay blue. *Any woman might marvel at a feather.* Walter said it with pride, standing by Iris's table, watching her work. *It takes a special turn of mind to appreciate a scale.* Rachel runs her finger along the line of overlap. Are they really such different structures after all? Lightweight, waterproof protection, endlessly adaptable, easily replaced.

"I wonder," she says, looking up, "if we might preserve the skin."

"You want birds?" da Silva says for the second time, calling up the memory of Paul's ill-considered hunt. It's a scene Rachel would prefer to forget: the lowered gun, the boyish humiliation writ plain.

"Not chiefly, no," Iris answers for her. "But Senhorita Weaver is right, the feathers will make a fine display."

As if in answer, the macaw stirs—a twist of the spine, a spasm along one wing. Without thinking, Rachel picks it up. Eyes open, it struggles against her. She cradles it and pulls its neck.

"Rachel!" Iris stares at her.

"The senhorita knows birds," da Silva says, grinning.

"I . . . we had chickens." Rachel stands, the bird pressed to her chest. "I'm sorry, Iris, I—"

"No, no," says Iris. "I'm just . . . surprised."

Da Silva holds out a hand for the macaw. Rachel would be inclined to wrap it in canvas, taking care to lay the plumage straight, but he just pushes it into his bag—an act Tuí takes as a signal. Turning on his heel, he shoulders the gravatana and sets off down the stream bed again.

23

The scene outside the porthole is calm: a drift of pollen across tea-coloured water, the ripples of mouthing fish. Rachel lets her gaze wander the bank. The resident turkey vultures behave much as they do back home, hunching by twos and threes in the high snags, croaking to the warming sun.

"Which do you prefer," Iris says behind her, "plain white or stripes?"

Rachel tips the washing water out the porthole and turns. Seated on her bunk in bloomers and chemise, Iris holds two pairs of pyjama trousers on her lap. Da Silva presented the unusual gifts last night, knocking at the cabin door moments after the women retired. *Forgive me, senhora, but tomorrow the track is not so easy. If you would be more comfortable . . .*

"I think I'll take the stripes," Iris says. "They'll go a treat with my blue blouse."

Rachel slips the enamel basin back beneath the jug. "Are you sure we ought to?"

"Why ever not? We'd hardly be more modest with our skirts torn to ribbons." Setting the white trousers aside, Iris bends to work a striped leg over her stockinged foot.

"Here," says Rachel, "let me help you."

In fact there's little to it. The legs are plenty wide enough to accommodate bloomers; the waist cinches with a simple drawstring. Rachel slips into her own pair and tries out a bent-over stride. Spinning round, she surprises them both by dropping into a deep knee bend.

"Oh-ho." Iris leans back on her bunk and lets fly with a kick, sending the jug and basin clattering. "Oh, Lord—"

"Tudo bem, senhora?" Deolindo's voice at the door.

Iris claps a hand to her mouth.

"Senhorita, está tudo bem?"

"Tudo bem," Rachel calls, but it's better than good—she's made her mistress laugh.

⌿

Eyes half-mast, Paul watches his aunt through the open side door. She stands at the waist-high bench, knife poised over a large yellow-green fruit. A swift chop exposes salmon-coloured flesh, a cluster of slick black seeds. The name comes to him: paw-paw. Then, from some back corner of his brain, *mamão*.

Its scent reaches him next, lush and troubling. He's not the only one with a nose; Vitor appears as though summoned, sidling close to his mother, his small hand tentative at her hip. The gaze she favours him with lasts only a few seconds—long enough to swamp Paul's heart. She cuts a slice and holds it up for her son. Paul closes his eyes, and for a moment wanting makes it so. He lifts his mouth to her—the scent, and now the touch of the fruit, sweet and slippery on his boy's small tongue.

Longing is not memory. The boy in the scene is his cousin, the woman, his aunt.

⌿

Tuí has already plunged away down the hunter's track. Much as Rachel wishes to follow, she judges it best to wait for the rest of the party. Deolindo has set to work along the wooded margin with the axe; it appears he'll be staying behind again. Da Silva is on his way back to the *Bridie Mac*. Despite his size, he sits easy in the montaria's shallow husk, paddling across the shallows to where Iris stands waiting at the launch's stern. Rachel's mistress was right, the striped trousers do look well with blue.

As he draws alongside the hull, Rachel turns back to the trail-head. She knows Iris won't fall in—da Silva is the last man to let such a thing happen—yet somehow it makes her anxious to watch. Faced with a screen of foliage, she allows her gaze to go soft. There. That twig there—it isn't a twig at all.

You've never seen anything hold so still. The nearer their departure date drew, the more often Walter spoke of that original trip. This time it was a simple narrative: the little Indian girl who fooled him with an insect that looked like a stick. The bug in the story was an astonishing six inches in length; the one Rachel now faces must be eight. They neither sting nor bite, she remembers, and so she grasps it gently about the thorax, plucking it from the tree.

Too long to rest in her palm, it sets the tips of its forelegs on her inner wrist. It's the simplest of designs, a stick-figure horse gifted with an extra pair of legs. The limbs are smoother, greener than the trunk, like new growth branching from the main. At its tail, a flare of what looks like bark where it might have been snapped from the tree.

Not flora, she reminds her eyes, fauna. How can it be? How can the skin—the exoskeleton, Walter would remind her—of a simple insect be so wise? Of course, it's not. The wisdom, the *intelligence*, belongs to all nature.

Under nature, Walter read to them from Mr. Darwin's inflammatory text, *the slightest difference of structure or constitution may well turn the nicely balanced scale in the struggle for life, and so be preserved.* It really is a matter of selection: when a bird spies one stick insect and not another, it preserves the more twig-like of the pair. In effect, its eye marks the survivor, imprinting the species with its surrounds.

It's not the first time Rachel has entertained the thought. Late last summer, a shipment of specimens from California transformed her corner of the library into a temporary warehouse. While she unpacked crates and catalogued their contents, her employers documented the new arrivals in watercolour and words.

"I do wish they'd take better notes," Iris said.

Walter looked up from his desk. "What's that, my love?"

Iris gestured to the jar before her, the specimen leached of colour by the spirits in which it was preserved. "'Granite Night Lizard,'" she read from the label. "'Black spots on a ground of yellow and grey.' Well, I mean."

Walter nodded. "I suppose you must think of the substrate."

"Hm?"

"Granite. More specifically, granite at night. If the creature takes its name from its environs—"

"Of course." Iris gazed into space. "Yes, of course."

Iris bent to apply the rock's pattern to the lizard's back, just as generations of predators had done. Prey, too, Rachel realized, unrolling the skin of a stout, sand-coloured snake. Keen-eyed mice had perfected its markings, painting the desert on its scales.

———

The stick insect shifts, a gentle tickle at Rachel's wrist. She glances back to find Iris and da Silva advancing toward her along the beach. Iris's stride in the trousers is easy, strong. Rachel considers the creature in her hand, the memory it will no doubt evoke. Returning it to its branch, she faces her mistress and smiles.

—

The pain wakes him; he's caught a toe in the gathers of his rede, twanging his injured foot. He breathes through the worst of it, resisting the impulse to moan. As it passes, his eyes adjust. A wedge of moonlight through the verandah doorway shows the others suspended in their beds. His aunt's leg dangles, girlish, strong. Tonight she's strung up her rede several paces from his—a sign, he can't help but feel, that his recovery is progressing well.

The children have piled into a single rede—not head to foot, as they do when talking or playing quietly, but heads together, Vitor tucked in tight under Lene's arm. An intimacy Paul can only imagine.

The rede is where he lives now. He'd wanted to hobble out to the backhouse, or at least behind the partition with a pot, but Carolina refused to let him try. The first time she worked the shallow basin beneath him, the relief was nothing to the shame. The following morning he feigned sleep, waiting until she and the children had descended to the beach. He succeeded in shifting the good leg, but the bad one balked. The hole in his foot seemed to scream; he broke an acrid, all-over sweat and lay still.

At least now he can manage the basin on his own. In the morning he might even attempt a smile when his aunt comes to carry it away.

24

Early light. Rachel follows the far islands with her eyes, Angelo pressed in tight against her. From time to time she passes a palm down the furred slope of his back.

Seated on the opposite bench, Iris twists to look shoreward. "What's that?"

Angelo rises as Rachel does, the pair of them crossing behind da Silva's back. Shading her eyes, Rachel sees what's attracted her mistress's gaze: there, on a distant praia, a bright orange patch. She digs in the carpet bag for the field glasses and hands them to Iris, who takes a long look.

"Are they flowers?"

"Flowers?" says da Silva. "No, senhora, not flowers."

"What, then?"

But he only smiles and turns the *Bridie Mac* toward shore.

Orange—a bed of it, a pool, hot as flame against the bone-white sand. It's not until they're in the montaria, yards from shore, that its meaning becomes clear. Iris's hand finds Rachel's on the gunwale. Just as da Silva said, not flowers. *Butterflies.* Hundreds, thousands of them, packed in tight, holding their bright wings erect.

Iris is the first ashore, soaking her boots, the bottom six inches of her skirts. She approaches on tiptoe, Rachel close behind. There's something breathless in the insects' collective posture, almost painful. Softly, softly, Rachel unrolls the mat. Not a flutter. She begins setting out Iris's things.

The flock stays put long enough for Iris to complete a handful of studies and one watercolour sketch. Liftoff begins with a flicker. A ripple along the margins and the whole mass rises, peeling away from the beach. Iris and Rachel stand to watch it float out over the river, where it unravels in a trailing cloud.

"Well," Iris says finally. Her expression is one Rachel has all but forgotten, the soft, secret look she wore on mornings when she and Walter rose late. Rachel stoops to retrieve an errant pencil, blowing sand from the lead.

"Leave all that." Iris looks up the beach to where the men have built a fire. "Come on."

Da Silva stands up as they approach. "Are you hungry?"

"Famished," Iris replies.

He grins. "Deolindo, café da manhã para a senhora e a senhorita."

"Certo, Capitão."

Deolindo pours out the coffee, then serves up fish and farinha with wedges of custard-coloured fruit. Rachel smiles to see the eagerness with which Iris reaches for her bowl.

"Delicioso," Rachel says upon trying the fruit. Then, thinking to include Tuí, "Como se diz em Língua Geral?"

"Delicioso?" says Deolindo. "Ikatu."

Tuí looks up, but before Rachel can speak, he's in motion, exploding to his feet. She turns to watch him go, pure spirit sprinting along the forest wall. It's over in seconds, Tuí airborne and arcing, coming down hard. Deolindo lets out a whistle.

"What is it?" says Iris. "What's he got?"

Da Silva watches for a moment more. "Iguana."

And so it is. Tuí trots toward them, a four-foot lizard twisting in his grip. "Wonderful," Iris calls out, "bravo!"

Holding the iguana firmly by the neck and the base of the tail, Tuí comes to a standstill a few paces away. Rachel rises for a better look.

"Careful, senhorita," says da Silva. "They bite."

"Nonsense," says Iris. "We had one about the house for years. She was gentle as a lamb."

"The males are different, senhora, trust me."

Rachel gets as close as she dares. Apart from a heavy crest of spines, the creature is a near twin to Lucy, whose portrait greeted her on that fateful day.

"Ikwe ú eō?" says Tuí.

Da Silva turns to Iris. "He wants to know, do you want it alive or dead?"

Rachel glances at her mistress. The effect of the butterflies is gone, in its place a sharper, more precarious joy.

"Oh, alive," says Iris. "Definitely alive."

—

Quiet in the house. Vitor and Lene are busy hauling up the day's water; Carolina sits sewing on the mat. Paul is watching Flor stalk a beetle along the wall when a frog drops from the thatch, bouncing off the floor nearby.

"Ai." Carolina rises, reaching beneath the shelf for a wooden club. The frog sits stunned on the mat. It looks harmless enough to Paul—grey-green and not two inches long—but his aunt must know otherwise. So why doesn't she strike?

Unlike Flor, who watches the frog with interest, Carolina fixes her gaze on the thatch. Paul looks up in time to see the snake's sharp nose emerge. A yard-long cord of green, it drops, roiling in the air. As the tamarin springs back, Paul's aunt swings with dispassionate accuracy, delivering a skull-crushing blow.

Vitor catches wind of the action on his way across the verandah. Setting his bucket down with a splash, he hurries to his mother's side, squats and inspects the kill.

"Bad snake," he says, looking at Paul.

Paul spreads a hand over his jumping heart. "So I gathered."

The boy looks at him quizzically.

"Yes," Paul agrees, "bad."

Just then the frog stirs, making a break for the door. As Vitor takes after it, his mother stoops to grab the dead snake by its tail. Paul should ask her to preserve it—a meagre contribution to the collection, but better than none. For the first time since Iris and Rachel departed, it occurs to him to wonder whether they left him any spirits, any jars.

He lets the question float, lets it follow his aunt outside to where she flings the offending specimen into the bush. In the meantime, Vitor corners the frog. He carries it back in closed hands, opening them a crack so Paul can see. The toe pads mark it as a species of tree frog, though it's relatively plain as they go. Soft dorsal stripes and silvery eyes—such odd, appealing creatures, frogs. Paul suffers a pang of conscience. How many of them has he dismantled on the laboratory bench?

The three of them form a triangle in the bow—da Silva seated on deck with his back to the prow, Iris and Rachel facing one another, each at the head of a bench. Deolindo and Tuí are already in their hammocks for the night, talking quietly and passing a clay pipe. Da Silva too is smoking. Now and then he holds his cigar out to Iris, who obliges him by taking a deep draw.

Rachel has the lantern close beside her on the bench, the wick turned up just enough to illuminate the page. She's decided to keep a record in one of Iris's smaller sketchbooks: date and location, species sighted, captured or killed. She'll have to do her best with local and common names, leaving the Latin for Paul. She winces inwardly, recalling the look on his face when Iris bent over his hammock to bid him farewell.

"Poor Paul." The words startle her, coming as they do from Iris's lips rather than her own. "I feel badly having left him."

"You saw how it was with him, senhora," da Silva says. "He could not come."

"Yes, but I could have stayed. I'm not a mother to him—I never have been—but with his father gone . . ."

Da Silva releases a stream of smoke. "He wanted you to come."

"Paul?"

"Paulo, yes, but I am speaking of Walter."

Iris nods, pressing her fingers to her brow. Rachel drops her gaze. The day's list complete, she folds the book shut and sets it aside. Angelo emerges from the shadows, brushing past her skirts. Ignoring the hand she pats in her lap, he crosses through lamplight to sit facing the captain.

"Ah, boa noite, Senhor Angelo."

Iris smiles. "Look at that golden coat."

"Onça dourada," da Silva murmurs.

"Isn't he handsome, Rachel?"

"He is, yes."

Da Silva flicks the stub of his cigar overboard. Quiet water, quarter moon. The sky is busy with night birds—goatsuckers or close cousins, some kind of swallow or swift. Among them, the fleeting forms of bats. Iris shies as one of them skims close.

"Don't concern yourself, senhora. These are not vampiros."

She turns her head after one. "How can you tell?"

"You see how they are feeding. These ones come for insetos, not blood. Anyway, you only have to look at this one." He lays a hand on Angelo's neck. "He is busy when there are vampiros. He knows his job."

25

again, Iris's bunk is empty. Rachel sits up, rubbing her eyes. She was awake in the night, shaken from sleep by a dream. Paul had shrunk to the tamarin's size. While the rest of them prepared for departure, he crouched in the rafters, large-eyed and alone.

She stands to banish the image. They've planned a morning ramble, and who knows how long Iris has been up and waiting. Winding her braid up under her bonnet, Rachel plucks her trousers down from their hook.

She finds her mistress at work. Dressed in her rose skirt and garibaldi blouse, Iris sits under the canopy with the painting board propped in her lap. Before her on a trunk, two creatures sit with gazes locked: the iguana in its cage of woven lianas, Angelo in a hunter's trance. Setting the rucksack down by the cabin door, Rachel approaches on quiet feet.

Iris has already sketched the big lizard in pencil and laid down the initial green wash. "What do you think of Lucifer," she says, glancing up, "you know, in memory of Lucy." She smiles. "Oh, Rachel, the look on your face. I'm joking. We can name him whatever you like."

Name him? Will they be christening every live specimen?

"Dressed for action, I see," Iris adds.

Rachel looks down at her trousers. "Aren't we going ashore?"

Iris rinses her brush. "Not this morning, dearest. I've made a proper start here." She touches the brush to a puddle of golden brown in the paintbox lid. "You must go, though."

"I . . . ?"

"Not on your own, silly." She drops the brown in along the dewlap's fringe. "Take Tuí with you, see what the pair of you can find."

"Oh, Iris, I don't—"

"Capitão," Iris calls.

"Aqui, senhora." He stands up at the stern, fishing pole in hand.

"Can Tuí go with Senhorita Weaver?"

"Certo, senhora. Tuí!"

The rest is lost on Rachel, a string of the repeated vowel sounds characteristic of Língua Geral. A soft splashing gives Tuí away; he's been hanging soundlessly in the water beside them. She leans out to watch him swim back to the tethered montaria and haul himself aboard.

Deolindo stands, handing his bamboo pole to da Silva before making his way forward to fetch Tuí's gear. He flashes a smile in passing. "A senhorita gosta da mata."

Rachel nods. She does like the jungle. She thought Iris did too.

There's no track as such, at least none Rachel can discern. For a time she snaps twigs at waist level, but when she looks back at the wild tangle, she finds her small signs lost. She keeps alert for landmarks. No stand-alone stumps, no stones. Spotting a distinctive palm tree ringed with thorns, she takes heart. Minutes later she meets its twin.

Nothing for it but to trust her guide. She may be surrounded by the trunks of strangers, but Tuí is among friends—one of

which catches his eye. Halting abruptly, he lays down the gravatana and steps in close to a tree. Rachel hangs back until he
beckons. She can't see what he means to show her—unless it's
the ants. Small and brown, they proceed in formation, headed
for the heights. Tuí points, and when she still doesn't see, he
purses his lips and blows. Rachel jumps back. Where there was
nothing but bark, the tree blinks a pair of bright eyes.

It's only when they lift away that she understands: eye-spots,
not eyes, folded beneath the moth's deceptive wings. Startle
response, Walter called it—an apt-enough term, judging by the
hammering of her heart. Tuí grins at her. No language between
them, but now they've shared a joke.

The next time he stops, the object of his attention is clear.
Rachel has known bears to mark trees in such a manner, but their
claws are nowhere near as sharp. Tuí drops into a squat, motioning
her down beside him. Pug marks show where the cat rose up
on its hind legs. Tuí stands to sniff at the scratches, and this too
Rachel copies, smelling nothing but raw wood.

"Onça?" she says.

He nods. "Yawara." Then, to be sure there's no misunder-
standing, he makes a circle of thumb and forefinger and marks
out a pattern on his chest. She can almost see it, a coat the colour
of sunlight dappled with black rosettes.

He breaks the spell with a gesture, indicating the bare
stretch of forearm where Rachel has rolled up her sleeve. Is there
something crawling on her? Nothing she can make out, but Tuí
persists, his finger shifting—*here, and here*. Again, a glimpse of
his teeth in that black circle. *Ah*. Rachel nods and mirrors his
smile. She too is a spotted creature—likely the first of her kind
he's seen.

Paul has been lying alone for perhaps an hour. Flor is out on her morning tour of the yard, the others gone down to bathe. For days he's been taken up with the family's domestic theatre, the drift from pain to discomfort, from present to memory to dream. This morning he woke wanting more.

Any thought of rising from the rede was short-lived. His foot may be a degree closer to its native colour and size, but when his aunt came at first light to bathe and dress the wound, he found himself looking away. His uncle had warned him to expect some loss of flesh, but the fact of it still came as a shock. *Necrosis.* Paul pushes the term from his mind.

Vitor is the first to return from the river.

"Hey, Vitor," Paul calls as the boy passes the verandah door, "come here, will you?"

His cousin presents himself, hair wet, skin shining. "Bom dia, Paulo."

"Bom dia." Paul reaches to touch the boy's arm. "Vitor, can you bring me my satchel?"

"Satcho?"

"My bag. My . . ." Not for the first time, he wishes Rachel had left the grammar behind. He points over his shoulder to the partitioned chambers, then mimes the outline of the satchel, the working of the hasp. Comprehension flares in Vitor's eyes. He's back in a matter of moments, lugging the laden bag.

"Obrigado." Paul rests the satchel on his belly, but the weight is too much. He lowers it to the floor. "Can you open it for me?"

His cousin grins and fiddles with the hasp. It pops open for him in seconds.

"Good boy. Now, there's a book—"

But Vitor has already made his choice. He holds out Walter's notebook. "Stories?"

"Not exactly," Paul says, but it's clear his cousin doesn't understand.

"Vitor." Carolina appears in the doorway, rubbing the wet ends of her hair in her shawl. "Não incomode Paulo."

"It's all right, Tia, he was helping me."

"Sim, eu estava ajudando," Vitor says in an injured tone.

Stepping inside, Carolina catches sight of the book in Vitor's hand. She freezes. "O que é isso?"

"É um livro, Mamãe," says Vitor. "O livro de Paulo."

"Não livro de Paulo," Paul corrects him. "Livro de Walter."

Paul's aunt glares at him. "Onde você conseguiu isso?"

"Foi na *satcho*—" Vitor begins.

"Silencio, Vitor."

Lene's light step on the verandah turns the boy's head.

"Onde você conseguiu isso, Paulo?" Carolina demands again.

The girl comes to stand beside her, mother and daughter wrapped in damp pink shawls. "Mamãe says where did you get it."

"What do you mean, where did I get it?" Paul says, confused. "It was my father's . . ."

His aunt's face darkens as Lene translates. In the ensuing silence, she stalks to the far corner of the room. Paul twists round to watch her kneel before a wooden chest. It's smaller than the other trunks, carved from a darker wood. It opens with a squawk.

When she rises to return, Paul can scarcely believe his eyes. In her hand, a yellow-backed volume—the twin to the one Vitor holds. "Where did you get that?"

Lene lowers her eyes to voice her mother's acid reply. "What do you mean, where did she get it?"

"But how— Did he give it to you?"

Lene murmurs. Carolina doesn't respond.

"Tia, please."

She watches him for a long moment before speaking.

"Mamãe says she takes the book—" Lene pauses. "She *took* the book when Walter took you."

"Took me?" Paul stares at his aunt. "He was my father."

"Certo." Carolina thrusts the second notebook at him and turns, her final word flung back as she disappears out the side door.

"He was your father," Lene says quietly, "but this was your home." She takes her brother's hand. "Venha, Vitor."

"Qual é o problema?"

"Nada. Venha."

Left alone, Paul lies with the notebook pressed between his hands. Isn't this what he's longed for—the other half of the story, the one his father wouldn't tell? The calfskin creaks as he eases it open. A waft of mould, the mineral impression of ink. His father's youthful script is unaltered. Incredibly, the narrative picks up where it left off.

December 2nd, 1844, Barra

After only a day's acquaintance, I cannot be certain whether Senhor Paulo da Silva is the *homem honrado* of Senhor Chryostomo's account. Thus far, however, he has proven a most agreeable companion. Rarely have I encountered so straightforward a manner paired with such a ready laugh. Of a different temperament altogether is our officious young host. Senhor Honório is the junior brother, yet he appears to have the running of the family's export concern. Save for a handful of servants, he lives alone in Casa da Silva, one of the finer homes in Barra. It is here that we are to be quartered while da Silva completes his business in town.

At dinner last night, Senhor Honório could talk of nothing but commerce. In light of my recent travels, he expected that I should quote him the current prices for everything from turtle oil to salsaparrilha in Óbidos, Santarém and Pará. Only after the young master retired did the talk proceed with ease.

Da Silva is, as hoped, a man given to conversation—though his unexpected facility with English may well stunt my improvement in Portuguese. Both brothers are fluent, their accents tinged with an Irish mother's lilt. Like myself, da Silva seeks to practise his second tongue, and so we have come to a bargain: when he draws me out on matters concerning life in the wider world, we converse in English; when the topic is local, we confine ourselves to Portuguese.

In this manner we talked late into the night, retiring in a merry state. I confess I hadn't the wherewithal to record the day's events before I slept. I set them down now by the grey light of a morning rain.

26

"Olá, Paulo."

"Olá, Lene." Paul lets the notebook fall shut, watching his cousin unhook one then another rede from the wall. "Where are you taking those?"

"On the verandah," she says lightly. "Mamãe said."

"Oh." What more can he say? It's only natural that the family should tire of the sickroom, opting for a breeze and a view. He'll be fine here on his own. Plenty to think about, plenty to read.

December 10th, 1844, Sitio da Silva

The wind kept in our favour all morning, rain falling in the white, sweeping curtains the locals call chuva branca. As fortune would have it, the sky cleared shortly before da Silva's sitio came into view. The house sat atop a steep bank, overlooking a bay. There remained only a sliver of beach, and da Silva informed me that the river would rise to within diving distance of the verandah over the coming months.

We had but little breeze upon entering the bay, so da Silva set all hands to the paddles—"all hands" consisting of four Indians, the mate Augustinho, the ship's naturalist and da Silva himself. This was a meagre crew to man the *Santa Carolina*, a galliota not much lighter than

Senhor C.'s *Sasurána*, but the current was negligible, and I could well mark our progress along the shore.

We were turning landward when a montaria rounded the bluff at the far end of the bay. Da Silva lifted an arm in greeting as the canoe cut toward us at an impressive speed. Its duo of paddlers plied their strokes as one. It wasn't until he hailed them with a cry of *Oi, Carolina!* that I understood them to be women rather than men.

As they drew up on our portside, the steerswoman in the stern held up a fish the length of her arm—a fine peacock bass or tucunaré, notorious for fighting the line. This was Senhora da Silva. The paddler in the bow— younger, with large, dark eyes and a distinctly pointed chin—was her sister, one Senhorita Zuleica Correia.

Paul shuts his eyes. Opens them and reads the sentence again. *Large, dark eyes. A distinctly pointed chin.*

His aunt startles him, slipping in by the side door. He closes the notebook as she comes to stand before him, holding out a heavy stick. Four feet long, sturdy, forked—could it be the mother of all snake sticks? He flashes on the *Boa constrictor* that flowed past his father's boots, sees Walter leap up and pin the snake's head, leaving the rest of it free to coil about him where he stands.

"Venha, Paulo." Carolina tucks the stick under her arm, and he sees it for the crutch it is.

Sitting up brings the blood to his foot, and with it a fresh wave of pain. Standing is like stepping into a campfire. He suffers a moment's gripping fantasy: the wound wrenched open like a spigot, his life's blood gushing away.

His aunt hovers close until he shows her he can manage. The children make a grave audience for his limping show, Vitor watchful, Lene cradling Flor. The first ten feet exhaust him; the second leave him trembling, close to tears. He's forgotten what it is to be outside. The view threatens to unbalance him: the dark extent of the river, the seeming safety of the bay.

The creek isn't deep enough to run black; even midstream, Rachel can make out the sand floor lying ridged and rust-coloured below. Tuí can easily manage the montaria from his seat in the stern, yet he makes no objection when she takes up a paddle to help. Already she's getting a feel for it. A dugout is subtler than a raft, more akin to the logs she straddled as a girl, riding the Neshaminy's spring flow.

Iris has stayed behind again. Absorbed in a series of foliage studies at the jungle's edge, she gave the briefest of waves when they pushed off. Rachel sets reason against disappointment: if she and Tuí concern themselves with the collecting, it leaves Iris free to observe and record. Da Silva and his mate have their work cut out maintaining the *Bridie Mac*—in addition to which, Deolindo must see to the meals. Besides, Tuí is the hunter, by far the most use in the field.

She's learning to listen for the click of his tongue, to glance over her shoulder, marking the tilt of his gaze. When she looks where he does, she sees things: the soaring form of a harpy eagle, a long-limbed monkey in retreat. This time it's what Walter would've called a significant find.

Tuí brings the montaria to a halt. Overhead, a high branch

wears a bracelet. Rachel has seen prints in Walter's books, but nothing to prepare her for the sight of a resting tree boa in its yellow morph. Coiled like a hearthside rug, the snake drapes neatly over the tree's thick limb. Rachel lays her paddle across the gunwales, steadying the dugout as Tuí stands. She turns in time to see him hoist the gravatana. A second's aim, his cheeks ballooning—*hwwwwt*.

The boa unfolds. Slow as sunlight, it follows the horizontal branch. Its bright head levers up, and with a quick cut of the paddle Tuí brings them in line. Rachel hears the whoosh, even feels—or fancies—the slim touch at her spine. She twists, shrinking, to find Tuí has already snatched the snake up.

Nothing to fear, he shows her, letting it hang. Gripping it by the neck and tail, he takes its measure, stretching his arms out wide. "Ikwe ú eõ?" The only words he's spoken since they set out—words she can't understand. Or can she? Recognition stirs as he speaks them again. "Ikwe ú eõ?"

"What do you mean? It's dead, isn't it? Morto?"

"Ikwe ú eõ?" He lowers his arms, the snake drooping in a brilliant U. What she wouldn't give for a grammar of Língua Geral. She searches her mind for which word da Silva returned in response.

"Ikwe," she says finally, animating her arm with a serpentine wriggle to be clear.

Tuí nods. Laying his quarry down over the rucksack, he withdraws a small pouch from his quiver and produces what looks like a generous pinch of salt. She watches as he plucks the dart from the boa's flank and rubs crystals into the wound. Taking hold of the creature by the head, he pries open its jaws.

"Careful, Tuí."

He glances at her.

"The teeth . . . nothing, nada."

He sprinkles a second, more generous pinch into the pink funnel of the mouth. Nothing for the space of a breath. Another. Then, scarcely perceptible, a twitch. Rachel gapes as the tree boa begins to writhe. Tuí nudges a basket with his foot. Of course. Yes, of course. She lifts its fitted lid.

It's hard to know how long he's been dozing. Rain surrounds the verandah, blurring the view. His aunt is nowhere in evidence, but the children sit facing each other in a nearby hammock, playing a wordless game. Paul watches them through his lashes. Lene makes a creature of her hand; it creeps and freezes, hunkers and hides. Vitor is the hunter. He must catch his sister's hand in his, keeping hold until it gives up and dies.

When Paul next surfaces, both the children and the rain are gone. The journey from one rede to another has left him stiff and sore. He stretches his arms out above him, turning his head from side to side. They've stationed him midway along the verandah, just outside the door. Down one end, the unruly gathering of fruit trees; down the other, the embowered head of the bankside path.

Movement catches his eye, a dark bird lighting, plunging into the arbour's crown. It reappears at a little distance, and this time Paul gets a better look. It's the size of a crow, with a grackle's blue-green shimmer and shapely tail. The heavy black bill is distinctive. *Ani*—yes, a greater ani. Walter wrote something about them, a note concerning communal nesting, collective broods.

Paul reaches down beside him for the notebook. Planting his good foot, he nudges the rede to a careful swing.

December 19th, 1844, Sitio da Silva

Today da Silva was to have acquainted me with the hunter's track that leads off his yard, but he was called away to mediate a dispute between two brothers in a neighbouring bay. I had resigned myself to a solitary ramble when Senhorita Correia kindly offered to act as my guide.

We followed the twisting tunnel of the path, occasionally drawing our tresados to clear some overweening branch or vine. After a mile or more, we emerged into a gallery of giants. Here we wound through open understorey, keeping our eyes to the ground. I had just flushed an anole from the litter, sending it scurrying up a trunk, when the senhorita called me with a click of her tongue. Her expression was mild, yet I noted her firm grip on her club.

A dozen feet from where she stood, a sizable snake lay sunning itself at the foot of a buttress root. It was a handsome creature, reddish-brown with a pattern of black rhomboids, thick as a man's arm and eight, perhaps nine feet in length. Here was *Lachesis mutus*, the bushmaster—largest of the venomous Viperidae known to man.

Certain members of the family, *L. mutus* among them, are furnished with heat-sensing pits located between the nostril and the eye. I cannot be certain whether the snake registered our warmth; it was, however, clearly aware of our presence, as evidenced by the vibration of its thorny tail in the leaves. The sound this produces is not a true rattle but a softer, more sinister buzz.

It seemed a shame to spoil the fine skin with a mess of shot. I was weighing the risks of pinning so large a specimen when the senhorita sprang. The crack of her club was decisive, though she followed it with a second to be sure.

"Um presente, senhor."

Her smile was a hunter's. Doing my utmost to mask my astonishment, I accepted her generous gift.

27

Rain hammers the cabin roof. A flash of lightning through the portholes reveals Iris, braid draped across her throat, hand at the corner of her mouth. Darkness again, and now thunder, a not so distant roar. How can she sleep so soundly? Rachel has been awake since the storm began.

The *Bridie Mac* rocks gently, tied in tight against the bushes with lines from her bow and stern. It's the montaria Rachel's worried about, thudding softly, rhythmically, against the hull. How long before it fills with rainwater? It can't be very deep here, but depth is beside the point. How does one raise up a dugout once it's discovered the river floor?

Daybreak. Rachel turns in her bunk to find what she's coming to expect: no Iris. Remembering the montaria, she sits up. The porthole at her shoulder looks out on leaves. She rises and leans over the mess of Iris's abandoned sheets, peering out. From this angle she can see only the dugout's stern, Tuí's back appearing and disappearing as he bails. *Oi, Tuí,* she comes close to calling—but what would she say next?

She's dressed in minutes, out the cabin door into the day. A bright-eyed Deolindo kneels on the far side of the cages, pumping out the bilge.

"O dia clareia, Deolindo."

He laughs. "Verdade, senhorita."

On her way forward, she steps over Angelo, tucked into a furry loaf. Still abed in his rede, da Silva lifts a lazy wave.

Iris perches at the head of the starboard bench, board in her lap, brushes, cup and paintbox at her feet. Not wishing to disturb her, Rachel halts at the canopy's verge. Iris bends to dip her brush, wicking up a bead of softest slate. She works quickly, confidently on the wet page, blotting a section to usher in dark, feathered borders, blossoms of light. Rachel looks on in wonder. *Clouds*.

It's been heavy going since they set out. Tuí leads her through a maze of fallen trunks and drooping lianas, repeatedly stopping to hack a way through. Just as she's wondering whether to turn back, the track delivers them. Sunlit clearing, sparkling stream.

The water in Rachel's flask is warm. She screws it shut and joins Tuí where he crouches, dipping her hand into the flow. The stream tastes of forest. When Tuí rises, she remains, untying her sweat-drenched bonnet and swishing it in the cool.

At the sound of metal striking wood, she looks round to where Tuí stands at the edge of the clearing, working his tresado down the trunk of a tree. Having freed a long strip of bark, he sets about shaving the rough cladding from the creamy inner skin. The result is a soft, fibrous ribbon. He splits it lengthwise with a slash of his blade.

Returning to squat on his heels beside her, he hands her the paired ends. He works quickly, efficiently, the soft bark sweating as he twists both halves to their tips. It's like magic when he touches them together, a flick of the fingers and they spiral into one.

Knotting the tail, he hands her the finished cord. Without thinking, she loops it twice about her wrist. This pleases him, his smile wider than she's known it, pulling the tattoo into a black ellipse. He takes hold of both ends and ties them—not so tight as to cut into her, just so it can't slip off. It's a pretty thing, slightly damp against her skin.

"Obrigada, Tuí."

He nods, his attention drawn to a bulky horned beetle struggling over the moss. This time Rachel is the one to see. There, among the grasses on the far side of the stream, a slithering glimpse of red.

Iris is delighted with the day's haul. She exclaims over the pair of pretty wood turtles, the anole lizard with its dewlap of midnight blue. Rachel saves the scarlet snake for last.

"Oh, Rachel." Iris's face lights up as she peers into the sack. "What a gorgeous red."

Rachel can't contain herself. "Tuí caught it, but I—" She hesitates, feeling suddenly foolish.

"You spotted it?"

She nods.

Iris touches her cheek. "Walter always said you had an eye."

Carolina has shooed Flor away from Paul's rede a dozen times, yet here she sits, grooming herself on his bare chest. She's a funny thing. Her little black hands are more paw than those of other monkeys—claws instead of nails, and no opposable thumbs. Her eyes are chestnut brown, her gaze curious, vaguely concerned. There's nothing masculine about her curved moustaches and silky beard; if anything, she resembles a whiskery grandmother in a grizzled smock. Her rufous tail shows beneath its hem, pumpkin-bright about her rump, fading to a sandy brown toward the tip. Running a lightly closed fist down its length, Paul holds the plush end to the light. The colour's familiar to him, an association he can't seem to place.

Unless . . . yes, the very shade.

He's never seen it loose. Even her braid is always hidden under a bonnet or cap—except when he chanced to see her swimming, and it tugged along on the surface, describing her backbone's line. And once before. He remembers now, the morning when he knocked bright and early on their cabin door. He'd looked past her then, determined to tempt Iris up on deck. Only now does he register the careful smile at the threshold, the long, sleep-softened braid.

Flor twitches her tail. Releasing it, Paul rests his hand on her back. He's surprised by the strength of her response, her slim spine arching against his palm. "Flor," he murmurs—not much of a sound, but enough to rouse his aunt from her siesta.

"Paulo?" She raises her head. "Flor, macaco mau!"

The tamarin tenses to escape, but Paul holds her to his chest. He can feel her breathing, her heartbeat racing against his own. "It's all right, Tia," he says. "Flor não é mau—" *She is clever, she is helpful, she is sweet.* "Flor é bom."

"Boa," Carolina corrects him. "Ela é boa."

"Sim," he agrees. *She is good.*

⌐

How long since anyone has spoken? As long as they've been sitting here—or reclining, in the captain's case—watching the supper fire die. The jungle whirrs with the onset of darkness. Around them the beach has shifted from ivory to amber, amber to stone.

Rachel can't be sure when Tuí left them; he has a cat's way of slipping into and out of a scene. "Onde está Tuí?" she asks.

"Não sei." Deolindo looks around mildly. "Na mata, talvez."

In the jungle? Rachel twists to survey its long, unbroken shadow. Where had he found a way in?

As if in answer, Tuí bursts from the trees, hitting the praia at a run. He sprints across the sand, his head obscured by what looks like a furry hood.

"What on earth—" Iris exclaims as he shoots past their little camp, flinging aside his tresado and a chunk of something dark. In his wake, a tail of sound—*vrrrrrrrrrrrrrrrr*. Not a hood, Rachel understands to her horror. A swarm.

"*Tuí!*" Her shout coincides with the splash of him hitting the river. She's on her feet before she realizes the others are laughing—da Silva and Deolindo, and now Iris too. Tuí pops up, slapping at himself, causing the men to roar.

"Stop it!" Rachel cries as he ducks down again. "Somebody help him!"

"Senhorita, senhorita, please—" Da Silva sits up, wiping at his eyes. "These bees have no sting."

"What do you mean? He—"

"Only little bites, I promise you."

To her amazement, it appears to be true. The next time Tuí surfaces, he too is laughing, shaking water from his hair.

"Rachel"—Iris tugs at the hem of her skirt—"sit down, dearest."

Chastened, Rachel resumes her seat. Da Silva reaches across Iris to pat her hand. Still chuckling, Deolindo takes up a branch and jabs at the coals, waking them before laying the branch down to burn. Tuí returns to them as the light licks up, no sign of any welts on his shimmering skin. He picks up his tresado. The chunk of what Rachel took to be wood, he holds out with a smile.

Deolindo warms the wax gently before breaking off portions and handing them round. Rachel smells the dark comb before tipping it to her lips. Not a hint of apple blossom or clover. This honey tastes of spices she has no names for, flowers she's never seen.

28

December 30th, 1844, Sitio da Silva

This morning I accompanied the senhora and her sister to the mandioca field—not, I confess, to assist them in gathering that staple root, but to engage in a harvest of my own.

The regional method of slash-and-burn farming creates soil that is soon depleted, driving those who would cultivate a successful crop ever deeper into the woods. So it is that the mandioca field lies a good mile along the right-hand fork of the track. The term "field" may be misleading. In these jungle clearings, the trees lie across each other every which way. When the mess is set alight, only the leaves and minor branches burn; the stumps and massive trunks lie blackened but whole. It is among this charred jumble that the locals plant their crop, and it is here that they must pick and wind—and indeed climb—a path, whenever they would dig it up.

Senhorita Correia had informed me that there are *muitas serpentes* to be found hunting or sunning themselves in the area, and her assurance proved to be true. While the sisters bent to their work, I set about stalking the perimeter of the burn. Within an hour I had bagged a juvenile giant bird snake and a liana snake. The latter, while of no great length, will undoubtedly command a good price for its plaited design.

The catch of the day, however, was a seven-foot *Spilotes pullatus*—the tiger rat snake. It gave me a good run along the field's margin and, when finally cornered, turned to present a series of sweeping strikes. The species is non-venomous, but known for its vigorous bite. I took aim from a safe distance and subdued it with my lightest shot.

Upon our return to the yard, we three went our separate ways—I to the hut da Silva had kindly put at my disposal, the women to the farinha shed, where they would begin the patient work of refining the mandioca roots.

I had my own work cut out in preserving the day's bag. Insects present a constant threat, and in these climes one hasn't long before putrefaction sets in. My *Spilotes pullatus* had sustained minimal damage, the stippling of the shot mitigated by dark scales scattered among the bright. I was seated on the little porch out front of my hut, tacking the skin to a board, when Senhorita Correia approached. She appeared to be at leisure, though her sister laboured on in the open shed. Having observed her skill in skinning the bushmaster, I indicated the liana snake and handed her a knife.

Paul looks up from the page as Lene rises into view. Seven years old and she appears at the top of the riverbank with a string of fish flung over her shoulder like a second braid. She catches his eye and grins.

"Muito—" he begins, but the word for "fish" takes a moment to surface. *Peixe*, he's about to add, when his cousin does him one better.

"Piranhas."

She comes to stand beside his rede, holding the string up in front of his face. They're not the prettiest of creatures; each of them wears the hard eye and underslung jaw of a stubborn old man. Lene pries open a large one's mouth. Its teeth are the stuff of nightmares, knife-tip triangles wedged into bloodied gums. Paul gets a whiff of something raw.

"Very nice."

Lene nods. "Very nice to eat."

Ducking beneath his rede's cord, she disappears inside. Paul shakes his head. The scariest fish he ever hooked was a two-foot muskie, and even that required his father's help. No matter how many suppers he and Walter caught, Paul preferred Mr. Coleridge's water snakes or Mr. Melville's white behemoth to any creature he might haul up from the depths himself.

He suspects Rachel's childhood had more in common with the one his cousins lead. There was something effortless, something ingrained, about the way she crouched at the river's edge, sharpening sticks. *She's a farm girl, you know. I stole her away to the city.* Having little to go on, Paul's mind paints a picture of willow-hung Quaker country, a modest farmhouse set on alluvial soil. The girl in the scene is a few years older than Lene, with a light brown braid and speckled skin. She walks up from the riverbank, skirts muddied, hands brilliant with fishy-smelling blood.

—

In her dream, Rachel leads Paul to the atrium. It happens as it did in life—in every respect but two. Halfway down the corridor, she takes his hand. She does this naturally, as a child might, and he accepts with corresponding ease. The second difference is where it all goes wrong. Upon opening the heavy doors, her dream-self is flooded with shame. She's forgotten to clean up. Walter lies untouched, glittering in his scarlet pool.

She wakes with the sensation of Paul's hand tearing from hers. The cabin is airless. Afraid she might have cried out, she lies rigid in the dark, listening. At first there is only the racket of her own blood. Then, with a wash of relief, there is Iris, snoring softly in the opposite bunk. Sitting up, Rachel feels for her trousers and shawl.

Outside, she draws the door shut and stands breathing. They lie at anchor in a warren of side channels; little current troubles either the water or the air. A rustling from the cages. Scent of snake musk, engine oil, trees. *Tobacco smoke*. Rachel squints into the canopied blackness, looking beyond the low-slung hammocks to where a cigar tip glows at the bow.

"Senhorita?"

The captain's voice is hushed. She picks a path forward, sidling past Tuí cocooned in his bed.

"Boa noite," da Silva greets her as she steps out into the open. "Please, join me."

"Obrigada." She sits down on the opposite bench.

"You cannot sleep?"

"I thought perhaps some air . . ."

"Yes." He brings the cigar to his lips, his broad face gleaming briefly as he inhales.

"I wonder," she says, "do you think it's safe to open the portholes?"

"Certo, senhorita. That is, yes, em princípio." He pauses. "But perhaps not tonight."

Glancing up, she can just make out the ship's cat perched at the canopy's edge. His ears swivel against a crescent moon. *You only have to look at this one.* An airborne shadow, a sudden thrum of wings. Angelo rears up and swipes at the bat, sending it tumbling off course.

"Bravo, onça dourada," da Silva says as Angelo sits back on his haunches.

"Was that—"

"A vampiro. Yes, but don't worry, senhorita, there are not so many here."

"Just enough to warrant keeping the portholes closed."

"Yes, well, I think one would be enough for the senhora."

Rachel nods, scanning the night sky. "She's afraid they'll fix on her. You know, like the carapanãs, the pium."

No, no, she expects him to say. Instead, he draws on his cigar. "This happens," he says, exhaling. "A girl in Deolindo's village was a favourite. They bothered the cattle there, but never the people—except her." He shakes his head. "Every morning, cuts on her toes, her cheeks, so many it made her weak. They had to find her a husband downriver. Somewhere with no vampiros."

"Sweet blood," Rachel murmurs.

"Eh?"

"That's what Walter used to say about Iris. About Senhora Ash."

"Walter." He makes a sound in his throat. "Senhorita, forgive me . . . Paulo wrote only that there was an accident . . ."

"Oh. Yes."

"If you prefer not to speak of it—"

"No, it's only that I haven't. Spoken of it." She takes a breath. "He was carrying a pane of glass—"

"Desculpa, senhorita, a 'pane'?"

"A sheet. Like a window, but with no frame." She looks at him. "He was carrying it and he fell. He was badly—"

"Yes. Entendo."

Grief in his voice. She casts about for an expression of comfort, finding none.

"He was a good man," da Silva says after a moment. "Brave, you know, and smart. He and I, we would talk all night." He shakes his head. "You see how it is with Honório. We grew up in the same house, but we were never close, never companheiros. The day I found out Walter was to become my brother . . ."

Rachel experiences a moment's dislocation, picturing a youthful Walter standing alongside his black-haired bride. In the darkness, she sees da Silva bring the heel of his hand to one eye.

She's about to rise, leaving him to his sorrow, when the ship's cat comes thudding down. No feline games—a burst of high-pitched squeaks, a leathery scuffle, and Angelo deposits the kill at his master's feet.

"You see how he looks after us?" Da Silva bends to pluck up the bat.

Rachel nods, following the arc of the winged body, the glint of fur before the splash. It must have swooped in at the canopy's far end and come crawling. She'd had no idea it was there.

29

Iris has been working on scale patterns since she got up— labials, temporals, parietals. Rachel sets the grammar aside and comes to stand beside her. "Iris, you should rest your eyes."

"Mm-hm."

"Just for a few minutes. You know what a difference it makes."

"Mm."

It's a gift, Rachel knows, to be possessed of a concentration so complete. A gift that sometimes results in a splitting head.

Iris lays down her number four sable round and takes up the two. Rachel stoops for the rinsing cup. Tipping the stained water over the side, she leans down with the long-handled dipper for fresh. She swishes the brush clean, plays the wet tuft over her palm. Funny to know the fur so well when she's never even glimpsed the creature. A variety of Russian marten, Walter told her once, essentially a big weasel. Can they really be that much finer than the species she knows?

Glancing up, she spots Tuí on his way back from shore, the montaria piled high with deadfall. He paddles one-handed toward the launch, holding up a wriggling sack.

"He's got something," Rachel says over her shoulder.

"Hm?"

"Tuí. He's brought something back."

"Mm."

He comes alongside on his way to tie up at the stern, slowing to hand Rachel the sack. Nothing dangerous, then; not much heft to it, either. She turns to find Iris still lost in her work. Da Silva, at least, takes an interest, rising from behind the boiler to stand beside her with grease-blackened hands.

She loosens the drawstring. Lizards—anoles, if she's not mistaken—half a dozen or so, twiggy and dull. They scramble in response to the light.

"Not so pretty," says da Silva. "These are for eating, I think."

She looks at him.

"Not for you, senhorita." He laughs. "For the snakes."

They've been under way for half an hour when Rachel raises the lid of the wood turtles' basket, releasing the sweet fetor of rot. She lifts out the smaller of the two creatures to examine it. Its left forefoot must have been injured during capture. Dark grey and dangling, it's clearly the source of the smell.

Standing amid the cages, she's downwind of a tranquil scene. Tuí has taken the helm while da Silva hunkers again by the boiler; Iris bends over the painting board. Rachel watches them for a long moment, turtle in hand. Then turns and squeezes aft along the cabin wall.

Seated at the stern, Deolindo is busy scraping the scales from a fat brown fish. He glances up. "O que se passa, senhorita?"

"O pé," she replies, turning the turtle's bad foot toward him. "É . . . ruim."

"Ai, que pena." Setting the fish down, he wipes his knife on his breeches and holds out a hand.

Of course, it must be killed—Rachel knows as much—but

she should at least try to salvage the shell. "Eu quero . . ." She taps the shell, then her own chest.

"Você quer que o casco?"

"Casco." *Cask*, yes. The container that holds the creature's life. She nods. "Por favor."

"Certo, senhorita." Again he holds out his hand, and this time she gives the turtle up.

She could leave him to it, but somehow she feels obliged to stay. Deolindo dispatches the wood turtle without ceremony, crushing its small striped head with the flat of his heavy blade. Severing the rotting foot, he chucks it overboard, where it slips away beneath the long wagging tail of the montaria. The head and three good feet go into his pail, after which he stands the shell on end. Nudging his tresado in between back and breast-plate, he lifts the whole works and brings it down. Once, twice—the blade dropping like a hatchet through wood.

In the end he carves out little meat. Having emptied the carapace, he passes it to Rachel, who turns it over in her hands. So much lighter. She sets it down like a bowl beside the scraped-clean breastplate, leaving the pair of them to cure in the sun.

January 3rd, 1845, Sitio da Silva

Upon waking from my siesta to an oppressive wet heat, I determined upon a dip in the bay. The yard I crossed was quiet, my hosts still in their redes. I was midway down the bank when the sky opened to throw down a heavy shower, and so I entered the river with little sense of the shift from one element to the next.

By the time I emerged, the rain had passed, leaving an agreeable coolness in its wake. I mounted the bank into a cloud of scent. At the verge of the mixed orchard there stood an orange tree in blossom. Fruit trees in this country flower to some extent the year round; the specimen that stood before me, however, was positively burdened with blooms.

Standing in the swell of its perfume, I became aware of the telltale hum that lends members of the family Trochilidae their common name. I saw only one bird at first, perhaps three and a half inches in length, with a white belly and an iridescent blue-green back. Within minutes the tree had drawn easily a score.

They followed no discernible course, darting from flower to flower, the speed of their wingbeats baffling to the eye. Occasionally one infringed upon another's trajectory, and the pair rose in a moment's heated battle before whirring apart. It was during one such skirmish that I became aware of the senhorita's presence. She stood observing from the end of the verandah.

"Como se diz em Inglês?" she asked.

Being unfamiliar with the species, I replied with the catch-all "hummingbird"—a term she mastered on the third attempt. I already knew the local name, but it seemed churlish not to inquire. Indeed, the senhorita appeared delighted to complete the exchange.

"Beija-flor," I repeated after her. The literal translation is "kiss-flower"—a charming name.

Beija-flor. Paul stares at the little bird's name in Portuguese, then in English—one born of the nectar-sipping moment, the other defined by sound. A noise comes between him and the page—a distinctly urgent squeak. Vitor rounds the corner of the house, showing himself, or rather the creature in his hands, to be its source.

"Well, now"—Paul closes the notebook—"what have we here?"

"Lizard," Vitor says proudly, his thin leg resting against Paul's.

"That's right."

Twice the size of the one at Senhor Felisberto's, this gecko is designed to disappear against tree bark rather than a white-washed wall. Vitor grips it firmly about the middle, its limbs and tail held rigid, mouth open to display a blue flag of tongue. Its feet mimic a child's flower drawing. Paul touches a finger to one and feels the toe pads shrink.

"Foot," Vitor says.

"Very good." Paul meets the boy's eager gaze. "And in Portuguese?"

"Pé."

"Pé."

Vitor nods. "Very good."

Paul laughs, transferring his finger to the gecko's chubby tail.

"Tail," Vitor says, grinning. "Cauda."

"Cauda." Keeping clear of the gecko's mouth, Paul taps its head.

"Head. Cabeça."

Paul points to an amber eye.

"Olho." The boy hesitates. "Eye!"

"Bom. Muito bom." Paul thinks for a moment, then works a finger through Vitor's clasp to touch the fine leather of the gecko's chest. He becomes sensible of a rapid ticking in his fingertip. Withdrawing his hand, he lays it to his cousin's breastbone and flutters a doubled beat.

Vitor can scarcely contain himself. "Heart!"

"Correto," Carolina says, stepping out onto the verandah. "E em Língua Geral?"

"Piá!"

Paul twists to see her in full. *The eye sinks inward,* Mr. Arnold wrote, *and the heart lies plain.*

"E em Português, meu amor?" Carolina asks her son.

The boy turns his face up to her. "Em Português dizemos coração."

A gentle rocking precedes the splash. Looking round, Rachel finds herself alone in the dugout, Tuí upturned behind her in the stream. She backpaddles, halting as he rights himself at her side.

At first glance he appears to be offering up a sheaf of mud-soaked leaves. The turtle is nothing like the one she lost. Its carapace is brown and bumpy, furred with growth. Its head is even stranger: a flat, snorkel-nosed triangle on a ribbon of neck.

"Matamata," says Tuí.

Of course. Walter made note of one, dubbing it the most outlandish chelonian he'd seen. Turning on her seat, Rachel retrieves a tin basin from beneath an empty cage. She dips it in the stream and balances it on the gunwale, whereupon Tuí delivers the turtle to its new home.

She waits while he climbs aboard before setting the basin at her feet. The matamata lies inert, the thin pipe of its nose upthrust. If it can retract its curious head, it chooses not to, even when she touches a quick finger to the neck's fleshy frill. Meantime, Tuí paddles—no longer upstream, but toward the nearer shore. His strokes are efficient, even urgent. Lifting her eyes, Rachel sees why.

The thunderhead hangs low behind them, as though positioned to block their return. Its underside flashes silver—light like a tree branch, a clap like the world cracking in two. The sky opens as they glide beneath the trees. While Tuí nudges the montaria in among the reeds, Rachel looks out on an impenetrable wall of rain. Five minutes out in that and they would've been swamped. She pictures the matamata floating up out of its basin, the dugout wallowing and going down.

Here in their green cave, the second lightning flash is muted, its clap a more distant threat. The forest sways. Overhead, a crashing of branches, a glimpse of rust-coloured fur. The roar of the rain contains untold voices, one of which rises to encompass the rest. Rachel meets Tuí's eye. The word is expected, apparent on his lips: *Guaribas.* They were close by that first night on the Rio Negro, but nothing like this. This time she's among them, inside their familial sound.

30

S cant breeze crosses the verandah, the smell of the river strong. Paul watches Lene work. She's weaving a small, neat mat, a miniature of the one on which she sits. He would doze if it wasn't for the racket in the yard. Half a dozen toucans sit yelping in a scraggly cecropia—dark, compact bodies with foot-long beaks, snow-white bibs slashed red across the breast.

"Are they always so loud?"

His cousin smiles. "Not always. Sometimes tucano comes just one. In the enchente—the flood—they fly many more together. They are good then, very fat."

Paul nods, picturing one of the curious creatures on a spit.

"Vovó was Tucano," Lene adds.

"Vovó?"

She thinks for a moment. "The mãe of Mamãe."

"Oh, your grandmother."

"Grandmother, yes. Your grandmother also."

No, he's about to say, when he realizes she's right. Grandmother. He's never known one—and if his cousin is conjugating properly, he never will. "Vovó, she's . . . gone?"

"Gone, yes. Morta."

"And she was Tucano."

"Certo. Not Vovô."

"*Not* Vovó? But I thought you said—"

"Vovô is the father of Mamãe—the grandfather."

"Vovô?" Paul struggles to hear the difference.

"He was from outside, a trader like Papai. Vovó left her village to live here on the Rio Negro with him."

"Oh, I see."

Just then, something spooks the toucans. A strident *yawp* and they're away, skimming the treetops in beak-heavy, undulating flight.

"Lene," Carolina calls from inside, "venha cá."

Ever mindful, the girl rises, leaving Paul alone.

Tucano. He's always known there was pure Indian in his bloodline—just not quite so close. The satchel lies on the floor beside him. Laying open the flap, he withdraws a thick brown book: *A Narrative of Travels on the Amazon and Rio Negro* by Alfred Russel Wallace. Paul is best acquainted with Chapter XVI, "Observations on the Zoology of the Amazon District." Today he turns to the following essay, entitled simply "On the Aborigines of the Amazon."

Skipping the first few pages, he skims for the list he dimly recalls: "The tribes which inhabit the Uaupés, as far as any of the traders ascend . . ." Paul runs a finger down to the subheading "On the River Apaporís," and further, to "19. Tucános (Toucans)":

. . . The men do not cut their hair, but gather it behind into a long tail, bound round with cord . . . The men have very little beard, and that little they eradicate by pulling it out; men and women also eradicate the hair of the eyebrows, the arm-pits, and the private parts. The colour of the skin is a light, uniform, glossy reddish-brown.

These were the men his grandmother left behind for her river trader—long-haired hunters who, like her, plucked their glossy skin smooth. Paul reads on through the details of the hunt, the alien bounty it affords: ". . . they prefer jabutis, or land-tortoises, monkeys, inambus (*Tinamus* sp.), toucans, and the smaller species of wild pig . . ."

He sees the elements of the feast laid out intact: tortoises upturned in their shells, monkeys grilled entire, their hands clasped as though in prayer. Walter ate monkey once—a sinewy, smoked limb that ended in a fist. *No weak stomachs in the jungle, Paulo.* A story told when the money box was low and the pair of them hunched over another supper of fish-head soup.

Paul reads on: "Their houses are the abode of numerous families, sometimes of a whole tribe . . . In times of feasts and dances, three or four hundred are accommodated in them."

Imagine, hundreds of bodies moving together in one communal home. Paul has been dancing exactly once in his life, an ill-advised trip via horse-drawn tram to a ball on Beacon Hill. Harvard men were expected to be versed in all the latest steps, but Paul could scarcely hold his own in a waltz. What a thing to dance as you had since childhood, not new steps but old.

> These people are as free from the encumbrances of dress as it is possible to conceive . . . While dancing in their festivals, the women wear a small tanga, or apron, made of beads, prettily arranged: it is only about six inches square, but is never worn at any other time, and immediately the dance is over, it is taken off.

Is that what Paul's grandfather saw, one near-naked girl dancing among a hundred—the one he felt moved to carry home?

We will now describe some peculiarities associated with their births, marriages, and deaths.

The women are generally delivered in the house, though sometimes in the forest. When a birth takes place in the house, everything is taken out of it, even the pans and pots, and bows and arrows, till the next day; the mother takes the child to the river, and washes herself and it . . .

Paul pictures his young grandmother brought to childbed in a rede. She insists her ribeirinho husband empty out the house. A woman paddles down from a neighbouring sitio only to be told she isn't required. Vovó manages the bloody business on her own, rising to carry Paul's newborn aunt—or is it his mother?—down to the water's edge.

Reading on through the ordeal of puberty and the theatre of marriage, Paul arrives at the final rite: "The dead are almost always buried in the houses . . ."

"Tudo bem?"

Carolina has the footstep of a cat. Forgetting the words on the page are meaningless to her, Paul slams the book shut.

"Tudo bem. Obrigado."

"Como está o pé?" She bends to inspect his foot. "Dói?"

Not as painful as yesterday, he realizes. "Um pouco."

She begins to unwind the bandage.

"Tia—"

"Sim, Paulito."

"Onde . . . onde Vovó?"

"Vovó?" She looks at him. "Vovó está na casa."

Grandmother is in the house. Paul hasn't the words for "buried," for "ground." He could call for Lene, but somehow this feels too private. He points to the verandah planks, then inside through the door.

Carolina nods. "Vovô também."

"Vovô?" Grandmother and Grandfather, both of them laid to rest under the swept-earth floor.

"Certo." She turns her attention back to his foot, peeling away the dressing of wilted leaves. "E Zuleica," she adds.

And Zuleica? Paul stares at his aunt.

She nods as though he's spoken. "Sim," she says sadly, "sua mãe."

⌐

It's a dark night for a glide. The moon is thin, but thankfully there are stars—overhead and in the water, even in the trees. These last appear in response to the lantern, swinging softly on its hook at the montaria's prow. Not nearly so numerous as those in the sky, the points of light among the foliage come in white, coal-orange, blue. And they come in pairs.

The waterway is narrow, an alley of sound. Croaks and gurgles, clicks and pings. A hoot. Another. A splash. Rachel misses what she's come to think of as her seat: da Silva sits up front, then Iris, then herself. Behind her, Tuí paddles in the stern.

The captain creates little disturbance with his strokes, Tuí even less. At a bend in the stream, they cease paddling. The montaria slows, lantern light spilling over a carpet of floating weeds.

Frogs dive to safety. When Iris looks round, her face is in shadow. Realizing her own expression must be visible, Rachel returns what she assumes is a smile.

Now they wait. Four of them in a line, listening. For a time they're among the quietest of jungle creatures—until Iris lets out a cry.

Not far off the bow, a pair of glowing red eyes. Six feet of disturbed surface angles toward them from the dark. Da Silva takes up his paddle. Reaching out with the wooden blade, he delivers a single, judicious shove. The caiman veers like a log diverted. Tuí sits poised with his paddle until the ripple is gone.

"I'm sorry," Iris says shakily. "I thought—"

"No, no." Da Silva turns in his seat. Backlit, he is without features. "This one is too big, though, I think. You want a young one, yes? One you can take home."

"A young one, yes. Was that a black caiman?"

"No, this is jacaré tinga. 'Spectacled,' you say." He brings a hand up as though holding a pair to his eyes.

Iris says nothing for a moment. Then, "Walter wanted a black one."

"A black one? Are you sure, senhora?"

"Certainly." A shift in tone—plain to Rachel, but seemingly lost on da Silva.

"Black caimans grow much bigger than this one," he says. "Fifteen, even twenty feet. You have room for this?"

"Capitão da Silva, I assure you my husband gave the matter a great deal of thought."

"Of course, senhora."

But da Silva has hit upon a point: the largest of Walter's ponds is only a dozen feet across. Rachel pictures the dark monster adapting to its confines, curving like a sickle moon. "Perhaps," she ventures, "we might take a spectacled caiman to begin—"

Da Silva holds up a hand. His head, suddenly in profile, cants forward like a hawk's. Iris hasn't time to cry out. Striking with a splash, he snatches up a caiman—this one a juvenile, half the adult's size. He brandishes it by its scruff.

"Venha, Tuí." Da Silva adds a phrase in Língua Geral that has Tuí standing and squeezing past.

Iris grips the gunwales as the dugout rocks. "Careful!"

Much as she longs for a better look, Rachel forces herself to shuffle back, distributing weight to the stern. While Tuí's silhouette produces a cord and forms a slip knot, da Silva's clamps a fist over the toothy snout. Together they secure the caiman's jaws.

Tuí makes his way back, Iris raising her arm briefly to allow him by. As Rachel trades places with him to kneel behind her mistress, da Silva proffers his catch. "You want to hold him?"

"Me?" says Iris. "Oh, no, I wouldn't—"

"I do," Rachel blurts. "If that's all right."

"Of course," says Iris, "if Capitão da Silva thinks it's safe."

"Certamente, senhorita."

Iris shrinks to the side as Rachel wriggles up beside her.

"Hold out your hands," says da Silva. "Take him here, at the neck, yes, and here."

The underbelly shocks her with its softness. *Kid leather*, her fingers tell her, *silk*. The caiman cycles its limbs.

"Atenção, senhorita, be careful of the claws."

He reaches round to lift the lantern from its hook. Light stuns the creature to stillness. There's a fineness to its design, something

Rachel has noticed in other hunters: foxes, peregrine falcons, minks.

"This one is jacaré tinga also," da Silva says. "See here." He indicates the bony ridge that crosses the snout.

"Spectacled," Rachel murmurs.

"Correto." He grins. "What do you think, senhora, you want to keep him?"

Rachel glances at her mistress. Iris's gaze has turned quiet; she's already sketching in her mind. "I do indeed," she says. "He's lovely."

Lovely, yes. Rachel looks closely at the creature in her hands—the olive-gold armour banded with black, the stippled, petrified eye.

31

"*st*, Flor."

Paul glances up from the notebook. His aunt sits in the next rede, braiding her daughter's hair. Flor crouches on Carolina's knee, her brown eyes fixed on the work in hand. She reaches again for Lene's scalp, and again Carolina swats her small hand away.

"Tia," Paul begins. He's planned to open with something simple—*My mother, how old was she?*—but something stops the question in his throat. He selects another, a generation removed. "How did Vovó and Vovô meet?"

Cross-legged on the mat, Lene passes the question back. In a moment she returns its response. "There was a festa in Vovó's village."

"And Vovô came?"

"He came, yes. For trading."

"And so . . . what did she see in him?"

Lene looks confused. "What did she see?"

"Like. What did she like about Vovô?"

"Oh."

Her mother smiles at the translation. "Minha mãe cresceu com homens bonitos . . ."

"Mamãe says her mãe was growing up with beautiful men. At the festa the men are the most beautiful, with the paint and the . . . coroas." Lene splays her fingers out at her temples.

"Crowns?"

"Crowns, yes, tucano feathers, arara feathers, and so many beads—on their necks and arms, on their feet. Some men, the best hunters, they wear onça teeth"—she indicates her waist—"here." She listens for a time before continuing. "And then comes this trader. He is mameluco—not a white man, but as white as they will see—and he has no paint, no feathers, no beads. Only short hair on his head, and his plain white shirt."

Carolina's smile broadens as she tells what followed.

"Mamãe says Vovô watches Vovó dance, and in the morning he sits up in his cuberta—his boat—and he watches her bathe. If the man is a Tucano from another village, he comes with his family and there will be a festa, two or three days, and then he steals the girl who will be his wife." Lene pauses while her mother clarifies a point. "It is a play, a game. But Vovô does not know this game. He is a negociante, so he goes to Vovó's father and he gives him everything he has for trade. He does not know he must carry his wife away, so he walks with her down to his cuberta. Vovó knows she is leaving everything—her mãe and pai, her village where everyone lives in one maloca—but she gets in the cuberta with her husband and she goes."

Paul is quiet. In his mind's eye, his grandfather is an amalgam of Walter and da Silva, his grandmother a younger Carolina with Zuleica's sharp little chin. Both of them take up their paddles when it's time to depart.

Reaching the end of Lene's braid, Carolina ties it off with a twist of string. "Era diferente com Walter."

"My father?" says Paul. "What about him?"

"Mamãe says at first Walter thinks he is taking Zuleica away, but the jungle is changing him."

"Mudando sua cabeça," Carolina adds.

Paul nods, the lesson of the gecko coming back to him. The little skull so definite under the thin brown skin—*cabeça*. The jungle changed his father's head.

⤳

In the buzzing heat, da Silva guides the *Bridie Mac* into the lee of a wooded bluff. They tie up in a sheltered spot—jungle overhanging the banks, the dark mouth of a stream. Rachel flushes happily at the thought of exploring its reaches; maybe this time she'll persuade Iris to come along.

They lunch on board, Deolindo sharing out a cluster of stubby bananas along with the second of two fowls he boiled at breakfast. Afterwards, he and Tuí take to their redes, while da Silva opts to stretch out on the portside bench.

Declaring herself wide awake, Iris lays open her sketchbook to a pristine page. Rachel sits close by, her eyelids heavy.

"For heaven's sake, Rachel, you're drooping. Go lie down."

"I'm all right." Rachel yawns. She only means to close her eyes, but Iris's hand at her shoulder wakes her. "What—"

"*Shh.*" Iris points.

Their mooring tree has been invaded, its boughs alive with a whistling crowd. Rachel catches sight of a diminutive face: white mask, black muzzle and cap. And now others—many others—running along the branches, peering out at them through the leaves. Squirrel monkeys.

The pencil flies in Iris's hand. In the time it takes the troop to pass through, she records a dozen gesture drawings—tilt of a head, lift of a bushy-tipped tail. As the last of the little visitors retreats, she scribbles notes between the ghostly forms. Rachel reads over her shoulder: *ears tufted with white fur, human in shape and placement; limbs mustard, trunk tawny; naked, nimble hands.*

Iris covers the top of the page. The bottom half is already home to a slower, more deliberate portrait, the one she was completing when the troop arrived. Da Silva sleeps convincingly on the page. Above him, monkeys float in various stages of becoming, as though he were dreaming them into existence, assembling them limb by limb. Rachel glances from the pencil portrait to its subject—somehow slighter in sleep, more of a buck than a bull. It's a subtle, unnerving change, and Iris has caught it. She has him, line for line.

~

Unable to sleep, Paul reaches down for the lamp and matchbox. His aunt stirs in her rede, then quietens. He turns the wick up as high as he dares.

He's retrieving the notebook when movement at the window catches his eye: Flor, returned from her nocturnal wanderings. Dropping down from the sill, she crosses to his rede in a series of silent bounds.

Her face is changed. At first he imagines it's a trick of the lamplight, but no, her moustaches are no longer white. Touching them, he dusts his finger with gold. Pollen. She's been out among the night-blooming branches, drinking nectar like a bat or a bee.

She nestles against him, tucking her face into the pit of his arm. He opens the notebook with care.

January 10th, 1845, igapó southeast of Sitio da Silva

In this season one may discover stretches of flooded forest in any number of locales, but da Silva is eager that I should become acquainted with the great tract that links the Rio Negro and the Rio Japurá. We are again a skeleton crew, with one addition. I had imagined da Silva would balk at his sister-in-law's request to join our party—or indeed that his wife might take exception to being left with the entire keeping of the house—but neither voiced any objection so far as I am aware. In any case, Senhorita Correia has proven her worth as ship's cook and more. Keen-eyed in the bow, she has spied out many a deadhead that might have breached the *Santa Carolina*'s hull.

Three days' sail downstream brought us to a wide lake dotted with islands. These proved to be the crowns of trees. We were girded round with forest, but nowhere was there any sign of land. Trees—among them species of palm, *Hevea* and representatives of the leguminous orders—rose directly from dark waters, the depth of which could not be told. I have often considered the manner in which the great river and its tributaries redraw their courses. Until now, however, I had not fully grasped the extent to which they can obliterate that most elemental of boundaries between water and land.

Da Silva bade his crew tie up to the stout limbs of an embaúba tree, the anchor being of no use, as it would have become tangled in the branches below. Once the boat was secured, we loaded the pair of montarias and set off down a narrow channel. Myself, the Indian Lontra and the senhorita took the lead canoe. Da Silva and Augustinho followed behind.

The black-water-flooded forest—the igapó—presents even the seasoned naturalist with divers challenges, not least of which being a disorientation that is quite complete. We followed one embowered waterway among hundreds. More often than not, upon turning round in the middle seat, I found it impossible to discern which way we had come. At such times, I took assurance from the senhorita's expression of concentrated calm.

The air cooled as we paddled deeper into the gloom. Through one solemn stretch the water was littered with small white flowers; others glowed eerily overhead in the firmament of leaves. Intermittent splashes alerted us to the presence of leaping fish. One could not help but envision a desperate chase going on beneath us—a multitude of finned species veering among the branches, botos weaving after them like naked birds of prey.

Smaller, more compact splashes spoke of dropping fruits and seeds. Beneath a well-stocked palm, fat tambaqui mouthed seeds from the surface like deer plucking apples from a tree. The light came and went in shafts. In places the water stood clear among the massive trunks, revealing leaves newly sprouted on branches a fathom submerged. Elsewhere the surface presented so perfect a reflection as to disappear.

In such an environment, it becomes difficult to trust the evidence of one's own eyes. Sticks masquerade as snakes; logs become caiman; the nub of a bobbing branch mimics a turtle's head. Then, in a watery clearing, actual turtles—perhaps a score of *Podocnemis expansa* paddling among a windfall of bobbing fruits. Lontra dispatched a large female, shooting his arrow upward so it might fall at the correct angle to penetrate the shell. The creature dove, but was restrained by a line fixed to the arrowhead. After a struggle of some minutes, da Silva and Augustinho dragged the dying creature aboard. It claimed a place mid-montaria parallel to my own.

There followed a quiet, winding stretch, Lontra working his paddle one-handed, occasionally pointing into the treetops to reveal the great bell of a wasps' nest or the hanging form of a sloth. At one point the senhorita tapped my shoulder, indicating that I should ship my paddle—a wordless directive I passed on to Lontra in the bow. In silence we glided beneath an airborne assembly of what I initially took to be hawk moths, but found upon closer examination to be miniature bats.

When at length we passed through a narrow aperture back into the open lake, a flock of green parrots exploded from a brake of buriti palms as if to announce our return. I thought I recognized the distant crown of an emergent ipê. After my sojourn in the igapó, however, I doubted my ability to tell one hardwood from the next, and so held my tongue, paddling on until I beheld the clear beacon of the *Santa Carolina*'s mast.

Careful not to disturb Flor, Paul lays the notebook down open against his chest. As a boy he'd learned to lie in wait for Walter's stories of the flooded forest. Such tales had to rise unbidden, and even then they were told haltingly, rife with

maddening holes. He can recall hearing of white blossoms floating on black water, but nothing about the ones that stood in for
stars overhead. Tambaqui were feeding fish, plain and simple—
no mention of apples, of deer. No mention of Senhorita Correia,
either. Not a one.

32

ow many entreaties on Rachel's part, and all da Silva has to say is, "You must come walking today, senhora— there is something you will wish to see."

Iris smiles and ducks away into the cabin, declining Rachel's offer of help. In minutes she's back, clad in striped trousers, blouse and sunbonnet, a crimson kerchief at her throat.

Da Silva takes the lead, in the montaria and on the path. Relieved of the responsibility, Tuí ranges freely through the half-light of the understorey, leaving Rachel to bring up the rear. Birds sound their presence: a racket of clacks and wows, the stroke of a brassy bell. They haven't gone far when Iris stoops suddenly, swatting frantically about her ears.

Rachel registers the whirr, the darting, blue-green glint. "Iris, *Iris*, it's all right." She smiles in spite of herself. "It's a hummingbird."

"Where?" Iris straightens, looking about. The little bird hangs in the air before her. "Oh!"

Da Silva turns. "It's your bandana, senhora. He thinks you are a flower."

And so it would seem. The hummingbird hovers, inches from Iris's chest. It's close in colouring to the ones Rachel knows, minus the ruby-red throat.

"Silly thing."

At the sound of Iris's voice, the little bird zips up into the canopy, as though somebody's yanked it on a string.

"Ai, senhora." Da Silva frowns. "You hurt his feelings."

The captain was right, Iris is delighted by the tree. It's not the first of its kind they've come across—the genus is common enough—but it's the largest by far. Indeed, "tree" in the singular falls woefully short. Scores of trunks make up the monster before them, as though an entire grove of saplings has converged.

"How marvellous," Iris says, gazing up. "What do you think, Rachel, for the mural?"

Rachel comes to stand beside her. The tree is a towering garden. Plants of all descriptions spill from its ridges and folds: ferns and philodendrons, an orchid with an ostrich-feather arc. "It's perfect."

Iris turns to da Silva. "Strangler fig?"

"Estranguladora, yes."

"It grows up around the host tree."

"Excuse me, senhora, not only up, but down."

Rachel looks past them, her eye drawn to movement among the trees. She's about to speak up when she spots the long antenna of the blowpipe. Tuí, stalking between the buttresses, running his eye over the heights.

"Think of the tree that came before," da Silva continues, "the—how did you call it?—the host. Somewhere up high, a bird passes—an arara, we will say, the one you call macaw. This arara, he has been eating figs, and, forgive me, senhora, but he is dropping seeds as he flies. One of these seeds is lucky—it lands where a branch grows from the host's trunk, and there it finds a . . ." He forms a bowl with his hands.

"Niche?" Iris offers.

"Niche, yes. And maybe there are some dead leaves there, just enough to make a little earth."

"It sprouts on the tree?"

He nods. "And you know what happens next—the leaf grows up, and the root—"

"Grows down."

"Exatamente. Only this root has a long way to go. To begin with, it is just another vine." He points to a slender S-curve in the trunk's pattern. "But when it finds the ground, it grows stronger. Another leaf, another root, and one day the roots are meeting and growing together, and the leaves are taking up the sky."

"And the host is finished," Iris says.

"Finished, yes. It rots, and there are termites."

Iris lays a hand to the buckled trunk. "It's gruesome, really."

"'Gruesome,' senhora?"

"Horrible. Cruel."

"Not really. The estranguladora needs a place like anyone, and it is a good tree. Not for wood—the wood is poor—but you will see how many animals come when there is fruit. Araras and parrots, monkeys—"

"Guaribas?" Rachel asks.

"Guaribas, yes, barrigudos, coaitas—all kinds of monkeys. And wild pigs come for the figs that fall, and pacas. Everyone comes, even the onças."

Iris looks doubtful. "Jaguars eat figs?"

"No, no." Da Silva grins at her. "The paca is his fruit. But you see how many the estranguladora feeds."

"And shelters," Rachel says. "All those nooks and crannies."

"The senhorita is right. Birds live in these places, and spiders.

Lizards too—one with an orange head. We will see if Tuí can find some."

Iris looks about. "Where is Tuí?"

"He will come." Da Silva turns. "Here, I will show you something."

He leads them to the far side of the trunk, where the ground is littered with feathers, bones. Above them, in the tree's ridged face, a hole.

"Morcego fantasma-grande." Da Silva humps his arms to form a sinister wingspan. "He is the king of bats."

Iris blanches, taking a step back.

"Ai, no." Da Silva drops his hands. "Don't worry, senhora, he is a hunter, not a vampiro. At night he goes looking for birds and lizards, rats. He finds them where they sleep." He knocks softly on the trunk. "He is sleeping himself now."

Rachel blinks. For a moment it's as though she can see through to the tree's hollow heart. The fantasma-grande hangs head-down, his eyes wide open in the dark.

It's Walter's fourth day in the igapó, and Paul is there with him, following along on the page. This morning Augustinho stayed behind, keeping watch over the paddlers after one of their number jumped ship to join a passing cuberta bound for Barra. Now they're two to a montaria: the captain and the Indian, the naturalist and his bride-to-be. Except Walter doesn't know he will marry Senhorita Correia—or if he does, he's giving nothing away.

... Travel by dugout through the treetops affords proximity to countless species ordinarily accessible by gunshot alone. Upon bringing the montaria to a halt alongside a cavity in an aged bole, the senhorita and I were rewarded by the bright eye ring of a trogon, followed by the flare of its yellow breast feathers as it emerged.

A nearby crevice, when probed with an arrow's shaft, produced a specimen of mygale spider reminiscent of a common house mouse in both colour and size. After a series of defensive feints, it climbed the trunk and proceeded along a limb. I stood up in the montaria and was following its progress with interest when the senhorita directed my attention downward. A slender fish hovered at the water's surface, chin whiskers extended, eyes turned to the sky. In a flash it leapt to a height equal to my own, snatching the spider in its jaws. In my surprise, I narrowly missed capsizing our little craft. Some minutes passed before the senhorita could contain her mirth.

About midday we came upon a floating meadow—a wide pond that harboured a flotilla of the celebrated *Victoria regia* lily. It was too early in the year to hope for the massive blooms, but the pads themselves—a yard across with turned-up rims and spiked undersides—presented an impressive display.

On one such platter, there stretched an immature spectacled caiman—the jacaré tinga. When I turned to point it out to Senhorita Correia, she brought us alongside the others and spoke a few low words in Língua Geral. Lontra nodded and began paddling softly toward the jacaré. The senhorita kept close behind. Not being privy to her plan, I followed da Silva's example and laid my paddle across my knees.

While Lontra flanked the quarry on the left, the senhorita sidled in from the right. The instant our montaria nudged the lily pad's rim, she snatched the jacaré up by the neck. After allowing me some minutes' observation of the creature in life, she swung it unceremoniously against the hull.

Taking care to preserve the hide, I butchered the caiman while the others hacked dead branches for a fire. There being no land, we roasted the kill upon the trunk of a fallen tree.

Paul knows this part: the tender meat of the tail savoured by a floating fire. He must have assumed his father shot the caiman. Walter wouldn't have lied to him outright.

The rest of the entry is taken up with collecting. Come nightfall, the little party is nowhere near the *Santa Carolina*, still deep in the watery wood. It seems no one, save Paul, is alarmed.

. . . As darkness gathered, we considered how best to make our camp. Loaded down as they were, the montarias could scarcely accommodate a single sleeper each. At a word from da Silva, Lontra set aside his paddle and stood. Taking hold of an overhead branch, he drew himself up among the leaves, where he proceeded to string up our redes over the flood. Senhorita Correia prepared a fine supper of cold caiman, farinha and palm fruits, after which we all four ascended to our beds.

33

With the sun's dip into afternoon, the Rio Negro takes a wide sweep to the west. Rachel lays a hand to Iris's back and points: in the branches of a bankside cecropia, a village of pendulous grass nests.

Da Silva glances over from the helm. "I hope you will not mind stopping," he says. "My brother has sent another boat for the shipment, but Senhor Brandão is an important trader. We have from him salsaparrilha, castanha nuts, also the cacao he grows on his plantação—"

"I understand, Capitão," says Iris. "It's a courtesy."

"A courtesy, exatamente."

Deolindo whistles from the bow, pointing to starboard, and da Silva guides them around a floating snarl. "We will have a good meal," he adds. "Senhor Brandão, he is a generous host."

"Lovely."

"And he can tell you all about this part of the river. No one knows more, eh, Deolindo?" The mate looks round. "Senhor Brandão entende o rio."

"Certo, Capitão." Deolindo grins. "Especialmente os jacarés."

"Ai, for shame." Da Silva smiles, shaking his head.

Iris looks to Rachel. "What did he say?"

"Something about a caiman."

"Deolindo is making a joke." Da Silva keeps his eyes trained on the river. "It happened many years ago. One night, Senhor Brandão was bathing, and there came a black caiman. Senhor Brandão, he doesn't hear a thing—this is an old jacaré, and smart. One moment the senhor is lying in the water, and the next moment the jacaré has him—" He makes a grabbing motion. "Like that, it bites his arm."

"How terrifying," Iris says.

Da Silva nods. "Already the jacaré is pulling him down, so he puts a hand out to feel for its eyes."

"Its eyes?"

"This is what you must do, senhora. You must find the eyes and—forgive me, but you must put in your thumbs."

"Oh!" Iris's hand flies to her mouth.

"Senhor Brandão, he could only put in one thumb, but it was enough."

"It let him go," Rachel says.

"It let him go." Da Silva nods ruefully. "But it kept his arm."

⌒

January 25th, 1845, Sitio da Silva
Senhorita Zuleica is proving a most able assistant.

Paul blinks. Somewhere between this entry and the last, Walter has made the shift to her given name. It suits her—strange in its loveliness, strong. Paul imagines his father giving voice to it for the first time. The pair of them work in companionable silence, Walter at his open-air table, his assistant cross-legged beside him on the little porch. "Senhorita Zuleica," he begins without thinking, and she looks up at him, her expression serious but in no way hard.

After a moment, Paul reads on.

Senhorita Zuleica is proving a most able assistant. She shares my interest in reptiles, exhibiting no hint of that prejudicial revulsion so common to members of her sex. Any woman might marvel at a feather, but it takes a special turn of mind to appreciate a scale.

Today we worked at preparing those specimens destined for sale. Da Silva has agreed to transport them to Barra; he assures me there is no better man than Senhor Honório to secure their safe passage to Pará. This is to be the second such shipment I have sent to the care and attention of Senhor Felisberto, who so kindly offered to forward them to Mr. Ingleby at the Academy of Natural Sciences.

When I shipped the first collection from Senhor Aracú's plantação, I could not help but accompany it in my mind. Óbidos, Santarém, Pará—I pictured every port that lay between myself and the safe arrival of those crates at Philadelphia's docks. Of late, however, I find my thoughts less inclined to drift downstream. Indeed, the more I think on it, the more I see no reason why a man of scientific disposition and enterprising spirit might not remain indefinitely in the field.

Paul looks out across the river. What if his father had stayed on? Paul can envision any number of ends: snakebite or fever, a jaguar on the path, a caiman in the quiet bay. Anything but a stumble, a shattered pane. Even more painful, he can picture Walter still among the living. Appearing at the jungle trailhead, raising his hand in a wave.

━━

From far off, Senhor Brandão's property resembles da Silva's sitio—a thatched and whitewashed casa, a yard carved from jungle atop a flood-cut bank. Rachel marks the discrepancies as they draw near: great swaths of yellow-green cacao trees beneath parasol banana palms; a small village of outbuildings—sheds and lean-tos, perhaps a dozen mud huts.

On the dock, two men in panama hats, the younger hulking a little behind. On shore, a chorus of dark-skinned women and children, a handful of men.

Da Silva waves. "It is Senhor Brandão and his son, Pinto."

The older man lifts his right and only hand. When the son raises his left, Rachel suffers a fleeting illusion of a two-headed man. They're close enough now to make out smiles—broad in the father's case, missing in the son's. Senhor Brandão barks something over his shoulder, causing the gathering on shore to disband.

"Where are they going?" says Iris. "I should like to meet the senhora—"

"There is no senhora," says da Silva. Deolindo has shut the dampers. As he quiets the *Bridie Mac* further, closing her wheezing main valve, da Silva lowers his voice. "She left after the jacaré—she went with a man who still had both hands. Little Pinto was his father's nurse."

Little Pinto? As the heavy-set son steps forward, making ready to catch their line, Rachel struggles to imagine him as a boy.

"Olá!" Senhor Brandão calls out. "Bem-vindo!"

It is indeed a good meal; Rachel only hopes Tuí and Deolindo are enjoying half such a feast by the fire among the mud huts. The women who carry plate after plate out to the verandah range in age. The eldest is tall, with a queenly stride; a pale blue head scarf gleams against her coal-black skin. Senhor Brandão says nothing as she kneels beside him to set down a platter of fried fish.

"É tambaqui, Joaquina?" da Silva asks her.

"Está certo, Capitão."

"Venha." Senhor Brandão holds the platter out to Iris. "Prova, Senhora Ash."

"Oh, thank you, senhor," says Iris, "obrigada, but I'm—"

"Here, senhora." Da Silva spears a chunk on his knife and transfers it to her bowl. "You like tambaqui."

"Joaquina"—the son holds up an empty jug—"mais cachaça." The only words he's spoken since the five of them sat down.

Their host has been talking for some time. To begin with, Rachel strained to understand, but as the evening wore on, Senhor Brandão's words ran together, shedding their individual forms. Now she waits for the breaks—a cigar fished out and lit one-handed, a muttered aside to the son—when da Silva does his best to bridge the divide.

"We are speaking of a difference in the country," he explains. "A small river not far upstream that has changed its course."

"Changed its course?" Iris says loudly.

Rachel glances at the cup in her mistress's hand.

"This happens," says da Silva. "A river floods, and when the water goes down, it finds a new way."

"É o trabalho da Cobra Grande," Senhor Pinto says darkly.

The work of the big snake? Rachel is unsure whether the

confusion is her own or a symptom of the cachaça in the son's blood.

"Verdade, meu filho." Senhor Brandão reaches across himself to pat his son's shoulder.

"Senhor Brandão and Senhor Pinto," says da Silva, "they speak of a spirit, a great snake—"

"An anaconda?" Iris stumbles ever so slightly on the word.

Da Silva shakes his head. "Much, much bigger."

"A Cobra Grande vive em lagos profundos . . ." their host continues, da Silva translating in the gaps. "The Cobra Grande lives in the deep lakes . . . His eyes are two lanterns . . . He can wrap around a boat and take everyone on board to the Encante."

The Encante. The world at the bottom of the river—wasn't that what Lene said? Rachel pictures the great lamp-eyed snake rising to lay claim to the *Bridie Mac.*

Da Silva listens for a long moment, nodding. "The Cobra Grande lies down on the land," he says finally, "and where he lies, this is where the rivers run."

"How lovely." Iris sets down her empty cup. "How perfectly . . . lovely. Capitão—" She pauses as Senhor Brandão holds out the jug. "Oh, yes, sim, obrigada, senhor."

"Iris—" Rachel murmurs, but Iris ignores her.

"Capitão, you must tell the senhores we are hoping for an anaconda."

He nods, relating Iris's request.

"Uma sucuruju?" Father and son exchange a look, a few low words. The one phrase Rachel catches sets her skin tingling. *Uma grande.*

"There is talk of one upriver," da Silva tells Iris. "Past Ramopreto."

"Alive? Tell him we want it alive."

Senhor Brandão laughs at da Silva's translation. "Você precisaria de um barco maior."

"What did he say?"

"He says for this one we would need a bigger boat."

Iris's smile is uneven. Rachel watches her look down into her cup and drain it. Again their host reaches for the jug. Finding it empty, he bellows, "Joaquina!"

One of the younger women comes running. As she stoops for the jug, Senhor Brandão catches hold of her wrist. "Onde está Joaquina?"

"Em sua rede, senhor."

"Hn." He keeps hold a moment longer before nodding and letting go.

Rachel takes her chance. "Perhaps we too should be going to our beds."

"I'm not tired," says Iris.

Rachel looks past her, catching da Silva's eye.

"The senhorita is right, Senhora Ash." He rises, holding out his hand. "It is late, and we will make an early start."

Senhor Pinto helps his father to stand. "Maria," the older man calls. "Maria!"

The young woman returns to the doorway, jug in hand.

He gestures grandly toward Iris and Rachel. "Leve as senhoras para as suas redes."

Maria nods. "Certo, senhor."

It isn't far to the guest hut, but the ground is rough, and Iris is unsteady on her feet. She pulls away when Rachel tries to take her arm.

"For pity's sake, Rachel, I'm *fine*."

Away among the gathered huts, the open fire burns low. At the threshold of one of the dwellings, Rachel glimpses the pale, twisted crown of Joaquina's scarf. And now a second, more familiar shape: Deolindo's grizzled head.

If Maria witnesses the embrace, she gives no sign, hurrying on with her lantern held high. It's Iris who stops. Swaying on her feet, she stares across the darkened yard. The sound she lets out is more painful, more private than any Rachel has known.

34

February 2nd, 1845, Sitio da Silva

There is a keenness of mind that comes of having fixed upon a course. This morning I rose at first light. I found da Silva on the verandah, and before he could call for Dona Carolina to bring café, I asked him outright for Zuleica's hand.

My friend is a man of perception; he betrayed no hint of surprise. Having secured his blessing, I proceeded in haste to where Zuleica stood half hidden among the fruit trees, her basket at her feet. I wasted no time in putting forth my proposal.

"Você vai me levar," came her response. You will take me away.

"Você está errada," I assured her. Never before have I known a woman to smile upon being told she was wrong.

Paul lingers at the bottom of the page, imagining what happened next. Perhaps they returned to the verandah to share the good news. Better yet, they slipped down to the bay, indulging in a shared swim as a married-couple-to-be. He'll never know. The following page offers a new heading, an entire fortnight gone by.

February 17th, 1845, Sitio da Silva

In dressing for today's ceremony, I realized my feet had become strangers to my shoes. Having shaken a host of cockroaches from the left, I walked a few pinched paces before stashing the offending articles in my trunk. I consoled myself that it would be churlish for the groom to stand shod alongside his barefoot bride.

The padre, an elderly Dominican by the name of Frei Sebastião, arrived by cuberta late in the day, having been delayed by a child's drowning in a village some miles upstream. So it was that the wedding began by the day's last rays and continued through the lighting of lamps. Frei Sebastião delivered a lengthy homily on the blessings and duties of matrimony, to which Zuleica attended with head bowed. Her attire was simple—feast-day white, the beads of her mother's people at her throat.

Paul shuts his eyes, picturing his mother in her dress. He begins with what little he knows: the eyes, the chin, the smile. The rest he pieces together, borrowing his aunt's firm build, his cousins' shimmering skin. "The beads of her mother's people" he bases on images recalled from a botany text: strings of glossy red seeds, the produce of a leguminous tree. For "feast-day white," he conjures up a garment startling in its purity. As the ceremony wears on into evening, the dress emits a cool, almost lunar, light.

The song comes through gradually. A thin, reiterative tune, it floats around the corner of the house from where the family are about their work. At first he hears only the children. Carolina sings at a lower frequency, her part reaching him only after he pricks up his ears.

He sets aside the notebook; time he was making himself useful. The crutch lies on the floor beneath him, at the ready for his nightly transfer back indoors. It's the first time he's struggled to stand unaided. As always, his foot yowls at the influx of blood. Gritting his teeth, he fits the crutch into the damp of his armpit. The good leg is rickety, but it holds.

His route along the verandah stands clear, the other redes hooked back against their beams. Swing and stand, swing and stand. Reaching the end, he leans against the wall. The song is clearer here, his cousins' voices sweet and high. He runs a hand through his hair before putting his face around the corner.

The three of them are busy in the open shed. Paul recognizes the scene from one he encountered on the page: the two sisters showing Walter how to press the poisonous juice from grated mandioca root, rendering the nutritious pulp. *Senhorita Zuleica demonstrated great patience, reviewing the process step by step.* Too many steps for Paul to manage. Vitor and Lene move about their mother like a pair of collies, responsive, alert. He'd only be in the way.

Drawing back, he turns to confront the verandah. The least he can do is work on regaining his strength.

The first length goes smoothly enough, notwithstanding the clumsy business of unhooking his rede and pinning it back. By the second pass he's steady, if maddeningly slow. The foot jabs at him. Three lengths of the verandah. Four.

His good leg goes on the turn. Lurching against the wall, he drives his knuckles into his thigh, subduing the spasming cramp. Suddenly he's back there, pinned to the verandah floor. The gash in his foot, the knife, the terror of the steaming tub. Rachel's hold on his leg is unyielding. Her face in his mind's eye is as clear as he's known it—serious grey gaze, sweat on her freckled brow. *Go on, Paul. Go on.*

—

Ramo-preto. Something black is all Rachel knows, until she digs out the grammar and looks up the other half. Black-branch. As they steam toward the Indian village, she looks out for the tree or stream that might have given rise to the name. No sign. Indeed, there's little evidence of the village itself, beyond a line of dugouts on the praia and a glimpse of grey thatch through the trees.

Tuí ferries them ashore then paddles back for Deolindo and the crates. It's a steep climb, made without the aid of stairs. Da Silva goes first, pausing intermittently to pull Iris up by the hand. Behind them, Rachel digs in with her boot tips, swinging and planting the carpet bag, finding handholds in the scrub.

Faced with a scattering of huts—some no more than a roof on poles—Rachel feels vaguely bereft. She's been imagining a longhouse, the image fixed in her mind since Walter read to them from Mr. Wallace's account of the great lodges on the Rio Uaupés. *Their houses are the abode of numerous families, sometimes of a whole tribe . . .*

The headman too defies expectation. A diminutive man in short breeches, he nods imperceptibly when introduced, then draws da Silva aside. As the two men confer, villagers begin to emerge. Naked children, men in breeches or breechcloths, women in petticoats and nothing more. Rachel has seen few bare breasts in her life. Her mother's had shrunk to sacs by the time Rachel had to bathe them; Iris's are full and shapely; her own are boyish and firm.

"Rachel," Iris says beside her, "you mustn't stare."

Breaking from da Silva, the headman calls his people in. The children gather close, bringing with them a scent of water, of fresh and floating plants. The women stand at a little distance, their men farther away still. The headman delivers a short address, the final syllables of which send a ripple through the group. The men are first to disperse, some making purposefully for their dwellings while others slip away down the bank—presumably to help Deolindo and Tuí unload. The women return to their work, but it's the children who draw Rachel's eye. At first they appear to follow their mothers, but like the men, they only pass by their huts for gravatanas, bows and arrows, clubs. One after another, they filter away into the woods.

"Come," says da Silva, "Senhor Lontra says you can work in his house."

The headman's dwelling is open on all sides, walls of grass matting rolled up beneath the eaves. Two women sit together on the swept-earth floor, one a wife's age, the other a daughter's. They rise at Senhor Lontra's bidding.

"Hello," says Iris. "Please don't let us disturb you—"

But the women are already on their way, walking single file down the beaten-grass track to a neighbouring hut. While Senhor Lontra hooks back a trio of redes, da Silva drags a long bench in under the roof. Setting down the carpet bag, Rachel begins unpacking Iris's things.

"This is most kind of you, Senhor Lontra, thank you." Iris waits while da Silva translates. The headman's reply is protracted. Da Silva bows his head, leaving a short silence before looking up.

"Senhor Lontra would like you to know that he knew your husband."

"—Oh."

"Senhor Lontra was with me in that time. He was part of my crew." Da Silva clears his throat. "He says to say Senhor Ash was a good man—"

"Yes. Yes, I see."

Rachel hears the catch in her mistress's voice. She steps around the bench to stand beside her.

"Oi, Capitão!" Deolindo shouts from the top of the bank.

"Desculpa, senhora." Da Silva gives a little bow and strides off, Senhor Lontra following suit. Iris stands frozen, save for the emotion working in her face. Rachel judges it best not to speak. Returning to the bench, she sets about arranging the brushes just so.

They haven't long to wait. Before anyone can return from the hunt, an old woman approaches, straight-backed but slow. Her hair is thick, cut in a heavy jet-black fringe. Standing before the bench, she sets her mouth, crossing her arms under flattened breasts. Rachel glances at da Silva, who signals patience with a slight lift of his hand.

At a word from the headman, the old woman reaches down inside her petticoat's waistband and produces a leather pouch. Rachel assumes the contents are alive, such is the delicacy with which the old woman unwinds the cord. In fact, the offering is long dead.

"Ah," says da Silva, "this is jararaca."

Iris peers at it. "Lancehead?"

"Correto."

Iron-dark and dusty, the dried snake head looks less like a natural history specimen than an archaeological find. Iris gives da

Silva the nod. He draws a length of red calico from a crate. At the sight of it, the old woman softens, her mouth buckling in a smile.

Rachel doubts whether the jararaca's glands harbour any venom; still, she avoids the fangs while measuring the desiccated head. Close by, Deolindo barters for a trio of chickens, making the woman who raised them laugh. Glancing up, Rachel catches sight of Tuí trotting along a pathway between two huts. Free as one of the village children, he ducks beneath a swag of lianas and disappears.

Iris is shading a sketch of the lancehead when the first of the hunters returns—a girl no older than Lene, lugging a tortoise the size of a wash bowl.

"Ah, jabuti!" Deolindo rubs his bare belly. *"Ikatu."* Accepting the tortoise, he deposits it in a wooden tub. The girl takes her payment—a few yards of calico plus a string of fish hooks—and carries it away. Minutes later she's back, lingering wordlessly, watching Iris draw.

The collection swells considerably over the following hours: a second tortoise, two-thirds the size of the first; a foot-long lizard marked with eye-spots; a snake da Silva identifies as a mussurana before dropping it into a basket with care. Of the men who come bearing quarry, some stay and smoke while others return to the jungle in search of further reward. The children tend to remain. Rachel keeps them out of Iris's light, occasionally checking a curious hand.

Some of the more dangerous finds come to them lifeless. Rachel measures a black coral snake ringed with white dots, then a fiery-red specimen with dark bands fringed in cream. *Red to yellow, kill a fellow,* Papa taught her when she was small, *red to black, venom lack.* A rhyme no earthly use to her now.

Compared with the coral snakes, the forest viper exhibits a quiet beauty, its turquoise skin flecked with shadow and light.

"This one sleeps in the day," da Silva tells them, translating for the boy who clubbed it. "It was on a branch in some bushes along the creek."

Nocturnal, Rachel scribbles in her book, *arboreal*. Meantime, the boy arranges the two-foot viper on the bench, demonstrating how he found it, coiled in sleep. If only Rachel could have seen it then—motionless, yes, but still rippling inwardly with life.

"Marvellous." Iris slips the tail of her paintbrush under its belly, lifting a bright coil. "Capitão, give this boy a knife."

"A knife, senhora? This is very—"

"I know." She turns her smile on him, and he complies.

Iris takes her time with the viper, working up three sketches in pencil before touching her brush to the paint. She proceeds with the system Walter preferred, augmenting the colours themselves with pencilled notes. Drawing a line to the pale blue-green, she writes, *robin's egg?*

Rachel leans in over her shoulder. "Maybe wood thrush?"

Iris nods, making the change. "Here," she says, passing the watercolour on its board. "You finish up while I make a start on the skinks."

Rachel looks from snake to image, image to snake. Iris has done justice to the markings: all down the dorsum, a delicate peppering of black; the occasional touch of soft orange, precisely four scales wide. The head is only partially crushed. The lips are a strange translucent shade; *greengages*, Rachel writes, underlining the word in her certainty. For the eye that remains whole: *pond-water (bronze)*.

Nothing left but to pack the specimen in a jar. She picks the viper up by the neck and lowers it in tail first. The jug of spirits is

unwieldy; she spills a little topping it off. She fills out a label—
Forest Viper, Village of Ramo-Preto, Rio Negro, Brazil—and ties it
about the neck of the jar. Paste is unreliable in these climes, and
a specimen without a label is soon worthless, just another fleshy
pickle on the shelf.

She's nestling the jar in straw when a youth comes jogging,
dragging a heavy branch. Children move in a shoal to meet him.
Men tip up out of redes, rise expectantly from low stools. Rachel
straightens. "Iris, look."

Wound like that around the branch, the *Boa constrictor*'s
length is difficult to judge. Five feet? Six? Deolindo sets a large
crate on end and lifts its barred door. As the youth lowers the
bound creature in headfirst, Senhor Lontra flicks a knife through
the cords about its throat and tail. Dropping the cage door,
Deolindo pushes the pin through the lock.

"Well done!" Iris cries.

Da Silva claps the young hunter on the shoulder. "Two
knives, senhora?"

"Whatever you think, Capitão. Two knives, three . . ."

Beneath their laughter, an almost imperceptible sound.
Rachel steps closer to the crate. Inside, the *Boa constrictor* is gasp-
ing, drawing breath after laboured breath. Rachel drops into what
feels like memory—though by rights the scene is Walter's, not
her own. A whoosh like the rush of water, of wind. As the naturalist watches, a snake twice the size of today's captive flows past.
Pursuit is futile. *Boa constrictor* outpaces *Homo sapiens*, effecting
its graceful escape.

35

Rachel sits up in the gloom. There was a thump. She's sure of it—something hitting the hull not far from her head. The montaria? Not likely. They're tied up in a glassy backwater, the *Bridie Mac* lying still.

There. There it is again. A thud, and now a dragging sound, passing beneath the keel. Rachel stands, wrapping herself hurriedly in her shawl. The cabin door sighs as she slips outside.

No sun yet, only the low, cold light it sends ahead. No one up. A rustle among the baskets, a scratching from the iguana's cage. And now a soft, unhappy cackling that lifts the hairs at the back of her neck.

Chickens, she remembers, only chickens. A sound she's known all her life.

Stepping over the tortoises in their tub, she kneels on the bench and looks aft along the hull to Deolindo's makeshift coop. He's passed a rope through the handles of a large covered basket, fixing it to the rail. Its bottom sits two feet above the river's surface. Or it did. Leaning out, Rachel sees where the wicker's been torn away.

The hen hangs by its claws. It should be squawking; like Rachel, it should be raising the alarm. Instead, it flaps and cackles. Instead, she grips the rail and stares.

The head that surfaces is larger than her own. Yard upon yard, the anaconda evolves from the shadows, hugging up against the launch. If she were to reach down with the dipper, she could touch it—its back is that close. Her skull buzzes, the weight of it threatening to upend her, send her toppling overboard.

The hen dangles. Drops. A second bird follows, a third. A moment's floundering, and the snake makes mouthfuls of all three.

Snake? Rachel blinks. It's as thick as her rib cage. Olive green with a motif of rotting leaves, it might be the riverbed itself, risen to confound her eyes.

A turn. A last fat S along the surface, and the anaconda drops away. *To what unseen lair does it retreat when not hunting?* Walter was right, one really could spend a lifetime studying them. But here, Rachel thinks, flashing on an image of the great snake overflowing its concrete pond. It would have to happen here.

Sitting back on her heels, she hears a soft, significant click. One eye on the water, she shuffles sideways on her knees to peer out from beneath the canopy's fringe. On the cabin roof, a pair of sentinels: the ship's cat, rigid with watching, and Tuí. Meeting her gaze, Tuí widens his eyes.

Iris doubts her at first—not about the fact of the sucuruju, but about its size. *You must be mistaken, dearest.* In the end, it's Tuí's account that sways her—da Silva nodding, *Yes, he says it was as long as the boat.* Even then, Iris appears more disconcerted than amazed. Still, she sets about documenting the incident, roughing in the surrounds as Rachel does her best to describe what she saw.

Having sketched a fair version of the snake, Iris opens her paintbox. The colour she mixes is all wrong.

"No," Rachel tells her, "it was darker than that. Still green, but"—she searches for a more helpful term—"dark."

Iris sets down her brush. "You should have woken me."

"I . . . it was over in moments—"

Iris's gaze narrows. "It didn't occur to you to call out?"

Rachel opens her mouth to protest, but in a sense her mistress is right. In those long, looping seconds, Rachel had no need—no awareness, even—of any gaze but her own. Her cheeks burn. Behind her, the engine spills heat.

"Are you ready, senhora?" da Silva says on his way past. "We must leave soon if you want to reach Ilha das Tartarugas before dark."

"Ready." Iris sets the painting board aside. "You must call me Iris, Capitão."

He turns, his smile uncertain.

She stands, obliging Rachel to take a step back. "Well?"

"Well, then. Iris." He says it the way she does, forcing the hard English *I*. Then again, as he did on the dock at Barra. "Íris."

"That's better . . ."

"Paulo."

"But you're still our captain. Capitão Paulo—yes?"

Rachel looks from one to the other, but neither will meet her eye.

"If you like, Dona Íris," says da Silva. "If you like."

⌒

Paul is embarking on his third length of the verandah when his aunt puts her head around the door. "Paulo, nós estamos indo pra roça de mandioca."

His cousins squeeze out past their mother, each bearing a large basket.

"Mamãe says—"

"I know." Paul smiles to cover the note of sharpness. "The manioc field." Hobbling closer, he sees Flor curled like a cat in Vitor's basket. The tamarin lifts her mustachioed face and blinks at him. He straightens on his crutch. "I'll come with you."

Lene and her mother share a glance, a murmured exchange. "Mamãe says it is too far."

Paul looks over the girl's head to meet her mother's gaze. "It's all right, Tia. I'll turn back if I get tired."

By the time they reach the forked trailhead, Paul has to stop and catch his breath. As he stands gazing down the leafy left-hand tunnel, Carolina and the children keep right, following the wider of the two tracks. After a moment he hitches along after them, eyes on the path, scanning for trip roots and worse.

In a hundred yards, he's beaten. The crutch bites at his armpit; the pulse tolls cruelly in his foot. His aunt turns before he can call out to her. He reads his own sorry state in the expression on her face.

"Lene," she says, "você volta com o primo Paulo."

The girl hands her basket to her mother and walks back to him. "I come with you, Paulo."

"Thank you, Lene." He fights an absurd urge to drop the crutch and lean on her—a child seven years of age.

She walks slowly, keeping to his invalid's pace. Halfway back to the trailhead, she stops.

"It's all right," he says, "I can make it." But Lene holds up her hand. Paul feels his heart shrink: there must be something on the path—or, worse, something watching them from the trees. Why didn't he think to bring the gun?

Lene smiles at him over her shoulder as, suddenly, they're surrounded by birds. Scores of them animate the understorey. Chirping, whistling, they flit through the bushes, lighting on branches and vines. Not one species, Paul realizes, but many. He's read of these mixed, insectivorous flocks—avian hunting parties comprising diverse individuals or pairs. He spots a robin-sized bird with a face striped like a badger's, the blue flash of a tanager's hood. A couple of little brown jobs—woodcreepers?—run up a tree trunk like rats.

Birds have never been his strong suit. Every Aves drawer he had cause to open at the museum filled him with a sense of defeat: tray upon tray of beaked skulls and feathered skins, dried, contracted claws. Some lay intact with legible tags. Others had succumbed to insects or crumbled to dust.

The flock is passing, driving deeper into the wood. Lene gestures after them. "They follow uirapuru."

"Uira—"

"Uirapuru. He is a small bird, not very beautiful, but his song is the most beautiful of all."

"His song? I don't think I heard it."

She looks at him, incredulous. "He does not sing now, Paulo. He is hunting."

"Of course, stupid of me."

She grins. "Venha." Something of her mother in the way she turns. "You must rest."

The rede welcomes him, his foot easing the moment he has it up. Lene rolls a blanket and tucks it beneath his ankle.

"Obrigado, prima Lene."

"De nada, primo Paulo."

"Could you please bring me some water?"

"Certo."

It takes her longer than it should. He's considering calling out to her when a sound reaches him from inside the house. The squawk is unmistakable: the lid of his aunt's wooden chest.

Sure enough, Lene brings something to show him—though not right away. She holds out a cup of water, one hand hidden behind her back.

He drinks. Sets the cup down on the verandah floor. "What have you got there, Lene?"

She steps forward, holding out her hand. If not for the russet cap and throat, it might be a mound of ashes in her palm.

He looks up at her. "Uirapuru?"

She nods.

"Yours?"

She shakes her head. "Mamãe says I will have one when I am older." She smiles shyly. "Uirapuru brings a husband."

"I see." A charm, then, a fetish. His father's caiman skull mined for its magical teeth. Paul wonders if his mother owned such a skin. Did she credit the plain little bird with Walter's arrival—and, more importantly, his decision to stay?

"Thank you for showing me, Lene," he says. "Best put it away now, keep it safe."

She nods, closing the bird skin in her hands and returning indoors. He shuts his eyes, finding his mind wakeful. Reaching down, he feels for the satchel's hasp.

April 13th, 1845, Sitio da Silva

Of late, my wife and I have broadened our explorations to include those waterways that lie within a few days' paddle of home. Today we had progressed a mile or more up one such stream when Zuleica noticed signs of a struggle on the bank. Beaching the montaria, we made an inspection of the site. Capybara tracks surrounded the drag mark of a serpent—*Eunectes murinus*, judging by its width and proximity to the stream. Zuleica confirmed this conclusion, uttering the local name of sucuruju.

Following the channel of its track, we found the anaconda stretched among a stand of palms. Tales of thirty-five- and even forty-foot specimens are not uncommon, but ours measured a modest fifteen feet. All the same, it had plainly succeeded in subduing a meal of considerable size. The swollen creature watched us from where it lay. Never the slenderest of snakes, *E. murinus* is capable of distending its stomach to a remarkable degree. Zuleica smiled when I caught her eye—her habitual response, or so I imagined, to a significant find. It was only when she laid both hands to her own belly that I understood.

36

Ilha das Tartarugas is cloaked in dark green growth, except for the vast, high-banked sandbar at its head. They cast anchor in a sheltered bay. Here they will camp ashore, making nightly sallies to the platform that overlooks the sand.

Rachel makes herself useful, helping Tuí gather firewood while Iris consults with da Silva about where best to string up the party's beds. The sun sinks as Deolindo builds the fire. Supper is a hushed affair, da Silva having warned them of the turtles' sensitivity to human sounds. *One gunshot is all it takes, Dona Íris. One shout and they are gone.* In any case, where Rachel is concerned, Iris has had little to say all day.

When the meal is done, Tuí returns to the trees, this time to cut lianas. He drags the woody lengths to the fire, where he and Deolindo set to work knotting a ladder. Da Silva busies himself with a greener, more pliable vine, ripping leaves from a trailing section before fashioning one end into a lasso.

"Rachel," says Iris, "what have you done with my sketchbook?"

"It's here." Rachel fumbles with the book, Iris cutting a glance at her before taking it from her hand. Rachel's used to the odd sharp word from her mistress, but she's never experienced this lasting chill. After a moment she stands and begins gathering up bowls. She half expects Iris to object; it's hard to know which tasks will be deemed inappropriate when the criteria shift from day to day. This time Iris ignores her efforts. Only Deolindo looks up, bobbing a grateful nod.

At the water's edge, Rachel removes her boots, rolling the grubby white trousers up above her knees. The bay gleams, polished by a rising moon. Rachel wades in and crouches. Taking up a handful of wet sand, she rubs it into the greased hollow of a bowl. For a time she scrubs and rinses on her own. Then, a little way out, a sudden moonlit spray. *Pahhhhhh*. She spies the pale, disappearing arc of a dorsal ridge.

Gathering up the dishes, she makes her way back to the fire. Tuí's still taken up with his knot work, but the others sit watching the water as though it's a stage.

"Boto solitário," Deolindo murmurs as Rachel resumes her seat.

Paaaahhhhhhh, comes the boto's breath.

Iris's eyes are full of firelight. "What do you think, Capitão Paulo?" she says. "Is this one a dolphin, or is it a man?"

The path along the shore is narrow. They proceed single file through the night, Deolindo dragging the ladder, Tuí balancing the gravatana and the coiled length of the lasso. By comparison, Rachel's rucksack is no weight—baskets and sacks, a couple of empty jars. Behind her, Iris walks unencumbered, having entrusted the captain with her bag.

For a short stretch jungle meets water, forcing them to wade. Soft, splashing steps, the thicket singing. Rounding a blind of brush, they come upon the praia's sudden rise. The five of them stand motionless in the shallows. Rachel fights a giddy impulse to shuck off the rucksack and run headlong up the glimmering bank. She glances at Iris, who, for the first time since the ana-conda, meets her look with a smile.

After helping Iris dry her feet and return them to their bal-morals, Rachel ties her own boots to the rucksack and carries on barefoot. The slope levels off in a high table, where the sand lies soft and cool. *Like walking on moonlight.* Not a rare romantic fancy, as Rachel supposed, but an authentic report.

They follow the jungle's border inland. At the foot of a tall, yellow-barked tree, da Silva looks up. High among the branches, a shape like a child's thin raft. The trunk stands bare—fifteen feet to the first low limbs—but Tuí turns his soles against it and climbs.

A shadow now, he comes level with the platform and strad-dles a supporting branch. Snatching the cord Deolindo tosses up to him, he hauls the ladder up after it and fixes it in place. At a click of Tuí's tongue, da Silva takes up the lasso and hurls the loop skywards. Tuí catches it and drapes it over the branch. Dragging up foot after foot of vine, he lowers the loop until da Silva has hold of both ends.

"Dona Íris," da Silva says quietly.

Iris understands before Rachel does. Ducking her head through the loop, she works it down over her bodice to rest against her behind.

"Ready?" da Silva murmurs, and she nods.

Deolindo moves in behind him, but it's clearly a one-man job. Hand over hand, da Silva hoists Iris into the air. With every soft jerk of the line, she ascends another few feet, skirts swaying, boot soles on view. At last glimpse, her grip on the vine is trust-ing, her expression serene.

Rachel holds her breath at the sound of Iris bumping against the branch, but Tuí is up there with her, and Rachel has never known him to be at a loss. Soon the vine slackens. A rust-ling of foliage and now, twenty feet above them, her mistress's familiar step.

It doesn't occur to Rachel to wait for the lasso-swing. There's a trick to the ladder: by the fifth rung she's gripping with fingers and toes only, the rest of her giving in to the sway. Above her, Tuí crouches. It's as though she hands him a baton—no sooner does she clamber up onto the branch than he begins his fluid descent.

The air is different among the leaves. Nudging in beside Iris on the narrow platform, Rachel rises to her feet. She can see clear to the tip of the island—open praia for some two hundred yards, then a carpet of living dark. She feels her gaze grow quiet. *You can't imagine. Thousands of them hauling up out of the river and dig-ging, depositing their hundred-some eggs.*

Iris turns to her. "Did you bring the field glasses?"

"Oh. Sorry, Iris, I'll fetch them."

Crabbing back along the branch, Rachel feels over the edge with her foot. The ladder's easy enough once she finds it; she backs down quickly, landing with a little spring. Looking about for the carpet bag, she spots it at da Silva's elbow. Already he's climbing, the ladder switching under his considerable weight. Taking hold of the bottom rung, she feels Deolindo's hand on her arm.

"Só há espaço para dois," he says gently.

"Oh." She nods. "Entendo." Only room for two.

~

Now that Zuleica is pregnant, weeks pass between Walter's hast-ily jotted notes. *Helped da Silva mend the dock. Zuleica working as ever, exhibiting no signs of fatigue.* Paul's getting used to filling in the gaps, folding open a phrase to discover an imagined scene. It's becoming second nature—so much so that it unnerves him to come upon the first substantial entry in months.

September 26th, 1845, Ilha das Tartarugas, Rio Negro
The island measures half a mile wide and perhaps two miles long. We anchored in a shoaly bay, not far downstream from where the great praia abuts the forest wall. Running ashore in the montaria, we took care to make as little commotion as we might, for in the waters off the island's head there gathered a great school of *Podocnemis expansa.*

The nesting takes place over the course of a fortnight, the turtles emerging nightly, wave upon wave. Each mature female lays a hundred or more eggs, often depositing them atop another's cache. The taboleiro, as such sites are known, is shaped to the purpose: safe from high water in all but the worst of flood years, it forms a natural incubator warmed by the sun.

A short walk along the shore brought us to the jungle's edge, and by sundown we had established our platform in the trees. The taboleiro lay beneath us. No evidence of turtles on the sand, but the distant water winked with a thousand pairs of nostrils breaking the surface to breathe.

We made camp at the base of our lookout. At first light I quitted my rede to find da Silva already aloft. Mounting the rough ladder, I joined him to witness an unforgettable scene: having spent the night excavating and filling their nests, the ranks of unburdened females were in retreat.

Full morning revealed a white expanse scribbled over with tracks. The thought came to me that the praia resembled an open book, and I turned to share this observation with my wife, only to realize afresh that she wasn't there. In light of her condition, all but Zuleica herself had judged it wise that she remain at home.

Her condition—which is to say, Paul. He lifts his gaze from the small circle of lamplight. That's him in there, breathing his mother's blood, helplessly holding her back. He can see her standing on the dock, watching the *Santa Carolina* round the headland out of sight. Her sister is already climbing the bank, but Zuleica lingers, hands on her belly, eyes on the last grey billow of the galliota's sail.

We'll be back before you know it. Iris had worn a fixed smile when she stooped to bid him goodbye. The thought of his step-mother is startling; it's been days since she entered his mind. Hard to imagine her climbing a "rough ladder," no matter how unforgettable the scene. Not Rachel, though. Rachel would be up it in a trice.

37

Tuí wakes her with his presence, standing close by her rede until she snaps open her eyes. The moon has set; stars falter in the pre-dawn gloom. The fire, kept alive all night, has sunk to flickering. She can just make him out by its glow.

He points northwest toward the praia, then up, his hand closing on an invisible rung. Rachel makes a quick survey of the camp: three full hammocks, all of them still. She's slept in her clothes—chemise, shirtwaist, trousers. Rising, she gives no thought to bonnet or boots.

They're halfway there before she realizes she's left the rucksack behind. No field glasses, no collecting sacks or jars. Tuí travels light as well, his only weapon the tresado, bouncing in its scabbard at his thigh.

By the time they reach the praia, the sand is turning silver in wasp-paper waves. Rachel spots the sentinel tree from a distance. Following close on Tuí's heels, she thinks suddenly, unexpectedly, of Paul. Maybe he really will be strong enough to return with them for the hatching-out. He'd never manage the ladder, but he might just submit to da Silva's lasso. She could climb up ahead of him and help.

The thought carries her, delivering her to the base of the yellow-barked tree. Taking hold of the ladder, she grapples for the heights. Tuí makes way as she rises, allowing her to gain the platform on her own.

The praia is changing its skin. Still grey along its western flank, its back has turned an ashy rose. It's covered with marks—scrapes and hollows, gouges and drags. In the distance, the last of the night's cohort retreats.

Here and there a straggler labours after the throng. One has other ideas: on the praia's high plain, a lone tartaruga drags herself toward the trees. *No*, Rachel thinks—only it's closer to hearing, her own voice whispering back at her from the leaves. *No*, it says again, *turn around*.

She's surprised to find Tuí no longer beside her. Peering over the edge, she sees the top of his head, already halfway down. *"Ikwe,"* she whispers harshly, unsure whether he's heard.

As he drops to the ground, she turns back to the brightening view. Tuí runs, an easy lope gauged to the depleted state of his prey. Spotting him, the tartaruga begins hauling herself round. Too late, she locates her intended direction, paddling desperately across the sand. Tuí lengthens his stride. He closes on her in moments, leaping to pin her flat.

Backing down the ladder, Rachel suffers a vague, vertiginous sickness. The ground is a comfort; so too the advancing light. It's true dawn now, the sand spreading golden around Tuí and his catch. The turtle's shell is smaller than the one Walter carried home, but Tuí's stature keeps the proportions true. Black hair, mouth hidden in a black circle akin to a beard. He jogs toward her, a rough double of the portrait she knows.

As luck would have it, Iris is spared the vision of Tuí and the tartaruga. She stands in the shallows beyond the camp, splashing her face and arms, oblivious to their return. In among the hammocks, the carpet bag sits open on the sand. On impulse, Rachel pulls out the sketchbook. Iris's time on the platform last night was productive. Several of the studies are long views, complete with leaf-framed foreground to locate the viewer in the trees. Others, made with the aid of the field glasses, reveal the tartarugas at work. Rachel lingers over a sketch of a weary female balanced at the edge of her nest. Foreclaws sunk in the sand, she labours. Behind her, the eggs mount up.

Closing the book, Rachel pushes it back into the bag. She takes up Iris's shawl from her rede and walks down the beach to meet her. "Bom dia."

Iris looks round. "Bom dia." No *Where were you?* No *Oh, good, you're back.*

"Tuí got a turtle," Rachel says after a moment.

"Did he? Good." Shaking water from her fingers, Iris smooths the wet hair from her brow. Her skirts are soaked to the knee; her blouse clings to her collarbones, the lace on her chemise showing through. Rachel glances behind her to where the men are busy about the fire. Da Silva lifts his gaze and almost immediately drops it. Keeping her back to him, Rachel opens the shawl.

They return to camp to find Tuí has laid the tartaruga on its back in the shade. Its flipper-feet curl. Its head cranes up, holds for a moment and falls back.

"Lovely," says Iris. "I'll make some studies after we eat." She moves toward the fire. "Café da manhã, Capitão?"

"Brava, Dona Íris." He smiles as she settles beside him. "O Português é muito bom."

Deolindo catches Rachel's eye. "Você está com fome, senhorita?"

And she realizes she is—very hungry. "Certamente, Deo-lindo."

He laughs. "Primeiro vamos alimentar as pessoas, depois"— he gestures to a bucket of fish guts—"alimentamos os animais."

He's right, of course. First thing after breakfast they must paddle out to the *Bridie Mac* and feed the collection. Tuí hasn't forgotten; he's tearing at a nearby thicket, amassing a rough salad of leaves.

An hour to sundown and still the praia holds the day's heat. They keep to the thin shade along the forest wall, Tuí trotting ahead, occasionally ducking into the trees. It no longer troubles Rachel when she can't see him; he invariably reappears.

She's just lost sight of him again when she stumbles on a buried branch. Glancing back, her eye catches on something not right. There is wood—bleached, bone-like—and then there is bone. Rachel's heart beats in her ears. Crouching down, she paws at the sand. In moments, the snag that tripped her reveals itself to be a rib.

Following the arc to its conclusion, she discovers a vertebra— and with it a notion of how to proceed. Peak after peak, the crea-ture's backbone leads her to its head. The skull is pristine, packed with fine white sand. Rachel carves out brainpan, eye holes, snout. Digging down, she catches her cord bracelet on the slick, pointed peg of a tooth. She frees it, measuring the head against her arm. Two and a half feet, easy. Which means the creature it belonged to was undoubtedly a jacaré nigra.

Caiman here, I think.

Walter's voice is clear in her mind. She can see him stand-ing in the atrium's twilight, surveying the newly finished ponds. "Turtles first," he added. "Save the anaconda for last."

Iris nodded, and Rachel with her.

"We ought to hold out for a *Jacaré nigra*—a black caiman." Walter smiled to himself. "I had a close call with one once."

"You did?" said Iris. "You never said."

"Yes, we . . . my assistant and I, we happened upon a nest. They make a great mound of leaves—this one had to be four feet across. I dug out an egg and held it to my ear. They chirp, you see, when they're ready to hatch." He shook his head. "Thank God my assistant heard the mother coming. We got up a tree, but just barely. I came close to losing a foot."

"Walter!" Iris laughed.

"It's true. She was huge, the mother. Thirteen, fourteen feet. We had to make our escape through the trees."

At the time, Rachel pictured it in comical terms: Walter and his nameless companion beating a monkey's retreat. Now, kneeling beside the buried caiman, it occurs to her that they could have stayed put.

What if you left the nest alone, climbing to safety before there was any threat? With the right provisions, a body could live among the branches for days. You could watch the mother come and go. You could be there when the young started calling for her through their shells.

Rachel sits back on her heels, considering. For now she can carry the skull back to camp; there's not enough daylight left to dig the skeleton out whole, and anyway, Iris may prefer to sketch it where it lies. Rachel can see how the thing should be done— the ribs and leg bones bundled, the feet parcelled out into sacks. The vertebrae will require special treatment; perhaps she might string them like beads on a series of Tuí's cords. *Jewellery-box collectors*—wasn't that what Walter called them? Feeling for the join to the backbone, she pushes the thought from her mind.

⌇

The night is still. Zuleica makes no sound as she rises, sifting up through the swept-earth floor. No one, not even Flor, wakes to see her hand Paul the forked shadow of the crutch. *Her smile was a hunter's.* He must tread softly; his mother wishes him to come alone.

Crossing the moonlit yard, he gets his first good look at her: broad, shapely back under a cream-coloured shift, muscular calves and arms. Her face when she turns is distinctly feline. Bright eyes and bone structure, that little pointed chin.

The trailhead gapes. Zuleica keeps left, dissolving to shadow as she sets off down the hunter's track. Paul follows close. One bend, then another, and the moon's pale influence is lost. There is the jungle—all it harbours, all it sustains—and there is his mãe.

An explosion wakes him where he stands. He cowers beneath a mad overhead scramble, terrified of what might drop on him from above. A whickering cry, a rush among the branches, as whatever it is panics and flees. For a moment he can't tell whether his eyes are open, the darkness is that complete. Heart in his throat, he puts a hand out to the side. Leaves. The same on the other side and, yes—he swipes gingerly at the low branches— overhead. Space before him, space behind. Not a dream, then. An actual path.

Spirit guide or no, he can't have come far. If he turns and advances slowly, he should be able to find his way back. A hobbled step brings him up against foliage. Stifling a cry, he reorients himself with a hand outstretched into blackness. Four steps unhindered. Five. Then a sound.

He freezes, straining his ears. *Not a true rattle. A softer, more sinister buzz.* It can't be. *Lachesis mutus* prefers the open understorey; remember, Zuleica led Walter out of the close-woven scruff into the mata virgem. On the other hand, where better to coil in wait for an unsuspecting mammal than beside its habitual trail? *Thick as a man's arm. Eight, perhaps nine feet in length.* The dark distorts Paul's hearing. Is it yards away? Feet? He can't be sure now whether he hears anything over the whanging of his own pulse. *Quiet, blood, the bushmaster will hear you.*

But sound is the least of his worries. If the great snake is near, it will have read his scent long since, tasting his fear on its flicking tongue. It might even be close enough to *register his warmth.* Either way, it knows him for the soft-skinned creature he is— something that ought to be tucked up in its tree hole, or hugging the furry saddle of its mother's back.

"Help." He can barely force breath into the word. Zuleica has left him, his father is gone. Paul opens his mouth, and this time it's the word he needs. "Tia!" he screams. *"Tia!"*

Nothing for a stretch of seconds. Then, in the distance, *"Paulo!"*

"I'm here," he cries, "aqui!"

He calls and calls. Time hollows out in the minutes it takes her to find him. Lamplight reaches through the boughs, the path glittering with the eye shine of spiders. They scatter as Carolina rounds the bend.

"Paulo!" She's not alone: Lene carries a second lantern, Vitor hard on her heels. At his shoulder, the ghostly glow of Flor's moustaches, the gleam of her two bright eyes.

"Atenção," Paul blurts, "serpente!"

"Onde?" His aunt holds up her lantern, casting light along the path.

He shakes his head, trembling. "I'm not sure."

"Venha," she says sharply, herding them all before her. "Vamos."

One bend in the path, another—it really isn't far.

"Meu Deus, Paulo," his aunt says as they emerge into moonlight. "O que você estava fazendo lá fora?"

God knows what she's asking. *Are you all right? What possessed you? What on earth were you hoping to find?*

"Não sei, Tia." And he doesn't. He really doesn't know.

38

achel feigns sleep as da Silva rouses Iris and gathers up her things. She watches them move off into the darkness through the slits of her eyes. It isn't fair. It should be Rachel up there on the platform beside her mistress. She understands wanting a man on hand, but surely the captain could keep watch from the ground.

Reaching down beside her rede, she locates the caiman skull. For a time she lies listening, her hand on its bony brow. She rises without deciding to. No chance to wake Tuí; one step toward his rede and he blinks to consciousness like a cat. Deolindo soughs in his sleep. They feed a fresh knot of deadfall to the fire before leaving him to slumber on alone.

The route is becoming known to her, the distance shrinking with every pass. To her right the jungle buzzes, to her left the river laps. Anticipation as they enter the shallows. The whistling, overweening thicket, then the rise of the praia, bathed in ambiguous light. The sentinel tree is a bronzed column. Hugging the jungle's margin, they make for it at a healthy pace.

They're steps from the base of the tree when Tuí draws up short. It takes a moment for Rachel to hear—high in the canopy, a repeated, keening note. Iris is weeping. Rachel is about to call out to her when Tuí looks round. His mouth is full of moonlight, the widest and most natural of grins.

Fool, Rachel Weaver. Child.

She can hear da Silva now—huff of an onça, a hunter's ragged breath. To her shame, the sound burns in Rachel's belly. "Oh," Iris whimpers, "oh, oh, oh—"Then a cry as though he's struck her, a prolonged and pitiable moan.

Tuí's gaze has turned serious in sympathy. Meeting it, Rachel takes a step back, then another, fitting her bare feet to their tracks.

October 14th, 1845, Ilha das Tartarugas, Rio Negro
Zuleica was even more put out to find herself excluded from this second trip. Both Dona Carolina and myself had to reason with her, repeatedly laying out the case against undertaking such a journey so close to her confinement. It is the only time I have known my wife to sulk.

We returned to the island to find the praia crowded with montarias and larger craft. Scores of locals had assembled from the surrounding villages and sitios— Indians and ribeirinhos alike. Their camps ranged along the jungle's margin, leaving the taboleiro clear.

Shortly after our arrival, da Silva took command of those gathered, bidding them form a ring at the taboleiro's edge. Upon his signal, man, woman and child set to digging with their paddles. Children filled their baskets and carried them back to camp. By nightfall a hill of eggs had grown up alongside every shelter, many in excess of six feet high.

Having toured the camp to inspect the proceedings, da Silva and I settled for a time by the fire of a venerable ribeirinho by the name of Senhor Carneiro. Given the scale of the harvest, I felt moved to inquire whether there would be eggs enough to sustain the next generation. Senhor Carneiro laughed. In a few weeks the praia would crawl with young, he assured me, for there are always those caches the people cannot find.

The lamplight flickers as Paul turns the page. The next entry catches him off guard. Its date is one he knows well—twenty-one subdued celebrations, a twenty-second soon to come.

November 14th, 1845, Sitio da Silva
Many a medical man has doubled as expedition natural-ist. Would that the reverse were true.

Here a black blot marks the place where Walter forgot him-self, resting his pen against the page. Paul can see him, hunched at his rough table, surrounded by skins and skulls. He manages a sentence more:

Zuleica died this night, not an hour after she was deliv-ered of our son.

Rachel has slept heavily, as though subject to a spell. She wakes to a bright morning, parrots squabbling in the overhead fronds. Then knowledge—the night's events rolling over her, more trou-bling than any dream.

She screws her eyes shut and reopens them. The scene is

peaceful. Iris sits bare-headed in the sun, her back to the camp, lost in her pencil's line. Down the far end of the beach, da Silva hacks branches from a fallen tree. Out in the bay, Tuí moves among the collection while Deolindo fishes for breakfast off the *Bridie Mac*'s stern. Between them on the roof of the cabin, the onça dourada stalks.

Rachel gets her feet beneath her and stands. Iris has left her sunbonnet hooked on the thicket. Retrieving it, Rachel smacks a line of leaf-cutter ants from the brim. She doesn't mean to sneak up; it's only natural, walking barefoot on the floury sand.

"Oh!" Iris looks up, startled.

"Sorry, I—" Rachel freezes, rendered speechless by the drawing in her mistress's lap. It's a better likeness than the one that hangs over the landing at home, the subject not quite as handsome but infinitely more alive. Iris has captured his every aspect—the devotion, the disappointment, the desire. And in that desire, something Rachel has hitherto failed to remark: an essential resemblance to his son.

Da Silva is coming back to them, his step heavy, his arms full. Rachel has made up her mind to be cold to him—a resolution that deserts her the moment he lifts his gaze.

"Senhora," he says formally. "Senhorita."

They answer as one: "Capitão."

Bending to lay down his branches, he catches sight of the open sketchbook. "Walter," he says in a tone of wonder, as though the man himself has appeared. He stoops over the drawing, hands braced on his knees. Eventually he straightens. "Life was kind to him. He was still the same man."

Iris stares up at him, tears sliding down her cheeks.

"Iris," Rachel says gently, "it's time we were under way."

39

aul wakes from his siesta to the sound of the family's collective breath. Vitor is the first to rise, tipping out of the rede he shares with his sister and standing at the verandah's edge to pee. Lene's up next, Flor bundled like a doll against her chest. She pauses alongside her mother's rede until Carolina opens her eyes, then climbs in to lie facing her, head to foot. As Flor settles along the seam between them, Carolina smiles, taking her daughter's feet in her hands.

Vitor returns to find his own rede empty, his mother's full. Rubbing his eyes, he turns to his cousin. Before Paul can speak, the boy hooks a knee up to nudge in beside him.

"Cuidadoso, Vitor," Carolina murmurs, and he is—as careful as a four-year-old can be. Paul holds the foot up until Vitor's arm comes to rest against his good leg. "Paulo," Carolina says, "o que você estava fazendo na mata?"

"Mamãe says what you are doing in the jungle."

"I was . . . dreaming." But that's not quite right. "I was following."

"Seguindo?" Carolina says in response to her daughter's translation. "Quem você estava seguindo?"

There's only one response, whether or not it's true. "Minha mãe."

The look on his aunt's face is heartbreaking. Until now he

hasn't known he will ask her. "How did it happen, Tia? Como minha mãe . . . morta?"

Carolina looks at him. "Walter não te conto?"

"Please, Tia."

"Ai, Paulito." She closes her eyes. "Ela sangrou."

"She bleeds," Lene says softly.

"Yes," says Paul. Vitor lies in quiet sympathy against him. "I see." But he doesn't. Children are born all over the world—how many, each and every day? Some of them content to let their mothers live, others demanding a life for a life.

"Did you name me?" Paul says finally.

Carolina smiles.

"After Tio Paulo?"

She gazes at him. "Havia um outro Paulo."

"Another Paulo?"

She nods. "Meu primeiro. Júnior."

"Júnior."

"Sim."

Lene steps in as her mother continues. "Mamãe says Júnior was not strong. He lived for nine days only." She pauses, listening. "For a long time she is thinking he is her only baby." Lene brightens, pointing to herself. "Até eu?"

Carolina nods, patting the girl's ankle. "Até você, meu coração."

Still Vitor says nothing, his eyes shifting between his mother and Paul.

"Você era forte, Paulo," Carolina says. "Sempre chorando por leite."

Leite. Why has it never occurred to him? No mother, no milk. "You? But—"

His aunt cuts him off.

"Mamãe says her milk came for you. Only one day of crying and it came."

When Carolina speaks again, Paul catches nothing but his father's name.

"In that time," Lene tells him, "Mamãe had a goat. One day she is feeding you and she sees Walter milk this goat."

Paul can see it too, his father kneeling beside the patient beast, resting his forehead on its back.

"This is when Mamãe knows what Walter is thinking," says Lene. "This is when she knows he will take you away."

Rachel sits surrounded by the collection, knees drawn up to her chest, back pressed to the cabin door. Iris has been lying down since late morning, when they steamed out into the main current, leaving the island behind. Da Silva keeps to his seat at the helm. Having refused his midday meal, he shows no sign of breaking for the siesta that's claimed his crew.

The Rio Negro runs at a measured pace; Rachel has a pleasant sense of being carried, now that they're travelling downstream. It's just as well they're heading back, given how the collection has grown. There's scarcely room to move amid the cages, baskets and tubs. She worries whether her charges are getting enough air.

Time she was seeing to them. She needn't feed the snakes— Tuí took care of them this morning, sharing out the contents of a rats' nest he'd raided at dawn—but she can't resist a peek at the tree boa. Lifting the lid of its basket, she wishes she had. Banana-bright when they caught it, the boa's colour has faded to match the fruit's insides. At least it's still eating—no wriggling rat pups to be seen.

The matamata's water stinks. She lifts the creature from its tepid pool, laying it on its back while she tips the water overboard and leans down with the dipper for more. Next, the tartaruga. Too large for the biggest tub, it lies in a crate lined with oilskin. All but an inch of its water has leaked away. Rachel adds another three, along with a fistful of river weeds.

The tortoises, huddled together in their tub, get fruit—as does the wood turtle, alone in its basket since its companion died. The iguana is hungry. It glares at Rachel though the cross-hatching of lianas, snatching at the greenery she pushes between the weave. The caiman hisses when she drops a fish through the barred lid of its crate. And now a second hiss, this one from the starboard bench. The jacaré skull is an object of fascination to the ship's cat. Rachel watches him bat the bone snout, dip a paw into the empty eye. Rising to join him on the bench, she passes a palm along his bristling spine.

It's hard to be certain where they are. Is that the small, still bay where the anaconda laid claim to their chickens, or has that particular backwater already passed them by? She need only close her eyes to see it: the dark, muscled dorsum, the great wedge of the head. *He can wrap around a boat and take everyone on board to the Encante.* It wouldn't be the first such collection sacrificed to the depths. Baron von Humboldt lost much of his haul to a storm off the African coast, and the unfortunate Mr. Wallace forfeited every specimen when the *Helen* caught fire and went down.

It's not difficult to imagine. Easier, in fact, than the prospect of carting it all home. Surely it makes more sense to stay—not forever, perhaps, but longer than a matter of months. Time enough to sit on the riverbank and listen. To shin up a tree and watch.

"Rachel?" Iris's voice through the cabin door.

Leaving Angelo to contend with the skull, Rachel ducks inside. It's stifling, both portholes sealed. "Iris, what are you doing?" She opens the porthole over her own bunk, then reaches to unlatch the one above Iris. "You'll make yourself ill."

Iris rolls over, showing her tear-stained face. "Is there any water?"

"Of course." Rachel pours out a cup and sits at the edge of the bunk. Iris rises on one elbow to drink. Lying back, she reaches for Rachel's hand. Such fine, pale fingers. Rachel closes them in her own.

"You've been very good," Iris says after a moment. "Looking after the collection the way you have."

Rachel squeezes her hand.

"Do you think he'll take it on?" Iris asks.

"Who?"

"Paul. Do you think he'll agree to run the *Domum Reptilium*?"

Rachel tries to picture it: starlight through the glass, the cramped forest and concrete pools. She can see Paul clearly—the way he shrank upon entering the atrium, the look on his face when he stood where his father had died. And now a different image, almost a different man. He was shining, that night on the *Tatatínga*'s upper deck—white shirt in the darkness, eyes turned to the sky. *Up goes my boat among the stars . . .*

"I don't know, Iris," she says finally. "He might have other ideas."

When it comes, there's almost too much of it. Paul lies with his eyes closed, scenes flashing through his mind. He sees the woman rise from the childbed, already gaining strength. Sees her fish and pick fruit and hunt, her son beside her, her husband never far. There are years of it, the little family moving together through the jungle, into and out of the bay. Paul isn't sure when the young woman joins them from the outside, or even how. For now he knows only that she arrives.

He sits up in his rede, reaching for the satchel, digging for his ink pot and pen. He'll need more paper—much, much more—but at present the untouched pages at the end of the notebook will suffice.

It's hard to know where to begin.

Only it's not. *Ela sangrou*, Tia told him, the verb fixed firmly in the past—but Lene's mistake in translation leaves the writer more room. Paul records it now, dipping his nib, pressing it to the waiting page.

She bleeds.

40

The children have gone down for their afternoon dip; doubtless Carolina will join them once she's finished inspecting Paul's foot. When she removes the dressing, he forces himself to look. The ulcer is still angry—the stone-shot pattern forming its third ring—but his aunt seems satisfied. She rises and sets the bandage aside, leaving the wound to air.

When she's gone, Paul reaches for his crutch. Flor watches him from the mango tree, chittering. It's the first time he's done his lengths with the foot undressed. To begin with, the breeze feels dangerous, but by the second pass he's coming to appreciate its touch.

He's completing his third length when a peal of Vitor's laughter reaches him from below. Flor trills and sits up on her branch. Stumping to the verandah's edge, Paul confronts an idyllic scene: the boy paddling circles around his sister, their mother floating on her back nearby. A little farther out, the memory of a slim, swimming figure in grey.

It's a matter of momentum. At the end of the verandah, he plants his crutch in the grass and proceeds to the top of the bank. Flor makes him jump, touching his good ankle with her paw. When he stoops awkwardly to pet her, she catches him off guard again, clambering up his arm. Her weight on his shoulder is welcome. Together they look down the long descent.

It's possible. So long as he's careful, so long as he takes his time. Crutch, hop. Crutch-hop. *Sway.* The tamarin knows enough to keep still.

He's halfway down, pausing to catch his breath, when Vitor spots him. "Oi, primo Paulo!"

Paul gives a cautious wave. "Oi, Vitor!"

His aunt rights herself, her hair a wet cloak. He expects her to scold him—at least bid him take care—but she only watches, holding him in her steady gaze. While Lene models on her mother, Vitor hurries up the praia, eager to help. A word from Carolina stops him in his tracks. Paul is left alone to manage. Forty-four steps—just as there were when he ascended them a month ago.

The moment his crutch touches sand, Flor springs from his shoulder and bounds over to the boy.

"Oi, Florzinha." Vitor scoops her up. "You miss me?"

The beach makes for slow going, the crutch sinking with every step. At length Paul reaches the hard-packed sand at the water's edge, and from there it's an easy hop onto the dock. Hobbling out past the cluster of montarias, he turns and looks down on his aunt.

"Bravo, Paulito." She smiles up at him. "Você está ficando mais forte."

"Mamãe says you are strong." Lene corrects herself: "Stronger."

He bows to woman and girl—a lopsided dip the best the crutch will allow. Beyond, Vitor stands in the shallows, coaxing a wary Flor to come in. "Vem, Flor. Venha pela água."

Paul carries on. Upon reaching the end of the dock, he considers dangling his feet. The water won't hurt him; it might even soothe the wound. But how to sit down, let alone rise again, without asking for help?

He watches a pair of macaws pass over the bay, calling to each other as they go. Beyond them, the vast, slow-flowing Negro really is black. It's the *Rio* part that seems like an illusion, an untruth.

At Paul's feet, the water is amber, the colour deepening to where it resists then refuses the light. Behind him, Vitor's thin, insistent call: "Venha pela água, meu coração. Venha."

They've been making good time, Deolindo feeding the engine, da Silva working the wheel. Iris has returned to her original seat beneath the canopy, she and the captain courteous with each other but no longer warm. Rachel sits with her back to them at the head of the portside bench.

They're rounding a headland when the macaws come squawking into view—a pair of red and blue beauties waving the bright ribbons of their tails. Rachel glances across at Tuí, the ship's cat seated at his feet. The pair of them follow the birds' progress, tracking them with their eyes.

She hadn't realized it was that headland, this particular bay. It's not strictly a homecoming, yet she feels her heart lift in recognition at the sight of the whitewashed casa perched atop the bank. The beach too looks familiar, as does the family in the shallows—a woman and her two children raising their distant hands.

And they're not alone. Rachel knows the river can fool you, but the longer she looks, the better she believes her eyes. The creature cutting toward her is no boto, no caiman, no snake.

"Paul," she says, rising. It's Paul.

ACKNOWLEDGEMENTS

Heartfelt thanks to those who shared their time and expertise. They are: poet and professor Ricardo Sternberg; consummate Amazon guide, Naresh (Anand) Pooran and his wife, Carolina; Captain Regildo of the *Camiiba* and his mate Júnior; Greg and Ron at The Steamboating Forum.

Without the following books, this one would be full of holes: *The Naturalist on the River Amazon(s): A Record of Adventures, Habits of Animals, Sketches of Brazilian and Indian Life, and Aspects of Nature under the Equator, during Eleven Years of Travel* by Henry Walter Bates; *A Narrative of Travels on the Amazon and Rio Negro: With an Account of the Native Tribes, and Observations on the Climate, Geology, and Natural History of the Amazon* by Alfred Russel Wallace; *Personal Narrative of Travels to the Equinoctial Regions of America: During the Years 1799–1804* by Alexander von Humboldt (translated by Thomasina Ross); *A Voyage up the River Amazon: Including a Residence at Pará* by William H. Edwards; *Viagem ao Brasil* by Alexandre Rodrigues Ferreira; *Don't Sleep, There Are Snakes: Life and Language in the Amazonian Jungle* by Daniel L. Everett; *Literary Amazonia: Modern Writing by Amazonian Authors*, edited by Nicomedes

Suárez-Araúz; *In Amazonia: A Natural History* by Hugh Raffles; *Entangled Edens: Visions of the Amazon* by Candace Slater; *Journey of the Pink Dolphins: An Amazon Quest* by Sy Montgomery; *Reptiles and Amphibians of the Amazon: An Ecotourist's Guide* by R.D. Bartlett and Patricia Bartlett; *Tropical Nature: Life and Death in the Rain Forests of Central and South America* by Adrian Forsyth and Ken Miyata; *The Smithsonian Atlas of the Amazon*, edited by Michael Goulding, Ronaldo Barthem, and Efrem Ferreira; *The River Sea: The Amazon in History, Myth, and Legend* by Marshall De Bruhl; *Explorers of the Amazon* by Anthony Smith; *The Lost Amazon: The Photographic Journey of Richard Evans Schultes* by Wade Davis; *The Species Seekers: Heroes, Fools, and the Mad Pursuit of Life on Earth* by Richard Conniff; *Field Notes on Science and Nature*, edited by Michael R. Canfield; *The Great Naturalists*, edited by Robert Huxley; *Chrysalis: Maria Sibylla Merian and the Secrets of Metamorphosis* by Kim Todd; *Women in the Field: America's Pioneering Women Naturalists* by Marcia Myers Bonta; *Margaret Mee's Amazon: The Diaries of an Artist Explorer* by Margaret Mee; *Tropical Renaissance: North American Artists Exploring Latin America, 1839–1879* by Katherine Manthorne; *Picturing Nature: American Nineteenth-Century Zoological Illustration* by Ann Shelby Blum; *A Brief History of Herpetology in North America before 1900* by Kraig Adler; *Animal Attractions: Nature on Display in American Zoos* by Elizabeth Hanson; *Old Philadelphia in Early Photographs 1839–1914* by Robert F. Looney; *Quaker Writings: An Anthology, 1650–1920*, edited by Thomas D. Hamm.

Two quotes, one from Humboldt, the other from Wallace, have been slightly abridged (*mea culpa*). The Latin binomials for some species are current; wherever possible, however, I've opted for the form in use at the time.

This novel was made possible by the support of the Ontario Arts Council's Chalmers Arts Fellowship; my thanks to them, as well as to the Canada Council for the Arts and the Toronto Public Library.

As ever, I'm deeply grateful to the good people of Penguin Random House Canada, especially Anne Collins, whose bright eye never fails. Thanks also to my agent, Ellen Levine, who doesn't let the grass grow, but brings the flowers along beautifully.

Family and friends, you know who you are, and you know what I'd be without you.

Last and best love to my husband, first reader and favourite creature, Clive.

ALISSA YORK's internationally acclaimed novels include *Mercy*, *Effigy* (shortlisted for the Scotiabank Giller Prize) and, most recently, *Fauna*. She is also the author of the short fiction collection *Any Given Power*, stories from which have won the Journey Prize and the Bronwen Wallace Award. Her essays and articles have appeared in *The Guardian*, *The Globe and Mail*, *Brick* magazine and elsewhere. York has lived all over Canada and now makes her home in Toronto with her husband, artist Clive Holden.